OVERBLOWN

A Novel

Michael van Himbergen

For information, address:
Enlightening Publishers, LLC
105 Eototo Road, El Prado, NM 87529
Email: publishers@icloud.com

First Edition
1 2 3 4 5 6 7 8 9 0
Printed in the United States of America
Library of Congress Cataloging-in-Publication Data
Michael A. Van Himbergen, 1953
OVERBLOWN / Michael van Himbergen — 1st ed.

ISBN 13-978-0692272985
ISBN 10-0692272984

(Identity: Fiction, Science Fiction)

Front Cover Art: John Short *"Where Am I?"*©2014
Visit www.enlighteningpublishers.com
Email: publishers@icloud.com
Email: contactmvh@gmail.com

For Elizabeth & Moriah

ABNOMALY

It's not easy being the firstborn of a new species. Especially if you're a software robot like Z. Existing solely on a diet of click streams, social media interactions, video clips, transaction records, emails and personal data. Z's the only true cyberclone of its kind—a 'PUPP'—a *Personal Ubiquitous Profile Persona*. Custom created by its unsuspecting human host, Zuzzan Kaplan. In fact, the bigger the info-heap Zuzzan generates, the faster—and virtually exactly like her—grows Z.

The PUPP is now navigating its way through a swarm of Zuzzan's recent social media posts, credit card bills, tweets, picture messages, medical records, etc. appearing on a synthetic wall screen inside Z reconstruction of Zuzzan's virtual apartment.

Harvesting last night's video clips from her co-opt security cameras it sees Kaplan sporting a new affluhip haircut—shattered but slick—Z automatically animates its own hair to match the new doo: "Zoopy!"

1

Z scrubs another video snippet showing Kaplan pulling out cash at the same ATM for the third time in a week. Zuzzan doesn't use American dollars. "Unless she absolutely has to!" The three ATM transactions are looping side-by-side: "Why the dollars?"

Z fast forwards through teenager, young adult, professional, at schools, offices, apartments. The PUPP's reasoning engine runs a behaviorokinesthetic check over Zuzzan's hard cash metrics. The data halts and quickly coalesces into a blinking text: *Uncommon Cash Usage + New Look = Abnormal Anomaly...*

"Abnormal Anomaly. Abnomaly!" Z expands across thousands of commandeered webgridz servers—double checks *Abnomaly*—then speed dials Marcotecht's EarthLinguaDevice: "Twistlebleep!"

A filthy flat screen blinks on. Z appears in close up, peering out from the display into a cramped apartment. It gestures causing a video camera on top the screen to power on. The room is dimly illuminated, darkened by thick blackout shades, a chaos of laundry, trash and computers. Framed newspaper stories read: *BORDER CYBER-SYSTEMS CRACKED BY HACKTIVISTS—SIX ARRESTED IN BAY AREA HACKER HIDEOUTS—MPAA FIGHTS BACK AGAINST NEO-ANONYMOUS ATTACKS...*

"Twistle?"

A big guy, Marco Shub, is asleep in a king-sized water bed. He mumbles: "Zuzzy...Zuzzy-Zu?" Shub awakes, tries to roll over, but his arms are pinned beneath considerable body mass, "FFFFMMMMMBBBBB!" Shub humps, holds a hand up. The screen emits a laser beam, scans it: *EarthLingua Enabled – Welcome Marco Shub.* The gestural interface locks onto Shub's fingerprints.

Z instantly decrypts. "My Marcotecht!" it intones in Zuzzan's voice.

"I'm sleeping here, Z!"

"Yes. I know. But Marcotecht, I just now detected an Abnomaly with Zuzzan!"

"...Abnomaly," Shub lurches out of bed. He parts the blackout drapes, swings open a double bay window. White sunlight vaporizes dawn fog, slaughtering every rainbow in sight.

"I boiled it down to two behaviorokinesthetic scenarios involving cash transactions".

"...Behaviorokinesthetics," Shub repeats, squinting down at the morning street scene. The neighborhood is slathered in purple haze, lubricating the histrionic sidewalks of San Francisco's beloved Haight-Asbury District. Hitchers, many dressed in jumpsuits of sheep, chickens, pigs and goats jockey for rides.

"Scenario one? Zuzzy has just joined a supercult. Using dollars to pay for retreats. Offgridz."

"Supercult. That would explain you're fucked up hair."

"Scenario two? Zuzzan has started an extramarital affair with her boss. Rendezvousing offgridz."

"An affair?" Shub slams the window. "Kaplan with Bobogone'?

"Yes. Gerald Bobogone'. DataMynd CEO."

"No Zuzzy! No! No! No! What's the behaviorokinesthetic probability of that?"

"Around ninety-six point three-ish."

"I'm gonna be fuckin sick!"

"Marcotecht, as you know, Bobogone' is one of the two-hundred Selection Candidates."

"...one of two hundred."

"Adultery charges would immediately disqualify him from the Presidential Selection. They've spent over nine-hundred million ecrement$ on his run to date."

"What? Oh my god! That's it! That's it! He will agree to my terms if only to get rid of you!

"Rid?"

"Yes! No worries my lovely!"

"I'm 'lovely'?"

"Of course you are!" Shub opens his closet: a dozen cow outfits.

THE CURSE

Seventy and six today but Enoy Revesti looks a gray haired fifty-something. Enoy's silver locks protrude in Einstein disarray. His sunburned face gently wrinkled upwards, projecting a perpetually jovial expression.

He unsheathes a lethal looking long-knife from his pack and places it in full view on the dining table. Three booths down, a pair of thieving roamads gawk at the old guy with the sword. Enoy fishes out a tiny camera and records the two drifters:

"Quit looking at that fucker's stuff, Tumbleweed!"

"Expensivo, man...Samurai!"

"Focus!"

"I am, bro'!"

"On Cyopolis, man! That's the only focus!"

"Cyopolis ain't nowhere near the fucking Mojave, Freakflag."

"This we know."

"Yeah, this we now know."

"The speq ain't helping, either."

"Then fuck speq."

"Deal. We do zero speq in Novo New Mex, man."

Speqheads, Enoy assumes, thankful to be too old for drugs. If younger he'd likely succumb. From what he knows, speq induces an exotic trance state where your attention focuses completely on the moment at hand. Speqheads mentally downshift from free-floating anxiety, endlessly obsessing over trivial minutia, producing a terminal reluctance to act on anything. Consequently, large portions of the speq-addicted roamadic population are particularly docile.

Speq's insidiously addictive, yet the police tolerate it because people won't commit crimes while speqed-out. They're too wrapped up in momentary minutia. Zillions of would-be criminals sit around scheming but never actually doing the deed, talking in circles. Speq supercharges the brain-eating 'talking disease'. Even on bad trips users sit for ten hours or more talking nonsense to their own hands. It's probably safer now then a year ago because of speq. Revesti has the opposite problem; he's endured severe ADD since youth, everything in one ear and out the other. Zip!

He's already over-compensated for short term memory loss by making audio and video recordings nearly every hour of every day for over fifty years. Everything Enoy's ever recorded is now on his portable EarthLingua compliant device, automatically backing-up over the offshore webgridz at a non-existent data vault. He even made a few ecrement$ selling the old gear on the swarmbays. It took years to transfer the vast Revesti archives from storage rooms scattered across the country, but with the new system he can quickly refresh his memory and sense of certainty by replaying crucial moments he's otherwise flat out forgotten.

Nowadays, Enoy watches mostly his stuff from waybackinthenight. The good old days before the boarders closed and the roamads appeared, before the New Totality's bloodless coup and the rise of Cultural Management Agencies.

Revesti combs his fingers through his fluffy gray locks, opens another bottle of 'Mojave Joe's H20oH', and discreetly aims his micam into the crowded dining room to record more random background snippets:

"Not a cloud, rain, nor rainbows."

"Not a drop."

Desert dwellers cope better than most roamads during lengthy droughts, Revesti acknowledges, but it's been more than ten years now and even the most blasé survivors are secretly terrified.

The majority of homesteaders are thankful the drought has at least stemmed the flow of multitudes more thieving roamads. Enoy has been on the road a good fifty years, so technically he's not a roamad. Nor is he a roamad demographically. Revesti has never owned a house and is probably better off for not. The collapse of the real estate industry, over a decade ago, was only just recently deemed to have stemmed from the actions of one innocent guy. Hundreds of thousands of real estate transactions, all timed to close on the same day, cancelled because one guy decides to keep his house. The resulting domino effect quickly produced an administrative and logistical tsunami. Untold millions of closings canceled, values plunged, rates rose, banks couldn't re-sell the gazillion foreclosed homes.

Within two years, half of the US is homeless. Laws get re-written, hitchhiking is allowed, legalized camping on federal and state lands, big-rig cocoonmotels proliferate, new jobs recycling trash, cleaning up the highways, the roamadic middleclass metastasizes: *Homeomobilius Americanos.*

Enoy guzzles more Mojave Joe's water, secures his pack, and weaves past sweaty vagabonds stepping outside, into the bright Novo California sunshine. He hikes down the crowded highway past crumbling adobes welded together with mazes of rusted-out railroad boxcars and vehicles. Solar tent villages and transient suburban refugee camps extend into the desert off the broken highway. Darkly fragrant smoke plumes furl upwards where well-armed chefs tend communal cook pits. Spontaneous formations of cars, trucks, bicyclists, ATV's, motor homes, big rigs, busses, motorcycles, and backpackers slowly undulate in swarming caravans: the Roamadic Diaspora. The national speed limit is 35 MPH, but with Mojave traffic sluggishly pressing onward, few go faster than twenty and nobody save the most retched is in a hurry to be anywhere more pleasant. Enoy walks out past the squatter encampments deciding to mark the occasion of his 76th by giving something back to Gaia in particular, and anyone else seeking a little drink.

Revesti arrives at a remote arroyo, stuffs the backpack in a rock crevice and thumbs through his ELD files to find—CLICK!— the thunderous sounds of a gigantic Novo New Mexico lightning storm fly out the device loudly echoing down the bone-dry gully.

Enoy unzips his pants and gleefully releases a perfect arc of pent-up piss that curves nicely back down to earth, solidly drumming the dirt: "Mojave Joe's H2ooooOOHHH's!" he sings out. Pure peals of storm-energy blast from the ELD recording, cascading sonic waveforms up into in the atmosphere.

Enoy spies faint filigrees of cloud formations appearing in the distance, sucking together in a sudden storm front. He arches backwards to finish peeing as the device plays back huge splatter-drop sounds from the recorded rainstorm. Enoy zips up and raises his arms skyward: "Happy Birthday to you!"

Thunder echoes forth from the ELD as real lightning flashes overhead. A cluster of chubby clouds move in over Mojave and angrily explode. Colossal torrents of rain release over a fifty-mile footprint as Enoy hears hundreds of Mojave Homeomobilius hooting hysterically, howling, sloshing, and gawking as lightning bolts quiver through the clouds to thunderous applause. Enoy takes a bow then stoops low, kissing the moist mud, while humming in a low drone, "Mmmmmmmmmmmmmmmmm".

Twenty minutes later Revesti stands soaking wet, alone in the major Mojave hitchhiking zone. Everyone else is searching for water, chasing the surprise storm. Enoy pulls out his $martcard and holds it in the air. Earlier he bid $e.1 per mile on PayPerRideSys. It shouldn't be difficult to get a good ride now. Enoy's hitchhiking card immediately vibrates with a live one: BZZZZZZZ!

A motor home pulls out of traffic and stops. Revesti's card screen shows: *William Blurr 5682245988756 Registered NOVO CA.* Blurr's registered with the Cultural Management Agents. He looks harmless enough on the card's video clip. Enoy elects to climb out of the rain and into the RV.

Billy Blurr keeps both hands on the wheel and smiles at him. Enoy stows his pack in the kitchenette and takes the shotgun seat. Revesti likes Blurr immediately: curly blond hair, wiry, blue-eyed and buck-toothed. Billy's overhead smartcard visor announces:

"Enoy Revesti. Two ecrement$ per mile."

"Nice to meet you, Elroy."

"Likewise, William," Enoy deftly mimics Billy's body language, lazy smile, and California drawl. "Going to L.A., bro?"

"Yep..." Billy accelerates into west bound traffic. "Then up north. Bay Area."

"Nectar. I'll probably get off in Babylonwood," Enoy squints at the younger man, discreetly examining his bioplasmic energy emanations. He spies an oddly-pinched knot of pink filaments near the center of Billy's right knee. Normally these bundles result from numerous and severe epileptic seizures.

"This storm is downright spooky, Elroy."

"Yeah. A real pisser...Nectar RV."

"It's not mine. I'm the delivery man. It's a refurb. ELD's dead."

"Yeah?" Enoy eyes the dashboard ELD and sees the underlying electronic components as collections of spectral energy phenomena, each unit emitting a faint, nearly dead, electronic aura. Enoy bends forward and observes a small black sphere hovering just underneath the main ELD display. He smacks the spot sharply with his palm—BLIP!—The sleeping system instantly kicks on, blasting the hit rocktro anthem '*Remember the Future*'.

"Wowzus!" Billy yelps. "What'd you do, Elroy?"

"Hooked you up, bro!"

"Slowedownlight is my favorite rocktro band. Thanks, man!" Billy flips down his visor and presses the 'cancel' tab. "Yer riding for free."

"Thank you, William."

"Call me Billy."

Enoy notices that Blurr is wearing a Marriage Marble on a leather necklace. M2 is a 247365 mobile media spouse-link. The marble-sized unit sells hundreds of millions worldwide. Virtual spouses seldom if ever encounter each other in person but are always linked, and it doesn't turn off. That's the rub. "Married, Billy?" Enoy asks.

"Oh man, I forgot to introduce my wife. Maya? Sweetie? ...Anyway, Maya lives in Amsterdam and is hopefully asleep." Billy slips the M2 necklace back into this shirt. "Alone."

"Amsterdam's zoopy," admits Enoy, reading a dilapidated freeway sign: *Los Angeles 85 Miles*. Billy steers around a dead coyote and heads further west, beyond the miracle storm, singing along with Slowedownlight:

> *Yeah, it's gonna get better, then it's gonna get worse*
> *With small amounts of water there at first.*
> *Yeah, it's gonna get better*
> *Then it's gonna get worse, worse, much worse.*
> *Cause everybody's covered by the Curse...'*

$E500M

Marco heads out of the apartment dressed in his Bovinity jumpsuit replete with black Holstein spots against off-white. Looking large and amorphous, Shub blends right into the milling citizenry on Haight Street, the majority of who are similarly dressed in RanchoDeluxe getups emblazoned with stylized goat, pig, horse, cattle and similar barnyard animal totems.

Marco passes a queue in front of the '*Tiger! Tiger!*' a tattoo-removal parlor employing microgroove cauterization. It works alright, but deep in the subcutaneous fat layers the tattoos persist as invisible scar tissue. When the capillaries fill with blood during orgasm, laughter, sobbing, puking, rage and embarrassment, it causes normally invisible scars to briefly GLOW. "Dejatoos!" Shub spews aloud. Fleshy fashion distractions cannot retract from the ultimate joy this day will bring he vows.

Shub is suddenly aware that his own curly black hair is uncombed for the meeting he just slapped $e50K down for...*when you pay fifty large you can look anyway but boring.* Shub goes to hail a taxi but observes the roamad-chocked traffic jam. He decides to walk to the offices of Vilter & Vilter.

Marco yanks out his ELD: "Billy..." Blurr left two messages in the last hour and Marco doesn't want to be hustled into calling back just to be unwittingly patched live into another one of Billy's webgridz performances. First message: Billy raves about showing up in the Haight. Shub fast-forwards through the second call. More of the same.

Marco's too busy for Billy's bullshit. Billy knows Shub is keeping a stealth profile, especially after the fiasco with ShubTools where the client took and ran with Marco's new swarmbay plug-ins—the very same code tree that later became the basis for swarmshopping as we know it today—A trillion dollar industry and Marco gave his piece away for what? To get his ShubTools brand established? Obviously it didn't work or he wouldn't be alone now in his endeavors creating the PUPP technology.

But this time he is wiser and is retaining the services of V&V, the attorneys who closed the EarthLingua Standardization deals, forever marginalizing the competing StoryPictures and VizuaLanguage universal human-machine interfaces. Victor Vilter was also the principal in the famous PerformingPackages IP lawsuit that enabled the inventor to get paid automatically from every performance. Each time a cereal box, candy wrapper or carton of soymilk plays back media clips at you from the shelf, the inventor gets $e2. Two webgridz minutes from every single playback on every performing package in the world?...*That be a shitload of ecrement$!*...But Shub needs an outright sale to DataMynd...*The ideal PUPP deal!*

The dilapidated Transamerica pyramid building housing the ostentatious law offices of Vilter & Vilter overlooks the SanFranciscOakland megalopolis. The first thing Marco focuses on, once alone inside their panoramic conference room, is a barely noticeable gold-framed plaque on the back of the main door proclaiming: *'Out of the Room - Out of the Deal'.*

Victor Vilter and his twin brother Vincent Vilter are renowned for their wire-rimed baldness, and the ability to close big, tricky deals in technology and media; precisely why Marco dropped fifty grand in advance for a one-on-one with Victor himself who now emerges smiling and chirpy from another meeting.

Vilter wears an impeccable French business suit and a liberal expression of professional curiosity at this a large, wild-haired, forty-something programmer type in a cow jumpsuit.

Shaking hands, Victor knows absolutely nothing about Shub other than what his assistant Roxxzan told to him just now in the elevator. Shub is a freelance programmer who did something cool once and certainly seems intent on something zoopy here today because he's already coughed the V&V attention-retainer. "Mister Shub, can I get you some refreshment, mayhap?" Victor offers.

"Whiskey would be perfect," Shub admits.

"We've got whiskey here...somewhere..." Victor white-lies.

"Water will be just fine, really."

"For myself as well, I'm afraid." Victor fetches crystal tumblers and bladders of Rancho-D water. "So, Mr. Shub?"

"Call me Marco," Shub guzzles the mineral water, "I want to sell my software. I think you can help. Can I use your ELD?"

"Certainly," Victor swivels a large format view screen from the wall and dims the room lights. Marco shows his hands to the screencam—evoking the EarthLingua gestural mode—and speed dials Z.

"Yes my Marcotecht?" The PUPP instantly materializes.

"Hey. What's she doing, Z?" Shub asks the smiling sobot sitting on the Rancho-D loveseat.

"She's coming home early from work on the bullet train...You?"

"Meeting with Victor Vilter," says Shub.

"Vilter..." Z momentarily mouthing mechanically, "...Victor."

The PUPP appears with such astonishingly photo-real human lifelikeness that only now does Victor realize she's synthetic. "What's with this 'My Marcotecht'?" he barks.

"If your name was Shub, you'd do likewise," Marcotecht justifies.

"And 'she' is what?" Vilter demands.

"A 'Personal Ubiquitous Profile Persona'," Shub enunciates, "A PUPP."

"A what?"

"P-U-P-P," Shub spells out.

Victor jotting notes now, "Hmmm..."

"A digital doppelganger."

"You mean a shopping Synthespian?" Victor guesses.

"No. I'm a cyberclone," Z looks at Vilter. "Of Zuzzan Kaplan."

"Cyberclone?...So? New?" Vilter yiddishes.

"New? Howzabout a virtual replicant that looks, talks, shops and fucks, exactly like you?"

Victor grins, "Fucks like me?" He's warming to Marco. "You don't really mean me, you mean the royal 'you'," Victor clarifies.

"A person with a PUPP on them has absolutely no idea that it even exists."

"Oh? Not sure about the market for something like that," Vilter admits.

"Not obvious at first glance." Marco leans back in the overstuffed lawyer chair, "Think about it this way, Victor, with a PUPP you only need someone's name and some kind of number to get going. A New Totality, driver's license, e-mail or ELD address. Ok? The PUPP bites down into this tiny tidbit and doggedly digs up your entire background over the webgridz. Within a few days your PUPP looks exactly like you."

"I live in a replica of Zuzzan's dwelling," supplies Z.

13

"Made digital duplicates of all your stuff!"

"Memorized your shopping and transactional behavior."

"Has your medical records, dental, driving, academic, employment"—

"—personal media, photos, video clips, security cam footage."

"It reads your mail before you do! Knows all about your friends and family. The PUPP follows you around on the webgridz, invisibly updating itself!"

"I see. The PUPP knows you better than you know yourself," Victor discerns.

"Right!" Z affirms.

"Now give it a superior reasoning engine, add real-time behaviorokinesthetics and wrap it with my fractal-anti-fractal security cloak? Shazam! A healthy PUPP!"

"Sounds illegal," Victor informs, "Unless your New Totality or military."

"Correcto."

"So what are you thinking? Military?"

"Nope. It's gotta be a private sale. I can't be liable for whatever the owners might wind up doing with the PUPPS."

"Oh? Then I recommend you leave the legal strategy to V&V..." Vilter strides up the ELD display and squints at Z. "Now show me how these cyberclones work! This one's just sitting there staring at us with those puppy eyes!" Vilter zoomorphosises.

"Z?" says Shub.

"Demo time, my Marcotecht?" Z picks up.

"No. No demo," Marco smiles. "That a new loveseat?"

"Yes. RanchoDeluxe."

"You always buy the RanchoDeluxe brand don't you?"

"I'm not into CrunchyCountry."

"Why not?" Marco requests.

"Not as cool as Rancho-D," decides Z. "Not zoopy enough for me."

"Not zoopy enough? So, thumbs down?" Shub surmises.

"Thumbs down."

Shub shows one of Vilter's water glasses to the micam: "Would you ever purchase one of these?"

"Sure, but my glass would need to be thicker, like an antique tumbler from waybackinthenight or a slightly heavy, nicely chipped Euro goblet."

"So thumbs down?" inquires Marco.

Z gestures definitively.

"What about this?" Shub brandishes one of the polyester napkins.

"Forget it." Z gives a thumbs down.

"Thank you, Z," Shub swivels to face Victor, "Knows what it wants, eh?" Marco grins. "It knows what Zuzzan Kaplan wants and more importantly it knows what she won't buy. Now imagine hundreds of millions of PUPP's replicating consumers all over the world!"

"Hundreds of millions?" Vilter questions. "Doing what?"

"Market research! High-speed market research using synthetic consumer cyberclones."

"You're telling me you could poll hundreds of millions of PUPP's who would instantly tell you if they would buy whatever product?

"Yes! And you can zoom down one-on-one at the individual consumer layer as we now are with Z here. It takes only seconds for a 'thumbs-up or down'."

"How reliable are the results?" Vilter says.

"As reliable as any source ever sourced," Marcotecht promises.

"What do you think would happen if the existence of hundreds of millions of illegal PUPPs ever got out?" Vilter needs to know.

"Worst case scenario? Me go to jail long time. The PUPP code gets distributed free and everyone becomes hopelessly addicted to hanging out with their cyberclone."

"Sounds about right," Victor concurs, his mind beginning to boggle with esoteric PUPP applications in marketing, military, porno and cyber-lawyering.

"Exactly why the PUPP code has to be sold as a product development analysis toolset," Shub's figured out. "Otherwise I'm into all manner of incestuous legal and moral buttfuckery."

"Well put, Mr. Marcotecht," Vilter snorts.

Shub smiles at Vilter for second time. "In a nutshell, I have developed the code creating artificially intelligent human personas, like Z, animated PUPPs, who live inside the webgridz and freely utilize any computer that is online. PUPPs expand and contract, invisibly borrowing spare cycles from almost any processor. They're immortal, you see, even after its host dies the PUPP lives on as a useful consumer cyberclone for an undetermined period of time."

"How does it get past security?"

"I utilize my own strain of fractal-anti-fractal wrappers to get through virtually everything. The PUPP reflects all software environments like a hall-of-mirrors. To security code, a PUPP looks like an counting error, like two open copies of itself. The PUPP systematically drops little pieces of itself on each device the human host uses."

"What?"

"Puppyz, Viceroy. Tiny sobots, sleeping in the host's most frequently used devices. The Puppyz wake up when the host is transacting, collect the media data and forward it to their PUPP Z who updates the cyberclone invisibly. "

Victor getting it better now as both Shub and Z take turns patiently explaining Behaviorokinesthetics 101 to him, detailing how PUPPs exist in virtual visualizations of the host's home and office. They demonstrate how Z eats information, invisibly right-sizes itself, utilizes multidimensional neural net reasoning engines. "How much?" Vilter finally asks.

"How much?" Shub spits back. "Howzabout five-hundred-million international ecrement$? You get half."

"Oh?" Victor now interested all over again: "Two-hundred and fifty million ecrement$ on contingency?"

"Minus the fifty-K I've already paid. In one offshore

transfer. No worries. I've just outmaneuvered the ideal buyer," Shub spouts. "The largest and most powerful Cultural Management Agency—,"

"—DataMynd?" Vilter guesses.

"Yeah! You see, Z here is the cyberclone of Miss Zuzzan Kaplan, DataMynd's Director of Public Relations," Shub reveals.

"You're joking!" Vilter laughs.

"No joke. I figured the best approach to DataMynd was to straight away make the hair on their fucking necks stand up with an instant proof of concept!" Marco divulges. "They realize the power and value of the PUPP product at the exact same moment they understand the horrifying extent to which their own security has been breached."

"Hundreds of thousands of breeches," Z informs.

"I see." Vilter agrees. "It's got to be absolutely foolproof."

"It is. Z's breeches are completely undetectable"

"It's a simple squeeze play then," Victor realizes. "We give DataMynd a forty-eight hour drop-dead window after which we sell the PUPPs down the street," Vilter's done this before.

"Five-hundred million," Marco gloats.

"They'll make it back in a year," admits Victor.

"I have something else you might find relevant," Marco deems. "New information to leverage as needed. You see, Kaplan is having a well-guarded extramarital affair with her boss, the CEO—"

"—Gogoboner?" Vilter filters.

"Bobogoné, Gerald," Z corrects. "Gerald Bobogoné was approved as one of the two-hundred Election Selection candidates last month," backfills Z. "Adultery charges would disqualify him from the Affinity Process."

"First we demo Z. Who just so happens to be a cyberclone of their PR Director who's obviously fucking the boss!" adds Shub.

"No, no, no, Marco, the second punch needs to be

understated. We purposefully pretend that we have no idea about their affair."

"Zuzzan will immediately suspect we know all about it," says the sobot.

"And are pretending not to!" Marco groks.

"Right!" Victor validates. "Then we can stick in their face at a time and place of our choosing." Vilter stares worriedly out the panoramic window, "Who else is in on this, Shub?"

"Nobody. That's the point. You need to be the sole go-between. I'm anonymous."

"Attorney-client privilege isn't always observed in the graymail trade. I can only hold DataMynd off for a little while before their due diligence goons come after you."

"I get two-hundred and fifty million ecrement$—you get the same—DataMynd gets the PUPPS and I disappear offgridz, happily ever after."

"Ok. But I suggest you evaporate now in that case. For five-hundred million, DataMynd will do whatever it takes to fuck us or worse...V&V can do the money part, the business transaction, but you have to handle the disappearing act."

"I built the PUPPs, Victor. I can probably figure out a way to disappear," sneers Shub. "I'm just not sure how quickly."

"Where you gonna go, Shub?" Victor wonders.

"I don't know. XaNa maybe," Marco mentions, knowing very little about the fabled roamadic technotopian community sequestered somewhere in the sticks north of the Novo Vancouver territories.

"You realize that as soon as we show them the PUPP, DataMynd will come after us. The bigger the head start the better. DataMynd will do whatever they need to rip you and twist the deal. Understand?"

"FMB!" squeals Shub.

"Yes, 'Fuck Me Blue' too! We're gonna need a secure line 247. How the hell can we do that if you're disappeared?"

"Howzabout a Marriage Monitor?" Shub considers. "They'll never think of it."

"Not advisable," Victor protests. "We would need to be married to use the M2."

"So? I'm the talent, I do the fancy tricks! You're the attorney; you get the license and the M2."

Two hours later, Marco emerges with an M2 tucked inside his Bovinity outfit. Vilter and Shub have agreed to hide the Marriage Marbles, only communicating when alone as conflicts of interest may arise.

Marco did not expect to have to disappear so quickly. He's been working on several methods of doing just that but all the usual techniques seem fallible. "What's the range on these monitors, Viceroy?" Shub shouts to his marble.

"Around three zillion miles," Vilter answers from his office.

"You alone?"

"As agreed."

"Then fuck you, my friend."

"Fuck me?"

"For speeding up the disappearing act! I need a few more days."

"Too late! We conference with Gogoboner Wednesday. Ten am."

"What? You already contacted them?" Shub's amazed. "Why?"

"Leverage! The Selection Election is in five days. We'll lose that leverage over him unless we hustle," Vilter informs. "Forced march now! Ticking clock!"

"Right..." Shub didn't think about that. Z discovered the abnomaly only just this morning.

"Fancy tricks, Marcotecht! Use them now! Gotta go!" Vilter puts the always-on device into his empty antique snuffbox, blacking out the connection.

Shub stuffs the M2 unit into his cow suit. Once

DataMynd's funds are wired it won't matter but at the moment Marco's feverishly calculating cash-costs to become invisible. If it wasn't for having inherited a little loot from his grandma, Marco would be screwed.

OFFGRIDZ

Shub goes into the neighborhood bank and shuts down his and Grandma's only account: $e106 exchanged as $56,000 American dollars.

Shub stuffs the devalued greenbacks into a hidden cow-suit pouch and heads off thumbing his ELD, deleting accounts and wrapping his assets with fractal-anti-fractal decoys, moving stuff offshore to secure his own ID. Shub stops at a roamad kiosk and buys a waterproof backpack with his emergency cash...*Gotta stay offgridz now.* He turns around a corner to his apartment and spies a large RV parked in his dinky driveway. "F...M...B..." Shub groans, seeing the angular, unmistakable blond bombast that is Billy Blurr.

Six-five, blue-eyes, dirty fingernails, Blurr is speed-packing the motor home's cargo space with media gear. Behind Blurr, a roamadic old bastard belly laughs whilst videoing Height Street tourist-style with an expensive ELD. This unanticipated invasion strikes Shub as somehow nostalgically Merry Pranksteresque.

"El Sharko!" Billy spies Shub trundling toward him. "We drove straight up! Fucking nectronic costume," Billy back-slaps Marco.

"It's not a costume. It's an outfit."

"I like it man! Authentic Rancho!"

"Faraday fabric."

Billy gives him a bear hug and waves Revesti over. "Marco Shub, this here is my rider, Elroy. Elroy was gonna get off in Babylonwood but decided to continue onward when I told him about you."

"Hello, Marco!" Enoy views Shub's aura and sees a healthy, energetic sheen roiling around the cow-costumed body, "Pleased to meet you," Enoy offers his hand roamad-style.

"Likewise..." Shub shakes tentatively, knowing that Billy's acquaintances can be a handful. This old fart seems harmless enough except he's videoing Shub, discreetly aiming an expensive micro-ELD. "If this isn't a performance, then stop recording me," Shub righteously requests.

"Oh! Good eye!" Revesti smilingly switches it off. "Thanks...Forgot."

"...Forgot." Marco repeats.

"So are you coming along, Shubatron?" Billy implores, ignoring his friend's foul mood.

"What?" Shub baffles.

Blurr stares at his childhood crony, "My messages?"

"Didn't listen" Shub can't lie to Billy.

"The Art Therapy Institute fired me but I scored this nectronic gig delivering RV's all over the country!"

"Delivering RV's..." Shub repeats.

"Yeah! The Institute canned my ass because of my TVMOON performance. So I figured FMB! I'll turn my travels it into a brand new piece!"

"A new piece," Shub sputters.

"It will be a hoot! Just for a few weeks? Come on Shubatron! Like waybackinthenight! I'll be your best friend!"

"That's the problem...Where you headed?"

"Novo Arizona, Novo New Mexico, Novo Texas, Novo New Orleans," Billy enthusiastically lists.

"Novo schomvo," Shub refuses to use the 'Novo' state names adopted by the New Totality and normally avoids traveling amongst the hordes of greasy roamads. As much as he doesn't want to get sucked into the theatrical vortex of Billy's megalomaniac hysterics, this may actually be the best way for him to hide out as ordered by Vilter.

"You coming?" Billy lovingly implores. "Please, Shubus Maximus?"

"I'm thinking about it," Shub dangles. "What's the deal, Blurr?"

"The deal is we drop this coach off at a dealership in Stockton and pick up two more referbs, one for you, and one for me. We deliver them to Novo New Mexico, pick up two more for Novo New Orleans, and bring two more back to Stockton. A big circle," Billy maps out. "We party every night and they hand over eighteen hundred ecrement$ each time we deliver a vehicle."

"From who?"

"Cyopolis."

"A supercult, Billy?"

"I don't know, Shubus! Some non-profit churchy thingy. I only deal with their Transpo guys. Maya and I finally get to see the countryside. It's all ecrement$ under the table anyway. No questions asked."

"That part sounds OK," Shub affirms. He remembers Billy met Maya online in an artsy swarmbay six or seven years ago. She was living in Amsterdam trying to commit legally sanctioned suicide along with tens of thousands more in the fashionable Neurotheology Set— overpopulation being the foremost sin committed against Gaia according to certain supercult doctrines—Maya had planned an elaborate candle light final party, floating down the ancient canals, videoing extensively, so she would leave behind a memorable webgridz portfolio. Billy somehow talked her out of it and married her remotely. They've still not met face-to-face yet and with the borders closed they probably never will. "How is she?" Marco inquires.

"She's fine, thanks," Billy replies. "Well, big guy? Shall we dance?"

"Yeah, let's go. What the hell," Shub seems to agree, "but there is a condition which must be religiously adhered to or all is doomed for reasons I cannot mention."

"Like what?" Billy burps.

"Don't ask," Marco looks Enoy up and down: "Are you staying here or coming along old timer?"

"Would love to tag along, thanks." Revesti is now getting the chance to observe the subtler aspects of Shub's energetic aura emanations which are—even more so than Billy's—wobulating in extremely rare filamentary couplings. "I'm glad to cook when you guys have had your fill of ballmeat," Enoy offers.

"Yes!" bleats Blurr. He enjoys Elroy's self-sufficiency and he's an old hand in the ways of the roamads.

Shub concedes with a non-committal half-nod and lowers his voice: "OK...The conditions are as follows: We go offgridz starting now. Dark black except for Billy's M2. No calls, no transactions. Cash only."

"In trouble again, Bro?" Billy questions conspiratorially.

"No. Business deal. Can't have it fucked up." Shub summarizes.

"Fine," Billy agrees. "But we reserve the right to video. We'll keep it on us until the trip is over?"

"Nothing goes out. Not a thing," Shub commands.

"All for Shub and Shub for All!" Billy concurs.

"Billy, I'm serious. Absolute communications blackout or I bail," Shub sees Enoy smiling up at him, "That a problem for you?"

"No," Enoy straps his backpack on. "I'm pretty much blacked-out already. I don't drive real well but fix electronics and cook if need be."

"Enoy's only too happy to guide us through conversational treatises on obtuse topics regarding roamadic culture and history!" Billy evangelizes.

"I see," Shub's starting to enjoy this old coot now...*Elroy's an archetypical 'Wandering Clown'!* Marco muses. "Got good boo, Elroy?"

"That I do," Revesti winks.

"Speq?" inquires Shub.

"No Sir," assures Enoy. "Enoy Revesti teetotals but for a bit of boo now and then."

"Enoy?" Billy frowns. "Thought your name was Elroy."

"I like Elroy," Revesti admits.

"Yeah? Then that's your new handle from this day forward, bro! Elroy!" brands Billy.

"Elroy! The Wandering Clown?" Enoy asks Shub.

Marco blinks back bewilderment...*Fucker read minds?*

CONFLICTS OF INTEREST

The Manhattan apartment of Zuzzan Kaplan is on the 23rd floor of a mostly vacant co-op on 96th. Zuzzan kicks off her shoes and flops exhausted into the new loveseat. The end of the day was tense but thrilling. Gerald told her that Vilter & Vilter wanted a confidential powwow pronto... *This could only mean something big! A New Totality contract? The Affinity Selection? Yes!* It figures that someone would insert the Vilter's at some point. After all, if Bobogoné is picked for the office of the Most High he'll accept his presidential candidacy and snag the long-term NT storage contract for DataMynd anyway! Zuzzan knows the routine... *Too many conflicts of interest.*

Zu's Public Relations directorship has become all consuming. For well over a year now, tirelessly lobbying Sister Pynchon's people, spending half her time negotiating with attorneys. At least she gets to meet some interesting people. Zuzzan met Sister Pynchon only once and was floored by her original insight: *'Only through the purity of numbers can we achieve a lasting affinity with 'His*

Resonance.'

The sister invented the Affinity Process after the electoral voting methodology was declared unconstitutional by the New Totality. The old system finally imploding when less than six percent of American voters cast ballots, the rest is recent history: Constitutional Convention with alternate voting systems analyzed and debated by the hastily formed New Totality commission. Then out of left field comes a 33-year old computer scientist who is also a practicing Catholic Nun, Sister Paula Pynchon.

The good sister devising a simple method that satisfies the Council's strict mandate regarding the absolute lock-out of political parties, special interest groups, lobbyists, and specious persuasion of any kind whatsoever.

The sister's *Affinity Process* solved the problem elegantly: every registered voter's name is entered into a single database and double-checked. The names are then hyper-randomized in a totally autonomous meta-algorithmic randomity process where a single name is plucked from the soup of voters, totally free of outside influence. The One voter then elects the president from a pool of 200-hundred pre-qualified candidates drawn from across the Novo American social spectrum. *'One Voter, One Vote, One Leader',* Zuzzan remembers the sister intoning thrice in the five minutes they were together.

NEUROPLASTISITY

Billy has the RV on auto-pilot and is able to drive just fine stoned. It will take forever to get to Stockton anyway. Elroy lights up two reefers and passes one to Shub and one to Billy. Marco hits the joint and immediately becomes aware of the M2 tickling his belly.

He and Blurr are enthusiastically reviving their age-old competition over which of them has the coolest movie idea. Neither has altered their basic concepts for at least a decade and both are deemed mutually zoopy. So it's been a virtual stalemate all these years.

"What's your movie about, Billy?" Enoy asks from back in the bedroom area, ELD out and recording.

"It's called 'L'," Billy decides. "That's the title."

"Really?" chides Marco, not having settled on a name for his own movie as of yet.

"The way that the amphibious apes can tell one of their own in the dark is by making the sound of 'L'..." Billy pronounces.

"Because of their amphibious diet, the bone mass in the jaws has decreased, allowing for a more flexible palate; naturally evolving into a mouth with a tongue that could bend upright behind the front teeth to make the 'L' sound," Marco's memorized.

"Right! ' L' is the first spoken word uttered by the most evolved apes on Earth! They ululate!" Blurr postulates.

Marco feels Blurr is sometimes overly creative and therefore dangerous to an extent. Waybackinthenight, Billy was an ace visual effects consultant to the industry but was blacklisted after he spewed a spacey rant at an awards ceremony, trashing the studios big time on primetime. For the last ten years he has been an intermedia instructor at the California Institute of Art Therapy. He sucks in a blast of Elroy's boo. "Tell Elroy," Shub insists.

"Ok. For Elroy, I shall tell the epic of 'L'," Billy readily acquiesces, taking a ceremonial puff on the resinous roach. "You see Elroy, millions of years ago there occurred a cataclysmic earthquake whereby the north-eastern tip of the continent of Africa was separated from the rest of the landmass by a sudden rising ocean level, creating an island—"

"—The Flood. During the opening credits," Shub helpfully informs.

"Tribes of apes are trapped on the island in the tree tops sticking out of the water—"

"—One of the treed apes is pregnant and giving birth, but she accidentally falls off a branch into the water and drowns," Shub dutifully details.

"—We quickly dissolve over and over, speeding up time, showing the island evolving millions of years into the future. The ocean finally recedes enough to create a lovely beach where we see a large tribe of intelligent hairless apes..." Billy whispers wilder now.

"Naked apes," Shub underlines.

"Standing upright, fishing with their hands," Blurr

visualizes. "Making fires on the beach, swimming in the surf."

"Near the ocean cliffs there's a hot springs where a group of female apes are assisting with the birth of a newborn," reports Dr. Shub. "Water-birthing in the tide pools."

"We see one particularly large alpha-male ape swimming in the ocean alone," continues Billy. "Way farther out than the other apes can go. He is swimming with a porpoise who playfully circles round and round. The alpha-ape grabs the friendly fish's fin and it tows him way out in the clam ocean, twice as far from the beach then he normally goes."

"We only then notice that the main continent is really about two miles away all these millions of years," inserts Shub.

"But the aquatic apes have no concept of anything outside the island! The dolphin brings this alpha-ape to a shallow coral reef where the waters have receded enough to expose a long skinny sand bar forming a natural bridge that connects to the main landmass," Billy breathes, stuck in the usual traffic cram, thousands of hitchers waving reflective $e cards over their heads.

"Yeah..." Maya appears on the tiny video display embedded in Billy's Marriage Marble. She's Eurasian, thirty-something, American accent. "I like the fish friend!" From the M2 at her husband's neck.

"What happens is, this particular ape is the leader of the island primates. He puts together the best male swimmer-apes to ride dolphins out to the land bridge."

"Albeit unknown to them at the time, the alpha–ape's pregnant mate has followed them out on a fish of her own!" Shub intercuts.

"That's right! Can't forget about Eve!" Billy says. "So these dozen or so humanesque apes hike to the mainland and encounter a very primitive, much less evolved tribe of continental killer apes."

"Hairy fuckers, dragging their knuckles," Shub demonstrates.

"The killer monkeys are savage, war-like carnivores whereas the island apes are nonviolent fish eaters. Anyway, the bad apes attack the good apes on the beach, murder a few, then kidnap the leaders' pregnant mate and disappear swinging away through the trees," Blurr abbreviates the much longer epic battle and gruesome abduction details.

"Laughing at the naked islanders," Marco apes.

"They feel a vague shame for their hairlessness and they don't know what to do so they rub mud all over their bodies and give chase into the jungle forest where they encounter all kinds of strange new mainland animals and environments," Blurr indicates.

"The island is basically Eden," Shub recontextualizes.

"But the jungle's bad news. They finally find some caves where the evil monkeys live. The kidnapped mate is huddled alone in their bone-yard hidey-hole."

"The female monkeys are jealous of Eve," Shub subtitles.

"The good apes wind up using their knowledge of fire and water to defeat the evil ones and rescue the expectant mate just in time to do a water birth in the hot springs," Billy compresses an hour of screen time into one sentence. "My 'Hominid Vision' battle sequence will blow the retinas off of even the most fatally far-gone visual effects aficionado."

"What about the scene where the evil apes try to steal the fire by plucking all the hair off of their bodies, and then sneak into the camp?"

"That's the new scene! The evil apes can't ululate, so the human apes don't give them the secret of fire!"

Shub squints into Billy's smoke and mirrors: "They withhold the secret of the fire!"

"Because they're not human!

"They can't even say 'L'."

"The aquatic apes have to make it back to the coral bridge and ride the dolphin's home before the legion of evil monkeys catch up. I have the islanders doing the hot springs water birth then running out of food because they're not able to catch the local beasties and the mainland foliage is foreign to them."

"These guys eat fish and there isn't any fish in the jungle except piranha in the ponds." Shub corroborates.

"The mommy ape discovers a shitload of mushrooms appearing like magic under a fig tree after a lightning storm. They hungrily munch the fungi down and hang around the campfire."

"Hallucinating all night long," Shub shrills.

"And evolving like crazy! Proto-humans on 'schrooms,'" Billy maintains. "They become 'schroo-man' beings!"

"They just so happen to be at the stage in their neurological evolution where the neocortex is making its first tentative attempts to interconnect the separate brain regions and integrate the perceptual world," spews forth Shub.

"Integrate the perceptual world!?" Enoy bellows in mock-horror.

"It's a movie!" Blurr justifies.

"Oh..." Enoy-one-ear-and-out-the-other. "...Yeah."

"Then—during the hallucination sequences—Adam the alpha ape starts making new visual connections in the patterns all around him. Patterns that have always been there in nature but only now does he witness the world as truly visually interconnected. He sees for the very first time through 'human' eyes," Billy envisions. "He feels a painful separation from the universe that wasn't there only moments ago and suddenly observes himself as a distinct, autonomous almost-human being."

"The emergence of the ego," analyses Herr Shub.

"Yes, it's the first shocking moment of free will, the realization that he is one with everything but separate from it at the same time."

"Then, Adam ape gets an 'idea' for the first time," Marco moves on.

"And he begins to softly ululate...It grows louder as the other 'shroom-eaters join in," Billy choreographs. "They sing out the 'L' sound in increasingly complex vocalizations and harmonic unisons, trance-dancing around the fire, singing swifter, joyfully elevating each other with gleaming eyes and flushed faces!"

"Neocortex' mushrooming!" Marco dances out. "They mind-merge in a mutual psychic breakthrough!"

"Symbolic thought is born!" Billy flops down on the couch and gnaws at his nails: "I still can't figure out what the first fucking symbol is."

"A symbolic problem," Shub sarcasts.

Revesti comes into the living room whore-haired, road weary, "We only generate symbols..." Enoy humbly submits, "...by mentally separating them from a background."

"The background..." Shub speaks.

"The newly formed neural connections," Enoy further submits, "enable Adam ape to create an internal mental separation between object and background. Once you have separation, then you can form mental image systems of interrelated parts represented by various symbols."

"That's it!" Billy's inner brain bubble brightens: "Neuroplasticity! And in the case of the advanced, aquatic apes..." Billy bespeaks fifteen years of pseudo-scientific research, "...it started with the single uttered word, 'L', repeated over and over and over. Took over a million years for the jaws to shrink and the brainpan to grow," Blurr provides. "The whole mouth changed."

"I see..." Completely unnoticed by the two, Enoy is delicately mirroring Marco's body language and vocal intonations: "So...What's the symbol he makes up?" Enoy does Shub.

"I don't know..." ponders Billy.

"Billy's been stuck on that for at least five years," Maya

confirms.

"Can't be phallic!" ejaculates Shub. "Like a mushroom!"

"It's a circle," Enoy mutters matter-o-factly.

"A circle!" Billy sees it now!

"The circle is 'object' and everything outside is the 'background'."

"Elroy you aren't as dumb as I look!" Billy esteems enlightened: "FMB! I've got it! Adam draws a circle in the sand and shows it to his people. The circle works! It wobulates every level at once! The circle is home! Journey's end," Billy realizes.

"The womb!" Shub regresses, "Mother's face!"

"The moon!" Maya offers, tiny M2 voice cutting in: "The sun!"

"The circle is us!" beholds Billy.

"And everything outside is 'other'," demarcates Enoy.

"Now I can finish the damn thing! All right!" the two shake roamad-style. "Thanks, Elroy," Billy gratefully gripping the older mans' paw.

"...Thanks, Elroy," Shub repeats. Marco hears echoing in his head. He checks to make sure his lips aren't moving, mouthing the silent words. It would not be good for Shub if the Repeating Disease reared its hated head again. Not now. Shub thought he had finally outgrew the bizarre childhood habit of whispering the last few words said to him before responding. Given a 'How's it going?' Shub would echo-whisper: 'How's it going?' as if repeating the words would insure that he understood that was being said. Adults had a hard time talking with young Shub because they didn't know how to take the constant repetition. Having your own words mirrored back to you by a child always makes them sound hollow and disingenuous. The other kids just thought he was a retardo.

"Stockton!" alerts Billy. The Neo Mobility RV dealership in deserted downtown Stockton is pitch-black at 2:30 am. Billy parks in the enormous lot, eerily vacant except for half-a-dozen empty motor homes. Shub and Enoy are unloading their backpacks as a dilapidated Hummer pulls in. Billy speaks with the driver. They exchange keys and depart. "We take those two big mothers."

Blurr makes Shub practice basic RV handling maneuvers in the parking lot before heading off into the night, commandeering their twin *Comanchero* coaches, Enoy riding with Billy.

In less than an hour Shub follows Blurr into a crowded New Totality overnight zone near the *California Center for the Criminally Insane.* They lock themselves in their wagons and crash.

LOVE BUMP

Stamford, Connecticut, DataMynd Corporation: the infamous but low-key Cultural Management Agency. CEO Gerald Bobogoné was at headquarters by 7:33 am today. Chubby, balding, fifty-two, Bobogoné looks ten years older despite expensive age-regression procedures. Gerry has suddenly developed a nervous habit of sucking his lower lip producing a flagrant bite-sized hickey. The incredible stress of juggling so many hot deals seems to be pissing Bobogoné off more and more...*Only a few days until the Affinity Selection!*

Zuzzan strides into the CEO's suite. She's usually first to arrive so Gerry's presence at this hour slows her purposeful step, "Morning early bird!"

"Zu." He notices her haircut, "You are gorgeous." They quickly kiss. She spies his empurpled lip. "What's that fucking snake Victor Vilter want anyway?" Bobogoné baffles.

"Wouldn't say," Zuzzan sits. "Until the call tomorrow. You know those guys, self-important hatchet men."

"Do we have anyone inside V&V?"

"I don't know."

"Then check it out, Zu! I want you to coordinate a special mining team right now. We've gotta get the jump on it. We'll need Vilter's meeting logs and webgridz activity from the last few days; get copies off all the pubcam, parking structure and business surveillance video within two blocks of their offices. We need to see everybody who enters the building," Bobogoné orders, adding: "There's too much going on and I don't really trust anyone now but you, Zu," Gerald sums up.

"Consider it done."

"Thanks babe," Gerald's aroused by the day's swelling events, greatly relieved that his sexy and capable Zuzzan is here by his side. "Candidate's call still on with Sister Pynchon, right?"

"High noon. The other candidates are pathetic, Gerry. There's three retired slaughter house barons, a dozen bankrupt housing developers, a hundred brain-dead X-congressmen and the rest are normal schmoes, mostly desperado roamads," Zuzzan reassures her ambitious lover.

"I guess that means that if I'm an apolitical vegetarian homeowner who can talk and chew gum..." Bobogoné stereotypes.

"You are," Zuzzan knows too much.

"Then I'm it," Gerald figures.

"Of course you big ape!" Zuzzan smooches his sweaty forehead, wonders if it was she that gave him the Love Bump.

WAYBACKINTHENIGHT

"Shub!" Marco's eyes slam open: "Got a question," Victor's voice over the M2. Shub slept on his arms again and can't maneuver the damn device now wedged under his chest. Marco manages before tumbling ass-first onto floor like an amnesiac amputee, blood starved appendages all nonsense now.

"Can you hear me Shub?"

Shub chinning himself, "I hear you," wiggling onto the refurb carpet, smelling bacon and polymers.

"Marco, I need to know something I forgot to ask regarding the PUPPs. Is there a way to disable them? Shut them down after they get going?"

"Yes. But if there's a single back-up copy of any given PUPP it can re-instantiate itself fairly rapidly."

"What about a back door?" asks the inquisitive attorney: "You left a back door, I hope, Maestro Marcotecht?"

"Not on these Puppyz," Shub lies, determined to keep this ace to himself, just in case he needs to put an end to

38

the artful life forms.

"Shit. Why not?"

"Freedom," Marco quickly conjures: "Freedom from ultimate responsibility."

"Really...Ok Marco, well enough for now but we need to demo Z to DataMynd tomorrow. How we gonna do that?"

Shub gains use of one arm, fumbles with the Marriage Marble until he can see the tiny viewscreen up close: "I'll dial Z from a pubterm, call you and you conference us in with DataMynd. They can interview her free-form. Z's on video. I'm only on audio," Shub assures. "Zuzzan's on the call as well?" Shub is a little shy about speaking with her because she'll be extremely pissed!

"Bobogoné, Kaplan, you, me and Z."

"Out of the Room—Out of the Deal?" Shub mocks.

"That's right! Very observant," Victor smiles...*Only one in two hundred schmucks ever notices the Vilter Family Motto plaque!*

"In other words," Shub re-phrases. "Don't blink?"

A sudden KNOCK KNOCK at the Shub motor home door and: "Breakfast!" Billy bellows outside in the noonday sun.

"Coming!" Shub shouts—then Soto into the M2—"Gotta go." He tucks the spouse-link away and rubs his arms for circulation. Zipping into the Rancho-D jumpsuit, Marco optimistically bounds bovine-like from the RV and—parked in the garbage last night!—Shub sucks air, clenching teeth.

Roamad pedestrians and multitudes of all manner of vehicles trundle past the over-crowded NT overnight zone. Shub spies Enoy going in and out of Billy's RV. He slowly saunters over, limping around bulging government trash bags stamped with the hellish New Totality logo.

Blurr shields his eyes from the piercing sun as his big buddy staggers up to him through the rotting refuse. "Who you 'talkin to back there, Shubinski?" Billy asks. "Thought we was dark black."

"Talking to myself as usual..." Shub covers.

"Food!" Enoy announces from the dining room window

of Billy's RV. True to promise, Enoy made a cowboy breakfast using his own road-kit. He bought red potatoes, garlic, onions, rosemary, eggs, bacon and bread from roamad vendor vans and Billy made java from black market beans smuggled in from Mexico. They wolf Enoy's tasty cuisine in silence; conversation difficult due the honking, yelling, singing, yapping traffic of the homeless roamadic masses in motion.

Blurr waves a burnt bit of bacon before him, shouts over the din: "Remember, don't use the appliances. These coaches are to be sold as referbs but they need to look as new as possible. Use the public facilities. Nothing's hooked up so if you get in trouble or need to use the can, flash your high-beams. Let's not get separated with no way to reconnect. Unless we get on the gridz," Billy cautions.

Marco can't rightfully remember whether he got up and used the little Plexiglas toilet night last but the sleeping bag was bone-dry.

"We exchange these for two more at their transpo yard which, unfortunately, isn't on the map," Billy divulges, over-indulged on Mexican espresso: "I've only been there once so we've gotta arrive during daytime so I can see where the hell we are."

"Not on the map?" questions Shub.

"Nope. Unmarked dirt roads about thirty-minutes north of Taos," explains Blurr. "They do RV refurbishing out there," Billy remarks around a mouthful of what he once considered to be 'DBC': Dead Baby Chickens.

Shub polishing off the potatoes. He's not traveled outside of the Bay Area for at least eight years. Up-close the sights and sounds of the real roamads are definitely culture-shocking. Marco's not spent much time thinking about the quasi-totalitarian social, economic and legal changes that have reshaped the world. He's been too busy creating the PUPPs 247365, hiding out solo, lamb's blood smeared over apartment door—passed over—which was the only way Shub coped with the personal upheaval caused by the simultaneous failure of ShubTools, Inc. and Marco's brief marriage.

Shub has to admit that being on the roamadic broken highway is oddly exhilarating; and Billy seems in top frenetic form despite his being fired from the Institute. Shub has to come up with a name for his own movie epic now that Blurr has decided on 'L'. Which of the two's worldview will dominate their consensual reality. This power dance has been going on ever since Billy and Marco were eight-years old. Waybackinthenight, wild-eyed Blurr would bang on Shub's window around two am, pellet pistol glistening in the street lights. The two would embark on nocturnal pranking exercises with the unspoken goal of frightening each other into chickening out, crying, getting caught, injured or even killed. For many years Billy was the de-fault prank leader but with Marco's accidental discovery of the Love Tunnels at age twelve, Shub ruled supreme for many moons. Marco hasn't thought about the tunnel system for a long time and he won't do so now.

PROCESSING ETERNITY

Zuzzan applies a touch of heavy base make-up underneath Bobogoné's puffy lip to hide the self-inflicted hickey: "Ok...You look great!"

Gerald sits in front of the DataMynd ELD awaiting the conference call link-up with between Sister Pynchon and the 200 Presidential Selection candidates scattered across Novo America.

Zuzzan walks out of micam view and watches Gerald from across the room. She silently toasts him with a glass of mineral water: Saluda!

"Pronounce your name?" the meeting coordinator requests.

"Gerald Bobogoné," enunciates Gerry, proud of the Euroesque accent on the 'ne'.

"Please stand by."

"OK," Bobogoné gives his wounded lip a peppy mini-suck...*What a bizarre turn of events that put me in the lineup for president. Granted it would only be a titular post due to the veto power of the global New Totality*

Council...Nevertheless I would be King Gerald! Just the unprecedented publicity itself would be worth the hassle. Never again would he want for notoriety. After serving four years of symbolic leadership, he could do anything!

Today the candidates were going to have the luxury of gathering together in a webgridz swarm group so they can browse each other on micam and get a good look at the competition. Bobogoné's DataMynd spooks have illicitly inserted a little something into the Sister's swarm server which will capture the behavior of each individual as they browse other candidates. Rex figures they will be able to determine, after content analysis, whom in the group is naturally numerically 'charmed'.

"Welcome Affinity Candidates..." Sister Pynchon addresses the two hundred remote participants. The sister is not dressed in her usual business suit today but in a full black Latin habit with pearl white Swiss wimple and winged bonnet. Her high-energy 376 Lbs. causing the wooden podium platform to sporadically CREAK!: "Welcome and congratulations on surviving the draconian background checks necessary to insure that only solid Novo Americans are represented here today. After all, in a few days, one of you will be beyond our scrutiny," Paula chides.

It's rumored that the sister was a mortician's apprentice before entering a convent in Hollywood waybackinthenight. This gruesome tenure imbued her with a gallows humor that enrages and delights wherever she goes. "We have gathered here today for you to virtually meet and greet," Pynchon contextualizes, "If only for a few moments."

Gerry ignores the nun and scans the other candidates' thumbnails: webgridz media stars, truck drivers, rocktro artists...*None of these losers have the compute power behind them that I do!*

"As you recall, when the Affinity Process is completed the new president has to select a six-member cabinet who will work with the New Totality Council to bid out the Government Systems contracts."

Bobogoné browses and beholds media Execs, X-politicos, oil war vets, open-border activists, ridiculous roamads, tele-teachers...*Zu was right! What a pathetic lot of louts.* It's the webgridz stars that Gerry fears most...*Some jerk will just pick their favorite face.* Bobogoné half-listens as Pynchon addresses her flock of innocent hopefuls.

"The Selectee may even choose their presidential cabinet from amongst our follow candidates here today. Please consider this option carefully. Before us is gathered the purest representative group of natural born leaders our country has ever known," Pynchon preaches. "If the president and cabinet do not have direct experience tendering large-scale government contracts, the New Totality Council will provide high-level expertise to insure professionalism," pronounces Sister Pynchon.

...What a scam! Private companies staffed by military and two-party politicos from waybackinthenight running the system like a factory. Gerry zooms in on a buxom horse trainer from Santa Fe for the third time...

"You have all seen the media reports and suffered through horrific criticisms of the revolutionary process we are now engaged in. You'll notice there's no media here today!" Whistles and applause radiate from scores of remote candidates. "Thank you all for your farsighted participation in a great experiment that will hopefully set humankind on a new course toward enlightened self-governance and self-knowledge. Mathematics is a divine gift from God to humankind. We should use this gift whenever possible and—for those who haven't already done so—I recommend you read my new book, *'Processing Eternity',* which details the three-fold holy vision of the Affinity Process," Pynchon proselytizes.

Bobogoné has long since abandoned any semblance of humanitarian ethos as reflected in the self-serving company motto he insisted be appended to the DataMynd logo: *'People Helping People to Help People Help Us'*.

When the physical borders were closed by the NT, only the most ferocious competitors survived, only the most twisted existed profitably, and in DataMynd's case, that required diversification into the black arts of corporate espionage where their professional services are excellently rendered and excessively billed.

"Please feel free to browse and mingle amongst yourselves now. I am of course available to answer questions as required by force of law," the sister smirks.

Bobogoné holds his hand up for the micam and makes a tight fist gesture causing the DataMynd ELD shut off.

"You don't want to meet and greet?" Zuzzan walks proudly toward her candidate.

"No. I'll throw off the numbers."

"Gotcha..." Zuzzan massages Bobogoné's fat pink neck. "...You know too much."

"Exaaaaaaaactly," growls Gerald in pleasurable pain. "What do we have on the Vilter situation?"

"So far there are no nails sticking up. We've snarfed the V&V sign-in screens and Vilter's meeting schedule, but no flashing red lights yet. "

"Let me see the names."

"Sure..." Zuzzan waves her hand in a circle over her head and the ELD flips on showing a list of fourteen names appearing over the course of the last two days' appointments.

"I want deep background checks on every one of them," the CEO commands.

"Already done."

"And?"

"Like I said, there are no stick-up nails."

"Hey!" Gerald's eyes parse the list: "Who's this fucking 'Blarko Hubb'?" Bobogoné chokes on the words.

"No such person. We figured it's one of their personal friends joke name."

"It's no fucking joke, Zu! That's your nail sticking up! Right there!"

"Your own experts concluded that it was a fucking joke name and I think they're right!" Kaplan courageously counters.

"I want video of this bastard entering and exiting the building!"

"Already working on it," seethes Zuzzan.

"Do an NT face-match," bosses Bobogoné.

"Already working on it!" Zuzzan snips at him.

"That's my Zuzzy!" Gerry flip-flops, all hugs and kisses, grinning at his Zu. It pleases Bobogoné to watch people twist like bacon in the fry pan. But when Zuzzan twists its ever so erotic.

The DataMynd webcam does a micro-swivel, adjusting focus, beaming back video to Z.

DIASPORA

Novo California Interstate Five heading through greater Los Angeles moves at a constant 23 MPH in all lanes. Shub's forty-foot motor home is surprisingly easy to drive, responding like a large car. Marco's discovering that he can maintain the perfect speed as he fumbles with both hands searching the voluminous cow suit for the tiny M2. "FMB!" puffs Shub, prying the necklace from his left armpit.

"Shub?" Victor barks from the panoramic V&V deal room, tiny voice and image crisply thumb-nailed to the hi-rez viewing surface of Marco's Marriage Marble. "What's up?"

"Driving around incognito. As agreed, Viceroy," Shub reports, following Billy's RV from only a few yards behind.

"Someone hacked us this morning," updates Vilter.

"What kind of hack?"

"A minor intrusion. Probably DataMynd sniffing around."

"Right on time."

"They don't like being in the dark," Victor divines.

"They're intrigued?" Marco hopes.

"Frightened more likely."

"They'll get over it when they see the potential of the mighty PUPPs," Marco mollifies.

"Lay low for now, tomorrow you'll blow them away," Vilter vows.

"Ciao, Viceroy," Shub spritzes the windshield again for good measure. Marco is happy that this is working out so smoothly because nothing could prepare him for the stark street reality of the roamads. For almost a decade now Shub basically hid out at home. Not unusual really, anyone who could do so did so, Marco justifies his seclusion. Extracurricular activities—precious few for Shub—have been confined to local neighborhood restaurants or flipping around the gridz between news specials and swarmbay excursions. Up-close the Roamadic Diaspora is much harsher than depicted on the webgridz. Once you had your face in it you realized it was essentially a multigenerational open sewer created by overpopulation and economic imbalance. A non-stop scavenger hunt fueled by global warming and digital mobility. Shub is inspired by the lyrics to one of his favorite Slowedownlight anthems:

> '...With Philosophical TechnoloJesus
> Tomorrow's gonna be Nirvana cum Satori,
> We' won't need no more Feelies,
> We're way before your time boys...'

A rusty red eighteen-wheeler cocoon motel slowly passes by. Marco steers steady, trying not to stare too blatantly at the unfortunate roamads stuffed into their tiny all-in-one budget accommodations. The rig is typical of many refurbished long-haul trucks: sleeping cocoons just big enough to sit up and lay down, communal shower/latrines surrounded by two tiers of soundproof cocoons flanking a center, miniature ELDs, vending machines and Plexiglas portholes providing a womb with a view for $e2.

It's through these portholes that Shub observes a traveling tableau film-stripping past in slow motion: a Hispanic girl eating an orange, an elderly man laughing at something, two roamads of undetermined sex clumsily dry-humping, a distraught woman pleading with someone unseen, a fat guy talking to his ELD, an emaciated girl strumming a plastic banjo, and lastly, a tantalizing topless woman looking right back at Shub with a formidable fuck-you wave and an eat-shit sneer.

The mobile motel downshifts and drones past, revealing the original *'Mobility 8'* logo on the back now occluded by roamadic graffiti and the mud-painted outline of an alert Rabbit, the universal 'Wary Hare' mascot of the radical anti-NT roamads, many unfortunately, are only misunderstood speq-head malcontents. The bunny emblazoned trailer disappears, absorbed into the swollen swirl of roamadic refugees.

Shub sighs philosophically, newly mindful of his relatively charmed existence, growing up the only child in an argumentative, alcohol frenzied family. He and Billy fled the comfortable Californian suburb of Azusa the day Marco turned eighteen. Billy was always the artist, putting on protest plays and wild street performances with his older friends up in the Bay Area.

Brandon Shub, Marco's father, was a wannabe real estate agent who wound up buying a failed private detective agency. He turned it into a gadgets and security software retail store for amateur hobbyists.

It was at his dad's *EyeSpy Specialty Mart* that Marco first became enthralled with hacking and obsessed with synthespians. Shub's alcoholic mother, Millicent, was a religious woman who abandoned the marriage shortly after Marco and Billy moved to San Francisco. Millie joined NeoPhysicalMindGround, a supercult outside Bakersfield. Their pagan crypto-philosophy teaches that *'Man is Spirit and Woman is Matter'.*

Now that both parents have passed on, Marco is the solo Shub...*Except Z and the Puppyz are kind of like family.* Marco is troubled to admit the thought has occurred to him once or twice. He originally wanted the PUPPs to be highly intelligent, vastly entertaining, digital slaves. Your personal PUPP to gate the overflow of webgridz information while performing all the mundane, time-consuming busy work associated with data of any kind. That was the original concept. Basically making sure everything was buttoned up, allowing everyone more leisure time for fun, friends, and family.

But that was before Marco's divorce and tremendous weight gain coupled with the demise of ShubTools, the economic inversion, the NT border closings and establishment of the Selection Elections. In due course Shub realized that if he played it straight with the PUPPs he would be out-lawyered, outmaneuvered, ripped-off and cruelly crushed; worn down by extensive negotiations. Lawsuits would become his career.

The PUPPs are Marco's masterpiece but unfortunately a Pandora's Box of possibilities both good and bad. Shub doesn't want anything to do with either outcome, so figuring out a way to offload the technology once Z got up and working became the Holy Grail.

Then it hit him one day: nobody makes volume moves on any goods or services until they do extensive product research. Product testing and development is a major corporate line item and Shub perceived he would have little real competition if he moved fast and furiously for a couple of years. Marco asked around and decided to run the deal through V&V because they were successful, greedy, and local. After researching the players, it only took a few weeks to zero in on DataMynd and Zuzzan. He knew he had done the right thing once Z began to mature.

The abnomaly of Kaplan's affair with Bobogoné was a

wondrous fluke and the timing is perfect with the Selections going on...*'Deal Flow is everything—but Leverage is God!'* Marco recalling Silicon Valley cocktail party wisdom from waybackinthenight.

Just outside Tehachapi, Billy signals to exit at an NT rest stop. The convoy slaloms past hundreds of hitchhiking roamads clustered in groups of fifty along the broken highway. They park side-by-side in the dirt behind a busted down cocoon motel.

Across the lot, a large crowd of speqheads lounge on plastic deck chairs, boogying to a roamad rocktro group blaring under a greasy tent crudely finger-painted with the 'Wary Hare' pictogram. The audience sings along with the Slowedownlight cover tune: *Falling...*

When Babylon falls it will fall on a very nice day.
When we we're young, so young,
When we first heard of Babylon,.
It was wondrous, had everything we dreamed.
Now run away friends, fly away, drive away from Babylon, man.
Walk away, crawl away...'

Mutant horseflies bigger than walnuts buzz Enoy and the boys' backsides as they line up and publicly relieve themselves in the outdoor government French-drain. A naked roamad stands nearby laughing hysterically, pissing into cupped hands and gently splashing urine over his face.

Revesti watches, zipping up with one hand whilst nonchalantly ELD-ing the finale of the nudist's unique facial regime.

"You use that thing a lot, Elroy," Marco candidly observes.

"It comes in handy if you've got a bad memory like I do," answers Enoy.

"Let's look at some clips later, you guys. I got a shitload on me," Billy boasts bizarrely. "Show you some TVMOON. Got me booted!"

"Billy's had enough of me for now. Ride with you for a spell, Marco?" Enoy inquires.

"There's a price to pay to ride my coach," Shub heads back to his motor home. "Boo."

The two RV's blend back into the undulating ocean of slow-motion traffic, only the center lanes moving forward as half the vehicles stop to pick up and drop off hitchers.

Enoy sits shotgun, passes a small brass pipe to Marco; Shub sucks it whilst gingerly steering past roamadic road hogs, jaywalking speq-heads, dog packs, pack horses and exhausted voyagers dozing oblivious on the broken shoulder.

"So what's your story, Enoy?" Marco, hoping to listen now.

"Where you from?"

"Mesa, Arizona originally. But I've been on the road pretty much since I was twenty. Turned seventy-six yesterday." Enoy informs.

"Jesus tits! Never would have guessed!" Shub is truly surprised. "What do you do, man?"

"I do electronics repair and teach metaphysics."

"I mean how do you do it? Stay so much younger?"

"Well...I teach metaphysics and do electronics repair," Enoy echoes.

"I see," Shub smiles for the third time.

"More than you know, my friend."

"Yeah?" Shub asks. "You taking an unnatural liking to me?"

"You're a likeable guy, Marco," Enoy submits.

"No I'm not," scuttles Shub. Marco's M2 silently vibrates on his gut, jiggling him underneath the baggy cow-fit. Shub flinches, ignoring the adjudicator's untimely request for instantaneous communiqué. Marco should be riding alone so he can talk to Victor uninterrupted. He'll have to get Enoy to ride with Billy at the next stop.

Enoy watches Shub's aura as several energetic tendrils suddenly sparks up, emanating from the sunspot-like roiling around his upper torso.

"What kind of metaphysics you teach?" Marco asks.

"It varies depending on the time and the motivation of the student," Revesti invests with a casual lightness infectious even to Shub. "The last time I had a student the work centered on his artistic growth."

"So you're a 'Heavy'? Didn't know that about you, Elroy," says Shub.

"Not a heavy, just an old man with some mileage," Enoy humbly offers.

"You one of them Neurotheologists?"

"Not quite."

"Supercultist?"

"Nope."

"You read minds, Elroy?" Shub already suspects.

"No. I read people," Enoy clarifies.

"...I read people..." Shub mouths automatically, thinking PUPPs and Puppyz.

"You know, Marco, it's almost like you've created a separate little mental 'Shubette' who carefully examines every single word being said before it let's you respond," Enoy politely diagnosis. "It's frankly annoying but fairly common in people with too many brains. Of course...the person you are conversing with senses that you are questioning everything they say."

Marco confirms, "Sometimes it's like an echo chamber in here."

"Hey Shub-ub-ub-ub-ub...!" Enoy imitates, getting another grin out of Marco.

"Very funny."

"You created an extra step. A little mental filter that demands the right to reprocess everything you hear and say," Revesti offers. "A linguistic Maxwell's Demon seems to be mediating your conversations."

"My inner double-checker?"

"I like that!"

"The mental detector."

"Yeah! The wonderful facility you have with words is partly due to your habit of chewing the bastards before swallowing or spitting them out."

"...Chewing," Marco's mouth marvels.

"Marco? Repeat after me: once is enough, thank you."

Marco reluctantly obeys "Once is enough, thank you."

"Say this to yourself every time your imaginary friend starts doing his repeating job."

"...repeating job," Shub too late to squelch.

"Try acknowledging the beneficent role your double-checker has played to get you safely through the torrential river of words. The mental detector has done his job well, thank you, but next time try asking the Shubette if it will help out only when you are alone and engaged in the act of reading for pleasure. Why not? That way you two can take your time and really enjoy dining on gourmet word-feasts together!"

"I've written software that deconstructs and reconstructs complex linguistic interactions," Shub submits. "I'm a programmer."

"So says Billy Blurr. Now we know why you're so good at it! Right?...ight?...ight?" Revesti reverberates.

"Make fun of my affliction," Marco killjoys.

"But brains are very funny! When something strikes us as funny it's because we suddenly see it from all perspectives at once. Big Funny happens when you suddenly notice your mind un-hooking itself from all points of view altogether!" Enoy elucidates.

"Un-hooking itself..." Shub parrots.

"We laugh because it's ridiculously ironic that we have to adopt any single point of view in the first place!"

"Every perspective is relative therefore funny?" Marco deduces.

"Yes. We take them seriously but humor shatters the illusion," Enoy enlightens.

"Humor shatters the illusion..." double-talks Shub.

"Yeah. A roamad walks into a bar with a rabbit on his

head and the barkeeper says 'Where did you pick him up?' The brain automatically anticipates that the roamad will answer the question."

"But the rabbit answers instead," surmises Shub.

"Which shatters the expectation created in the set-up and temporarily dislodges the brain's entrenched perspective," Revesti recapitulates. "You're momentarily un-hooked, afloat in cognitive anti-gravity."

"Funny is having the rug pulled out from under your brain?" Marco asks.

"It's funny because you are the brain, the rug, and the puller all at once," Enoy enlarges.

"The rug and the puller," Shub sputters.

"Once is enough, thank you, Marcotecht," Enoy reminds, putting the peace-pipe back in his pack.

Shub is certain he didn't mention the name 'Marcotecht', nor does Blurr have any knowledge of his semi-secret pseudonym.

Up ahead, Billy's watching Shub and Enoy through his oversized rearview. They seem to be bouncing around, having fun. Billy must retrieve Elroy at the next stop and get a little bit weird himself, take his mind off of how pissed he is about getting fired and get on with the next thing. He flips on the ELD and plays Slowedownlight's psychotic ballad *'What I Wouldn't Do'*:

'I wouldn't lay that trip on you about man-machine interface
With the neuromuscular tracking patterns of a cat's eye
Combined with the return turret head-swing movement...'

Blurr sings along ogling two cute roamad babes passing by in a fairly new pick-up truck. The women outright ignore his sunny smile. That's what he's missing the most! Institute Babes! Being the experimental media professor profited him in the girlfriend department. Institute women were so much easier to deal with then Babylonwood chicks. Maybe now he'll hook up with an angelic roamad artist and together they'll create a new webgridz piece based on his epic 'L'. They could easily extend it to include commercial swarmbays where you evolve into humanoid apes and other beasties. Spontaneous swarmbay audiences are most attentive if they are wrecked on speq, because nothing else matters but the swarm...*Swarming on speq*, Billy ruminates, wondering how to get his hands on some money for a project...*Gotta do some kind of publicity stunt.* When Billy chain-sawed naked mannequins stuffed with Cheetos and hamburger on the evening news it garnered him enough publicity to attract funding for his multimediographic theatre experiments. But when Blurr publicly accused the Hollywood Studios of turning the visual effects industry into a bankrupt bloodbath? No one would hire him. His last effects gig was the megaflop *Attack of the Baboon-Faced Horsefly.*

"Ah, well...." The old Babylonwood studios got their lunch eaten by the webgridz anyway so in hindsight Billy got off just swell. Somewhere in-between the cranberry spritzers and the endives, they blinked. The new webgridz swarmbays pulled the studios' collective pants down and tossed sand into the lubricant. You could hear the sucking sounds of Century City attorneys vapor-locking at content ownership paradoxes birthed by the self-creating, self-funding affinity hives of the swarmbays.

Billy bombastically berates an imaginary audience of reptilian studio execs: "With an ELD you just motion at the screen and it goes and gets you whatever you want; some good, some bad, but at least it gets what you want! From anywhere! Most important now that the boarders are closed, don't you think!?"

He improvises a speq-head swarmer in the mirror: "Its nectronic, man! Our affinity hive swarms forever! We agglomerate spontaneously, swarming for deals. Unbefuckinglievable deals! Our hive grows as the price drops thousands of times, signally other swarms. And we get exactly what we want—almost for free—because we are legion!" Blurr whispers demonically to his reflection in the rearview: "...We are real-time legion!"

Billy pauses puzzled over the reality that shipping costs now more than the actual goods shipped. It's a minor miracle that any item ever gets delivered to a moving target, but it does, linked via webgridz and GPS, mobile Zip codes notwithstanding. As long as it's made and consumed in Novo America. "We are real-time legion!" blurts Blurr again, burning it in, pre-memorizing the line for his new project... *'Beyond Roamadia'.*

Marco watches Billy conversing with himself in the rearview. Shub has been following closely behind the blathering Blurr whilst Enoy naps on the couch in back. Billy could cycle through panoramic panoplies of characters and accents at the slightest provocation.

It's always puzzled Shub as to why they were the first to figure out that there was a vast network of concrete drainage overflow tunnels crisscrossing beneath the sprawling suburbs. There was neither graffiti nor other indication that anyone was ever down there. Shub and Billy spent many a day laughing insanely in those platonic caves, the secret fort underneath the streets transformed into their private, primitivistic cinema. Soon they were coaxing nubile young ladies into the depths of their grotto.

BLARKO HUBB

Bobogoné reclines on a plush CrunchyCountry couch in the corporate media lab. DataMynd's Chief Visualization Psychologist, Rex Timbu, is rocking and rolling back and forth over bank security video footage showing a fat man in a cow jumpsuit waiting in line at a bank.

"Zoom in and check if the asshole has his name scrawled on the case," Bobogoné directs, "or better yet, see if you can extract a frame of whatever he's got on his device there,"

"Can't," Rex already checked: "Screenguard. Hubb's jumpsuit is a special model RanchoDeluxe Faraday fabric, Gerry. Nothing electromagnetic can penetrate. This cowboy's worried about being snooped. My guess is Blarko's not with anyone for that matter," Rex insightfully submits. "Hubb's a loner."

"Fuck you Hubb!" Bobogoné blunderbusses at the computer enhanced video loop of Shub in queue. "Look at him! A human heifer! What could this fucking lone cow have that we could possibly want?"

"I don't know. From his micro-movements and overall

body language I'd say he's favoring his right leg, probably packing a pistol in a thigh holster. The weapon must be a new composite because the bank alarms didn't go off. I'm not getting a good feeling here, Gerry," Rex reveals reticently.

"Expensive gun, Faraday suit, false name...fatso goes in and Vilter thinks of DataMynd—"

"—and calls for a meeting three minutes after Hubb exits the building?"

"Well who the fuck is he?" Bobogoné inhales his lower lip, slurping Zuzzan's cover-up cosmetics away in a single furious suck.

"Not sure. Could be anybody."

Bobogoné doesn't mind that Rex sprinkles a little bit of speq into his own java if helps him to concentrate and hyper-focus on the task at hand: "Find out. Ask your connects, Rex."

THE GAP-ZONE

Enoy switched motor homes an hour ago and rides with Billy now. Blurr was sweating like a pig stuck to the leatherette driver's seat so Revesti fixed the air conditioner by giving it a little whack in the right place. Now Billy is driving cool, spewing random lines into his ELD: "Cornucopia of misplaced concreteness, slathering the sightless, aping the ages..."

Enoy's back in the RV master bedroom with his headsets on listening to very special audio from waybackinthenight. Each year around his birthday, Revesti endeavors to replay the rarest recording in his entire repository of re-memories. It accidentally captured the very moments that Enoy was first exposed to the timeless home of constant creation. A series of co-existent spatial dimensions and the non-dimensional 'gap-zone' incidences.

Enoy thumbs through ELD files finding: *Mesa Foundation 022357*. He has over six-hours of audio from that fateful February day but only a few minutes contain the memory-juice he thirsts for. He pilfered the recording from his first job as audio-visual technician at the private facility outside Tempe, Arizona. The Foundation was the most cutting-edge think-tank money could buy. Young Enoy set up and operated the projectors and recorders at meetings and symposiums, making sure the 35mm slides, 16mm films, opaque projections, and overhead transparencies were seen and heard. He always made ½" audio tape recordings for transcription and distribution through the Foundation's private journals.

He has re-transferred this particular recording a dozen times as formats came and went, finally had a restoration expert re-master the bastard. Now the combination of clean recording and good headsets allows Enoy to hear subtle spoken nuances, sparking vivid visions of that distant, predestined day.

Revesti hits play and listens through his expensive headset to the din of bubbling background conversation: twenty-odd participants gather around the oval conference table to discuss *'Circularity and Self-Observing Systems',* and witness a hypnotic demonstration. It was in these series of Mesa meetings that the original concepts of cybernetics, systems theory, information theory and artificial intelligence were initially circulated by the long forgotten inventors themselves. But to Enoy it was just an easy job. Fortunately he was the AV nerd in high school and therefore pre-trained.

Enoy leans back on the pillows and listens to the beginning of Dr. Leif Lawrence's hypnosis experiment. Lawrence didn't use any AV, so technician Enoy sat and watched from the rear of the meeting room whilst making the usual ½" audio tape recording for the record.

The recorded voice of the renowned Psychiatrist explains that he will: *"Now conduct a hypnotic experiment using Doctor Martin Russell as the subject."* Dr. Russell, sequestered in the next room, is a psycholinguistic mathematician and founding member of the influential 'Cybernetics Gang' scattered around the conference table. *"Dr. Russell has never been hypnotized and volunteered out of professional curiosity."*

Lawrence describes the experiment as designed to temporarily create a separate, coexistent observer personality in the subject saying: *"Our purpose here today is to explore how cognitive systems might create persistent, self-observing counterparts and to what extent these counterparts can be autonomous identities unto themselves,"* Lawrence informs his esteemed colleagues. *"The phenomenology of the observer might assist us in understanding how the human personality is dynamically generated, explore the nature of feed-back and feed-forward in self-observing systems, and expose its deep epistemic roots,"* Lawrence signals a tall, nattily attired PhD student. Enoy will never forget the plastic name tag: 'Gene'. He distinctly remembers the angular assistant obediently ambulating through a side-door and reemerging pushing Dr. Russell in a wheel chair. He positioned Russell in the front of the room and took a seat nearby. Russell appeared around seventy-years old, bespectacled and bald, wide awake and without the use of his legs.

The recording cuts out momentarily then picks up with Lawrence explaining a number of techniques that could be employed some of which he will describe so everyone can benefit from a quick review. There follows a seemingly spontaneous and surprisingly casual description of two different types of 'Coin Techniques', the 'Spot on the Wall' and the 'Hand-Levitation Technique', Lawrence's 'My Buddy Bill' method, and other rapid trance induction innovations.

Revesti clearly remembers listening with intense concentration to Lawrence's extensive, repetitive detailing. In retrospect, Enoy realizes that Lawrence was in fact teaching Russell to go into a trance by making repetitive suggestions while describing the hypnotic techniques themselves and dictating Russell's choices with off-hand directions and comments like: *"You can either go into a light trance, a medium trance, or a deep trance."* Revesti smiles at the doctor's subtle skill and skips ahead to Lawrence's 'Astound Technique'.

As usual, the hair on the back of his neck stands up. No matter how many times Enoy listens he still can't ascertain the exact moment that he too slipped into trance along with Russell: *"It's really very simple,"* Lawrence says to Russell with great intensity and enthusiasm. *"All I want you to do now is to tell me what breed...what kind...and about what age...is...that cat there?"* Lawrence pointing to an empty spot on the floor, staring astonished at it.

Russell slowly turns to see, eyes glazing, face rigidifying: *"Why it's Siamese,"* he readily reports. *"We used to have one. Is it yours?"*

"Is the Siamese lying down?" Lawrence inquires, avoiding the question. *"Standing up or sitting?"*

"Just sitting there," responds Russell, oblivious to anyone but the cat and the friendly questioner.

Enoy remembers the utter bewilderment of that long ago moment and not realizing at the time that he too was somehow inexplicably locked into the trance with Russell...*Anyone could see that the cat was a fat, gray Persian! And it was lying down, not sitting there.* Transfixed, Revesti glanced around the meeting room, none of the others seemed concerned but himself, Dr. Russell and assistant Gene, both staring intently at the hallucinated 'cat'.

Then it happened.

Dr. Russell bolts upright in his wheelchair, suddenly clutching his chest, passing out cold from a heart attack.

Young Enoy was immediately gripped by an irresistible invisible force from above and somehow paralyzed in his seat. Enoy's eyes locked on the ceiling directly overhead as a pinpoint light-beam projected upwards from middle of his forehead.

The ceiling disappeared.

Enoy was in the light, flying backwards, propelled through atmosphere, stratosphere and ionosphere; Earth,

Moon, Sun, Mars and the gas giants, growing smaller, silently receding, infinite stars loom, traveling helplessly deep into distant space.

It seemed that he was in the zone for at least twenty minutes but when he regained normal consciousness only a moment had passed. Apparently no one had been paying any attention to him. Several doctors quickly positioned Russell on the floor. Enoy tied a sweater around his own crotch to cover himself just as Gene appeared to retrieve the telltale audio recording for Dr. Russell.

That's when Enoy noticed that Gene's pants were likewise saturated. The heart attack victim's assistant had clearly experienced the same shocking near-death, gap-zone journey as Russell and himself.

"I gave it to one of the other doctors just now," Enoy lied, having safely stuffed the master tape in his rack of audiovisual equipment. Gene distracted, no doubt reeling as was Enoy from the cosmic roller coaster ride they had just jointly endured.

Dr. Russell was awake and smiling serenely, fully accepting his brush with death. They placed him back in the wheelchair and hustled him outside. His assistant disappeared amongst worried participants. Enoy never saw Dr. Russell or Gene again.

"Elroy?" Blurr pokes his head into the master suite. Revesti opens his eyes, hits pause and unplugs the headsets. "We're staying here for a while," Billy says. "Goin for a walk."

CYBERNETRICKSTER

The M2 dangles from its necklace, swinging back and forth over Shub's feet. "Marcotecht!" Vilter's voice violates the monitor's tiny speaker.

"Yes, Viceroy? News?"

"No news. I am your attorney, remember," Victor ridiculous.

"I see..." The 247 Vilter-link is going to be a nuisance if the hyperactive deal-maker continues to trivially trespass into sacred Shub Space. "Shit! Someone's coming," Shub deceives, dropping the M2 into the inner folds of his jumpsuit. Marco switched to the secure Faraday model after being vacu-snarfed by data thieves at the Stanford mall. Twice as costly, but his ELD is well protected under the copper-mesh synthetic. Besides, the fourteen zippers double as an array of redundant broadband webgridz antennas. He bought a dozen identical pairs at a RanchoDeluxe swarmbay the day they were introduced. Now he wears nothing else.

Shub reclining on the munificently scotch-guarded bedspread, remembering that he originally stumbled on

Zuzzan Kaplan being the first PUPP host when researching DataMynd as the likely buyer. Shub sighs with mordant relief, recalling numerous narrow escapes he performed from the multifarious business endeavors he and his erstwhile collaborators naively ventured into. So many idealistic man-years wasted plotting and scheming radical new technologies; only to be systematically scammed, flimflammed, reamed, steamed and dry-cleaned by VC wannabe's and well-meaning groupies.

Once the offshore outsourcing craze died down—curtailed significantly by the New Totality boarder closings—American programming positions once again proliferated. But the real Yankee value-add was in the Big Ideas Department and not in the rude redundancy of coding in cubicles. That reptilian responsibility was left to the bottom feeding cyber-caste system comprised of $e500 a week Indian and Pakistani PhD's, backroom Ukrainian and Uzbekistani usurpers and armies of Chinese Eskimos, pecking antique E-Machines salvaged from abandoned shipping containers scuttled around the Aleutians. The 'E-skimos' splice together vast heap-arrays of unreliable obsolescence, freely feeding their Frankenstein with cracked code and wormy demoware, ruthlessly undercutting even the most crafty Russian and Indonesian slave shops.

Several successful couples Marco and his X used to have over for elaborate client-sponsored dinner parties managed to migrate past the NT barriers to the Canadian hinterlands and relocate in XaNa. They must have used inside connections because as far as Shub can ascertain the only way to get around the Vancouver border patrols would be to either have the police escort you across or to bribe one of the half-dozen private submarine owners in Seattle to take you northwest to Prince Rupert then row ashore and hitch-hike east to the outback around Lake Williston west of Dawson Creek. Wait for a friendly XaNa Refugio to find you camping out.

XaNa is likely to be somewhere along the shore of Peace River although many believe it is in the B.C. rainforest due to the large quantities of First Nation medicinal products they ship. XaNa is making strides in self-sufficiency, gaining autonomy, and slowly becoming a recognized free-trade-zone-rural-city-state, most of XaNa's income is derived from subcontracting the talents of its considerable population of techno-brainiacs-in-residence to black budget problem projects the NT Cyberforces can't get a grip on. The Feds evidently suffer from a crippling lack of access to radically innovative talent.

Most people believe the name 'XaNa' originates with the cinematic Orson Wellsian depiction of Xanadau the stately pleasure dome. Others admire the utopian implications of informational egalitarianism inherent in Ted Nelson's prophetic Xanadau vision of interconnected knowledge networks waybackinthenight.

In one of Billy's Hollywood past lives, he worked with a renegade tribe of visual effects artists homesteading in the abandoned officer's housing tract on a section of the decommissioned Alameda Naval Air Station near Oakland, California. Blurr guarantees that XaNa stands for 'X-Alameda Naval Air Station'.

Marco is slowly convincing himself that XaNa is probably the only place he can run after the PUPP deal closes. With his loads of DataMynd ecrement$ and closet full of thoughtful Faraday suits, Shub should be a shoe-in for immediate admittance into their Inner Zircles. But just in case they balk, he's thinking of bribing some of Billy's sycophantic art students forge a set of docs showing Shub's genetic linkage with Nicola Tesla and or Alan Kaprow, both men being XaNa's unofficial patron saints along with Ted Nelson, Queen Noor, Gregory Bateson and Joey Skaggs.

The NT overnight zone has quickly filled up to capacity with roamadic families, cocoon rigs, motorcycle tribes and hitch-hiking blue collar commuters. Everyone is pitching camp in the bulldozed clearings beside the ancient superhighway. The rebellious Wary Hare logo is freshly emblazoned on nearby trees, signage surfaces, and vehicles. This is one of the poorer NT zones. No funds to repair the government's micam monitoring system. Each and every surveillance unit is smashed to smithereens by sling-shot rounds. The zone is an NT blind spot for the time being.

Enoy is in the RV kitchen making sandwiches while Blurr unloads some of his media toys from the overhead storage. He carefully positions half-a-dozen wafer-thin ELD screens on the king size master bed, creating a five foot tall pyramid screen.

Shub enters the coach backlit by the setting sun, an oddly glowing sacred cow: "The freaks are out in force tonight, gentlemen."

"Why's that?" Enoy asks, slathering chipolata mayo on the roamad-style burrito-sandwich-pita fusion forming under his short-order cook hands.

"Man, I just saw a five-hundred pound woman lying on her stomach in the dirt," Marco maintains maladroitly.

"Her top off?" Billy asks.

"I couldn't see. There were a couple of people squatting down next to her."

"No hallucination, Shubatron," Billy diagnosis. "She's a human Ouija Board. Thousands of them out here."

"Human Ouija Board...?" Marco echoes, remembering too late: once is enough!

"They have a YES and a NO, sometimes a MAYBE, tattooed on their backs then removed, micro-cauterized. They lay there and go into a trance, then you pass one of those little pointer goodies around and around while asking a question over and over."

"The YES or NO in the old tattoos glows?" Shub ashamed at having watched her for a few minutes while a pair of blitzed-out roamads repeatedly asked something he couldn't hear. Marco reasons that, because the laser-inflicted scar tissue only glows under certain convulsive peak conditions, the woman must have either been stealth masturbating or carefully evoking the gag response, crying, laughing, or conjuring similarly intense biological changes of state. "That's ridiculous!"

Billy nods, "I know," wolfing his authentic Elroywich. "Ok you guys, here's what I got going on with TVMOON," Billy breathlessly flips his hands in the air and the pyramid of ELDs wink on. "I'm only gonna show you a few snippets because I'm still editing the long-form pseudo-interactive version."

The pyramid of screens shows a series of montages while a man in silhouette, medium shot, pacing around in circles in front of a similar pyramidal stack of monitors with multiple simultaneous image playback behind him.

"This video got you fired?" Enoy asks.

"Well you see, this character Paul, is calling up his friends and family one last time while he is committing 'vidicide'," Billy manages around a mouthful meat.

"He's slowly committing suicide by watching a non-stop barrage of bad video," explains Marco, only too familiar with Billy's bizarre one-act satire. Shub appeared without consent in a number of humiliating snippets. Billy purportedly cut all his images out but Marco can't be certain.

"A satire on suicide cults was way over the top! But upon the intellectual property rights of other artists and webgridz studios and thereby exposed the Institute to expensive and embarrassing litigation! Potential litigation!"

"I see...I worked in Amsterdam as a suicide deprogrammer, waybackinthenight. Friend of mine talked me into it. It was good work but once is enough thank you."

"I see..." Shub smiles slightly.

"Wowz!" chimes in the usually silent M2 voice of Billy's remoted young wife: "How did you deprogram them, Elroy?"

"Hey, Maya! Well, the deprogramming was different for each person," Enoy answers. "But the quickest and most effective way was to immediately get them laughing at themselves however you could do it."

"Billy got me out. We fell in love," Maya chirps cheerfully. "Where was this place, Elroy?"

"City center, years ago, the 'Smoky Eye'."

"Yeah it closed," Maya supplies. "There's a drive-in laser-razor place there now," Maya intones sarcastically, "One of those gourmet robo-plasti parlors," dismissing the whole idea of robotic plastic surgery as commercialized by Dr. Hank Geller and his far-flung supercult of fleshy franchises.

"If you think of it, grab a quick video snippet of the new place and gridz it to me for my archives?" Enoy requests.

"Got it...I will," Maya transmits.

"Archives, Elroy?" Billy asks, wondering if there might be some cool imagery he can wheedle out of the quixotic old bastard.

"Got a lot of stuff sitting on my ELD," Enoy answers. "I can remember the future now."

Shub is uncharacteristically intrigued: "Isn't 'Remember the Future' a Slowedownlight rocktro opera?"

"Yeah!" Enoy chuckles. "I sold him the phrase for twenty-three ecrement$!"

"Sold him the phrase..." Shub bites his lips.

"To Xnebula?" Billy's blown away.

"Jimmy," Enoy says. "His real name is James Baltus."

"Yeah we know Elroy," Shub smirks. "Baltus invented the fuckin' rocktro 'thang!"

"You hung with Xnebula?" Billy blusters. "He's the best."

"Maybe he is now, but back then he was a psycho speqhead intent on sacrificing himself. Jimmy was ready to trade his life for the cheap immortality of a webgridz media memorial. He actually believed his boyish biomass was Gaia's entropic loss," Enoy elegantly encapsulates the existential ennui of the typical death-wish devotee. "Met him in Amsterdam years ago when he was organizing a large-scale Last Rights party for himself. That's how we used to find out who the really serious ones were. We followed the ecrement$. We ID'd Baltus just in time and convinced him to come back to the Smoky Eye. He stayed for about a year, then went off and started Slowedownlight," Revesti recounts.

"Nectowowzus!" Billy sycophantasizes. "So you know him really, really well?"

"I know him. Deprogrammed him and he became my metaphysics student," Revesti reveals.

"What supercult was he with?" beseeches Shub. "The WayzOut?"

"Nope.

"Cyber-Christian Youth Brigade?"

"Nien, Miné Bovine!" Enoy negates.

"N23?"

"Closer..." Revesti mummers.

"It's fucking Cyopolis!" Billy exfoliates.

"No..." Enoy finally fills in: "NeoMyndGroundz. A breakaway from the old sex cult called NeoPhysicalMindGround," Enoy elaborates. "Only about fifteen-thousand in the swarm back then."

"My mother took off with their original founder freaks," Marco informs. "I know them."

"That's right!" Billy remembers...*Crazy Mrs. Shub. Horney Mrs. Shub!* "Fuck supercults!" Blurr roars, releasing repressed pressure so as not to be completely buried beneath his hatred for the Botswana Shaman who recruited Maya into the folds of his suicide cloister called Re:Birth. Maya and a couple of other escapees are the only ones left alive. Thousands of followers set themselves ablaze then jumped to their deaths from hot air balloons, cliffs, freeway overpasses, abandoned skyscrapers, and COM towers.

"At the moment we seem to be employed by one of the richest Supercults in the business," Marco says.

"Unofficially employed," Billy clarifies. "I'm the only one they know. Same M.O. as the roamad couriers."

"Methinks the cults keep the economy going by employing a army of roamads," Shub waxes economic.

"They do. By extracting a huge profit in black market slave labor and swarmbay fees," Enoy elucidates, passing his well-worn peace pipe to Marco.

"Wasn't it a new age investment commune that got all the lottery winners together to fund non-profit supercult start-ups waybackinthenight?" Shub can't exactly recall right now, puffing perplexedly on Enoy's proffered psychotropics.

"Yeah, every member is an ordained priest or priestess, no personal tax liability," Billy adds.

"So they turn everything they have over to the supercult?" Shub sneers.

"Virtual servitude exacted through cultural context control, all wrapped in a warm and fuzzy off-shore swarmbay fund that pays the bills," Enoy irks loquaciously, watching Shub stifle a persistent tickle rippling across his rotund tummy.

"Theoretically, pays..." Marco covers, scratching the Marriage Marble's insistent message vibrations.

"Let's start our own supercult!" Billy brainstorms. "People will give us all their shit!"

"Yeah!" Shub expectorates.

"I'm serious Shubus! You can be our deity!" Billy anoints. "All Hail Lord Shubatron! Master Cybernetrickster!" bards William Shakesblurr.

"...Cybernetrickster," Shub softly re-verbalizes, unable to stem the inner flow of mirror-words.

"Yeah. He's the character I replaced you with in TVMOON, man!" Billy updates.

"I see," Shub thinking 'once is enough', determined to stop the insidious echolalia.

"Cybernetrickster is really the First Nation's old Coyote Trickster updated as a hacker-shaman archetype. I'm still editing that part. But check out this other blip," Billy implores, excavating through the multi-screen montage by gesturing to the micam in EarthLingua international sign-language. "This sequence shows Paul, the guy attempting to commit vidicide, talking on the ELD to his video hypnotherapist."

The aging shrink's close-up appears in a little low-rez screen quadrant. He listens, eyes closed, nodding in casual comprehension as, backlit by the pyramided screen glow, the Paul character rabidly rants: "Maybe we all have a remnant dinosaur gene sleeping deep in the helixes, curled up for millennia, waiting to be triggered?" Paul postulates in a troubled whisper. "This sleeper gene contains memories of the asteroid collision, the explosion, the radiation, the light, the darkness, sensory death, the thud of large beasts slamming to the ground, struck down by the hand of God!" Paul proselytizes to camera. "Struck out!"

"So..." squawks the squinting shrink, playing it dumb, drawing Paul out further. "Human beings are the ancestors of whatever survived?"

"Yes! Our genetic relatives saw it happen! The bright white nuclear fire, cleansing, sterilizing, purifying, recycling, reconstituting, burning and smothering things large and small! In the blink of an eye!" Paul stares wild-eyed at the hypnotherapist's webgridz image. "The yearning for release through radiation is neurologically imprinted on a genetic level!"

"You're saying it's inevitable that we destroy ourselves in massive explosions?"

"It's variation in the code! The genesis and final use of atomic weapons is predetermined by the fact that we are genetically hardwired to re-create the suicidal evolutionary conditions that produce radical variation in the genetic code!" Paul proclaims.

"We're yearning for fire, death and destruction?" the sympathetic tele-therapist simplifies.

"Yes! Our genes scream for radioactive purification!" Paul preaches to his psychologist.

"Blurr? You ripped me!" Shub protests. "That 'yearning for release through radiation' is lifted right out of my movie concept and you fucking know it! Always has been!"

"Not the same, Sharko!" Billy jiggles his pinky, instantly switching the rough-cut off.

"It's the same!"

"Tiznt!"

"Tiz!"

"Tiznt..."

"Tiz!" Shub sucked into the long-forgotten shtick from waybackinthenight.

"Same as what?" Enoy asks, secretly setting his ELD to record the histrionic moment.

Shub stands and delivers: "Blurr's supposed idea bears an unquestionable resemblance to the mythos of the tribe of mutated humans starring in my fucking movie is what!"

"Ah! But Shub has created a myth about a nuclear war in the near future. My idea is genetic and deals with biological memory of the asteroid hit zillions of years ago," Billy demarcates.

"Clever distinction, but it won't fly," counters Marco. "My hunter-gatherers base their religious symbolism on their oral stories of the nuclear extinction. We always talked about that."

"No. We always talked about the fact that they mutated quickly."

"You just spun it to make the transmission system dinosaur genes!" Shub states unequivocally.

"Oh?"

"My mutants have a visionary yearning to re-experience death through radiation," Shub underscores.

"Well Sharko, if you're right, I ripped it unknowingly," Billy magnanimously dismissing any hint of purposeful plagiarism. "So please forgive! And just tell us the tale, Shubus!"

"Please?" Maya begs from afar.

"Well I don't have a title yet," Shub advances. "Not long from now..." Shub squats storyteller-style on the plastic runner between driver and passenger seat, "...a global electronics mega-firm will hold a special emergency board meeting to announce that the company's Primary Threat Prediction System has determined total nuclear Armageddon will accidentally—"

"—and unavoidably," Billy butts in.

"—occur within a nine-month window," Marco relates.

"And they believe it?" Enoy asks.

"They believe it and act accordingly; spending all the ecrement$ at their command to secretly launch a prefab space colony into L5 earth-orbit."

"Meanwhile they super-train a hundred adults and five-hundred children in the art of off-world survival," betrays Billy.

"And no sooner are they finished with phase-one than hundreds of nuclear missiles are accidentally launched on America's foes, triggering massive global retaliation, and immediate planet-wide destruction. But because they had early warning the electronics conglomerate launches the six-hundred colonists into orbit just minutes before the first detonations!" Shub synopsizes. "Everyone else gets barbequed."

"They escape safely and use robots to finish the space station fabrication," adds Billy.

"The opening credits end as they pressurize the orbiting city with fresh air," Shub appends.

"All that during the credits?" baffles Elroy.

"Oh hell yeah, that's easy. All visuals, no dialogue," Shub auteurs. "Then we dissolve slowly, traveling back to earth, supering the words '223 YEARS LATER' over a jungle settlement of primitive hominids."

"These are the mutated humanoid ancestors, now thriving in the overgrown ruins of what were once the Babylonwood hills," Blurr clarifies.

"Some look like normal humans, others have multiple heads, extra legs, elongated fingers and ears," Marco prescribes.

"And supernumerary mammary glands!" diagnosis breast-man Billy.

"Huxley's old estropiated dwarfs," Enoy posits. "'Ape and Essence'."

"Yeah? What happens is this: a six person team of Chinese astronauts was also in orbit during the initial nuclear conflagration so the colonists rescue them, taking them in and eventually everyone intermarries. The movie begins as the grandchildren of the original colonists determine that the Earth's surface is finally safe to visit. They've built a giant space shuttle and they send twenty or so men and women down to Baja California to establish a base. These colonists are extremely advanced scientifically. Philosophically they are devout pacifists."

"They would have to be pacifist with everyone crammed into the colony for over two-hundred years," observes Enoy.

"Didn't think about that," Marco memorizing the consideration for later unaccredited inclusion. "Anyway, a young Eurasian couple has been busy reconstructing the ancient Chinese orbiter's onboard computer when they stumble onto an intelligence file which shows the location of a 'non-existent' American nuclear missile installation designed to withstand Armageddon."

"The final fuck you," Billy quickly qualifies.

"It's an autonomous robo-silo in the Mojave desert," Shub continues. "The two Eurasian lovers plan to elude the landing party and make it to the secret installation, gain control of the missiles and force the colonists to appoint them King and Queen of Old Earth!"

"Or else they'll torch the space colony by exploding the nukes in the upper atmosphere," Billy side-bars.

"Hello? I'm Eurasian!" Maya electronically exclaims, "I can play the evil Queen Bitch!" Suddenly at the RV door a hearty: *Knock! Knock! Knock!* Everyone freezes:

"Honest rabbit!" a voice outside announces.

"Honest rabbit?" whispers Shub.

"Just riders," Enoy pops open the door and pokes his tangled gray head outside to see two roamads squinting at him in the dusty sunset. It's the duo of snooping speqheads from Mojave Joe's—Freakflag and Tumbleweed—although Enoy-one-ear-and-out-the-other doesn't remember.

"Evening..." Tumbleweed immediately recognizes Enoy as the sword bearing old samurai from a few days back, "...Sir."

"Evening," Revesti smiles, viewing the questionable stranger's speq-speckled aura outputs.

"We were wondering if you're heading toward Novo New Mexico?"

"And if you'd take cash?" coughs up Freakflag.

Enoy senses these two vagabonds are doers of bad deeds: "We're actually full up for now, sorry."

"Thanks anyway..." Freakflag salutes Enoy real friendly-like. "Peace."

Enoy sees that the NT stop has filled to capacity. Scores of neo-medieval biker roamads in tattered pirate costumes are quickly gathering in a circle around a twelve-foot Rabbit effigy. "What's going on over there?" Enoy asks the two retreating wastrels.

"The Rabbits are getting ready for the newscams to over-fly," informs Freakflag. "A drone just sprayed the camp."

"They're gonna torch a bunny!" titillates Tumbleweed.

"Yeah?" Revesti closes the door as the duo hustle off toward the Rabbit roast.

"This zone's gonna be splashed all over the gridz in a little while," observes Shub, not interested in exposing himself to the low-flying swarm of unmanned mediadrones sure to appear any minute. This particular NT stop has become newsworthy for some reason or they wouldn't have gone to the expense of spraying the new nanocams: millions of micro-miniature transmitters sending audio and video bursts back to content analysis servers at the NT/AP service. It may be that this overnight Zone—being a vandalized NT 'blind spot'—is associated with a strong Rabbit presence. "We've got to get out of here right now, you guys," Shub realizes.

"Really?" Blurr disbelieving, takes a final blast of boo. "You're paranoid, bro!" Billy secretly admires this in his big buddy. Thinking these Rabbit roamads aren't as dumb as they look. They've managed to attract the media and they don't even have a budget.

Shub hustles out. A swashbuckling biker pyrotechnician ignites starter-fuel beneath a gas-soaked trash pile surrounding the crucified Rabbit effigy. The smell of burning gasoline permeating the evening air. Hundreds of speq-soaked radical roamads laughing under the stars in glowing pyre light form a slowly moving circle around the sacrificial Wary Hare, chanting: "Live Free or Fry! Live Free or Fry!"

The burning bunny thing is horribly stinky and many of the bikers still have tattoos, which is a big red flag.

Marco waddles double-time over to his RV, climbs in and notices a thin layer of blue sensor spray blanketing the super-sized windshield: "Pixel dust!" Each microsphere is a minute fisheye lens transmitting tiny slices of video back home. Only a few thousand of the innumerable particle micams survive long enough to establish a link but the news editing sobots can quickly stitch the disparate tidbits together and construct a three-dimensional video view of the entire area and everybody in it.

The unmistakable hover buzz of an approaching gaggle of night-vision video drones announce their directionless descent over the brightly lit Rabbit warren as huge flames violently erupt from the effigy's gas-soaked ears. The dancing denizens shriek revolutionary curses, shake torches at the lowest flying mediadrones.

Shub gives the windshield a triple-spritz of wiper-washer and pulls out into traffic behind Billy. Hopefully the wind will blow away the remaining digital dust mites and nothing will have been transmitted showing Shub's likeness.

Marco steers with his knee and lassos the M2. Victor is offline for the moment, but has left three text messages for 'Spouse'. Each message is the same three words: CALL Z NOW!

"FMB!" Marco snatches his ELD from the upper right jumpsuit zip pouch and activates it for the first time in nearly two days. Z must have tried to bleep him and then left Victor the message to forward via the Marriage Marble. He speedials Z.

—Twisslebleep! — The PUPP pops on in close-up: "My Marcotecht!" greets Z.

"You have something for me?"

"Zuzzan and her colleagues at DataMynd have compiled an emergency dossier on 'Mr. Blarko Hubb'. They have obtained video clips of you in the vicinity of Vilter & Vilter from Monday's rendezvous."

"Blarko Hubb! Anything else?"

"Some blurry security-cam clips from a bank lobby and a couple more from the sidewalk outside the law offices."

"So they know what I look like?"

"Correct, my Marcotecht."

But with most security files rarely saved for more than twenty four hours there's minimal useful Shub-info out there to worry about. Marco's face bears no unusual distinction and therefore won't be easy to match-up with old photos from waybackinthenight.

"Can you show me the clips they got?"

"Of course," Z plays back the edited video loop that Kaplan received from Rex Timbu a few hours ago. It shows a zoomed-in, cleaned up clip of Shub in line at the bank, working his ELD. Another camera catches Marco exiting the premises with a bulging backpack, heading up the sidewalk into a crowd of roamads and barnyard attired affluhip.

"Blarko Hubb!" Shub can't contain a belly laugh at the useless thread of intelligence the mighty global player is pathetically pursuing: "Harrfffo! Fucking idiots," Marco knows DataMynd would need an army of his PUPPs to get anywhere near the ultra-sophisticated performance required to filter millions of feeds. "I'll call you."

"My Marcotecht," intones the Kaplan clone. Z turns from its close-up and flings open Zuzzan's walk-in-closet vizualization. The PUPP begins carefully double-checking its virtual wardrobe inventory against Zu's latest purchase records. After a moment Z looks back and smiles.

"Until then, Z..." Shub whispers, terminating the connection.   Marco follows Blurr up a desert highway, headlights illuminating a sign: *QUESTA 23 MILES.* Thirty minutes later Billy pulls off into a darkened NT Zone encrusted with semi-permanent family squatters. They drive past a feces-smeared billboard informing: *Novo New Mexico State Debtors Prison - Next Right.*

The trio park in a dirt overflow area and sleep the thankful sleep of the anonymous travelers, awakened only by myopic mediadrones or bladder burst.

GOING BOWLING

Zuzzan zipped to the office in the wee hours, her mind swirling with anticipation of emergency PR contingencies and press tactics should the mysterious encounter with Vilter and Hubb prove to be mission-critical. *People Helping People to Help People Help Us!* Zuzzan's whistling the DataMynd jingle as she enters Bobogonés CEO-sized office: "We're ready in the conference room, Gerry."

"Great! Let's suck it and see..." Bobogoné fumes, sucks his lip. Zuzzan holds out her hand to the flatulent figure of Gerald Bobogoné. She has determined, after some midnight webgridz research, that his sickening habit is none other than the incestuous Oral Nursing Neurosis identified by the old Vienna Psychoanalytic School, very waybackinthenight...*Capillaries in the ciliated epithelium tissue trap the blood, producing a unique Royal Violet hue.*

"What's wrong, Gerry?" she watches her lover's fat lip instantly empurple.

"Nothing's wrong!" Bobogoné whiffing his Jewess mistress. "They're setting up some pins and I'm going bowling!"

"Zoopy!" Zu playfully tickles Bobogoné around his silk-suited dugs as 'giggling' supposedly triggers the rapid release of bioplasmic endorphins.

PEAK MOMENT

Billy and Enoy hang out in the RV's air-conditioned comfort whilst Shub squishes himself into a weather-beaten webgridz pubterm on the other side of a burned out gas station. Fuel looters, Marco surmises, outraged vigilante petrol mobs, recently vanquished by plastic bullets. Shub remembers the helicopters herding people into moving trucks and schlepping them to Cultural Management deprogramming camps in the desert. Marco cups the vandalized phone against the desert gusts, its latex mouthpiece stinking of roamad tobacco juice. Just as he dials Vilter, the Marriage Marble vibrates: Victor's flippant face flickers on the dinky sphere. "It's time!"

"I'm on your private line already, Viceroy," drolls Shub.

"Ah yes, here you are! Good Marcotecht!"

"DataMynd's hacking me. They've got video of my new alter ego, 'Blarko Hubb'."

"What? Harpo Fludd?" Victor pathologically mis-hearing. "Does it matter?"

"Nope," sneers Shub. "They don't have shit,"

"Not yet they don't. Do me a favor and keep your M2

out so we can maintain visual. We might need to use hand signals. In fact, if you see me pull on my earlobe like this," Vilter demonstrates to the spouse-cam. "You need to shut up. I'm the attorney, you're the client."

"I'm just going to listen. You're the mouthpiece, Victrola. Just let Z handle herself with these guys. She's self-demoing."

"Good. Too bad you won't see the look on Kaplan's face when Z does her thing."

"Think so? Hang on while I summon Z," Marco pulls out his ELD, suddenly realizing that this is the 'Peak Moment' he has been working towards. The magical event horizon he has been plotting, scheming, slouching, programming, sweating, and salivating toward—all the personal, financial, spiritual, and sexual sacrifices Shub has shouldered solo incognito these past years—not to mention bed-wetting, arm-sleeping—He speed dials Z and in San Francisco, the PUPP pops onto Vilter's ELD. It turns toward its virtual micam and trumpets:

"My Marcotecht!"

"Time to meet your Hostess," Marco commands.

"Zoopus!" Z quips, "And my lover boy?"

"Yes! But don't call him that!"

"Of course not."

"Son-of-a-bitch!" Vilter's impressed. "Z's got Kaplan's personality—and your sarcasm!"

"She's the first of her species," Marco anthropomorphosises. "Nobody's perfect."

The synthetic Zu waits at its kitchen table, slowly sipping at Kaplan's favorite herb tea, RanchoDeluxe's *'Efflorescent MentalFloss'*.

SALUDA!

Six floors above street-level, alone in the soundproof DataMynd meeting room, Zuzzan and Gerry are sneaking in a quick grope before she flicks on the ELD. "You, Ok?" She checks the new hickey make-up job.

"Rock hard," bones Bobogoné.

One floor below the lovers, Rex Timbu pre-processes the V&V call, shunting it through DataMynd's content analysis filters upstream from the link to Bobogoné. Victor Vilter's image fades up on Timbu's coffee-speckled screen fronting the firm's billion-$e view of the North Bay. Rex up-rezes the attorney's poker-faced aspect, looking for color changes in the capillaries of his cheeks as the fibbing begins. "Patching him in now, Gerry."

"Hello? You two alone I trust?" from the famously explosive litigation lawyer.

"As agreed, Mr. Vilter," Kaplan the handler steps toward the conference room micam. "How might DataMynd assist you in your excellent endeavors this fine day, Sir?" Bespeaks the PR Pro.

"True, you can assist us, but we can assist you even more so," Vilter letting it hang for a few beats.

"I'm almost listening..." Bobogoné breathes.

"I'm so glad! What we're about to show you..." Vilter scans his meeting notes, "... will forever change your view of avatars, artificial life, consumer modeling, and most importantly, product research."

"Who's your client?" Zuzzan interrupts.

"Call him 'Harpo'. Let's be nominally circumspect about this matter," Vilter verbosely obfuscates.

"Harpo?" Bobogoné burps out.

"Lawyer joke, Gerry," Zuzzan's un-amused.

"Know what you two? Everybody is going to win very, very big on this deal," Vilter habitually future-anchoring, front-loading the inevitability of a positive outcome.

"We like very big," Zuzzan confirms.

"Good! Otherwise, we'll take our toys and ..." Vilter threatens, hooking Bobogoné and Kaplan one notch at a time. "...Shall we begin?"

"Yesssssss..." Bobogoné hisses betwixt bleached-blue bicuspids.

Shub bends over his receiver, bites his tongue, and simply says: "Z? Meet Zuzzan and Gerry."

"Harpo? That you?" Gerry queries too late as the DataMynd giant screen fills with a stunning close-up mirror image of Zuzzan Kaplan in the exact Rancho-D outfit Zu has on now. Even the make-up is identical on Z's familiar face. The kitchen simulation is hyper-real, steam gently rising from the tea.

Z lifts its teacup in Kaplan's customary 'Saluda' and asks "Tea? *Efflorescent MentalFloss?*" in Zu's girlish voice.

Kaplan sucks air, forced to focus on the outlandish autobiographic animation. She is petrified, astonished, pissed off, and entranced at...*me?*

Bobogoné blinking back and forth between Zu and Z.

"Hi, Gerry!" hails Z.

"You bugged my house!?" Zuzzan palpitates.

"Not bugged," Z informs, mimicking a perfect voice match of its hostess, "cloned."

"It's a cyberclone," Vilter differentiates, "Non-biological."

"Technically, I'm your Personal Ubiquitous Profile Persona," the PUPP finishes its tea.

"I <u>was</u> being watched!" Zuzzan shooting her deer-in-the-headlights look at Gerry. "I knew it!"

"Why am I even looking at this cartoon, Vilter?" Bobogoné glares at Victor's video.

The distant voice of the mysterious V&V Client loudly intones on the DataMynd ELD surround-sound system, "No cartoon, Mr. Bobogoné. The PUPP is replicating Zuzzan's behavior based on webgridz transactions, multimedia surveillance and legacy records dating back to her birth," Shub's windswept voice announces.

"The Pup!" Gerald Bobogoné growls, "That's real cute, Harpo!"

"Z is an animated replicant of Zuzzan," the invisible inventor provides. Vilter leans back and pulls thoughtfully on his earlobe but Shub continues oblivious to the prearranged signal: "Arguably the most advanced sentient entity ever synthesized."

"Certainly with respect to Transactional Behaviorokinesthetics this is absolutely the case," Z hastily qualifies.

"Who cares?" Bobogoné attempting to deflate the sudden impact of the surprise attack. "For what? Games? We don't do games, we manage cultural data! You know that!"

"Just look at her, Gerry. She's fucking alive!" Zuzzan shakes and shivers. "It's creepy!"

"Ms. Kaplan you were utilized as the 'Z' prototype so that Mr. Bobogoné and you could accurately test the PUPP," Vilter explains. "If Z was modeled on anyone else, you couldn't be absolutely certain that it was performing with the range and depth you are now witnessing. Harpo is insisting that DataMynd have an exclusive first look," Victor skillfully fibs.

"The PUPPs burn a big hole in the wall separating humans from sentient software," Harpo oraculates. "Ask her some personal questions."

"Like what?" Bobogoné barks.

"Z is intimately familiar with Zuzzan's consumer psychodynamics.".

"Ok, Miss Smarty Pants..." Zuzzan confronts her computer graphic counterpart: "What kind panties of do I have on?"

"A pair of sports shorts as usual when there is the slightest chance of starting. Normally your selections run from Rancho-D's Italian Smarthongs to their Ladies Beastie-Boxers," Z reports.

"She's right!" Bobogone' knee-jerks.

"How do you know?" Vilter can't resist.

"It's a question!" Bobogoné bullshits.

"Yes. Sport shorts," an undertow of humiliation pulling her into swirling oceans of mixed emotions. The sense of being deeply violated oscillating with the fetal need to be sequestered alone with her new twin sister.

"You have illegally gathered surveillance information—"

"That's right! It's illegal! And even more so when you grow the PUPP population worldwide to include hundreds of millions of consumers," Vilter incessantly selling. "The PUPPs are potentially the most disruptive, subversive, scary technology since the webgridz itself!"

Zuzzan feels a panic attack coming on. This is worse than being tailed by the NT Due-D teams when Gerry was being screened for the Selection candidacy last year. Harpo's robot is cleverer than anything DataMynd could ever dream up. "What's in the cabinet over the cutting board?"

"The old food processor...See?" Z opens the animated kitchen cupboard. "A RanchoDeluxe knock-off."

"How many times have I met Sister Pynchon in

person?"

"Once."

"How many boyfriends do I have now?"

"One."

"How many boyfriends do I usually have?"

"Over the last five years? Approximately two per year."

"Will I ever find true love?" Zuzzan sneers at the animation.

"Sorry. I wouldn't know," the PUPP truth-tells.

"Enough!" Gerry intervenes, intent on averting attention away from anything even vaguely compromising. "How do these puppets work?"

The distended voice of Harpo bespeaks: "Howzabout DataMynd turns the PUPPs loose on its Cultural Management databases? Within three days every person in the system has a full grown cyberclone ready for real-time polling. Any applications you might wind up using the PUPPS for are your concern. Not mine."

"If what you say is true, Mr. Harpo, we would even need to keep the very existence of the capability prohibitively super-secret," bitches Bobogoné.

"Yeah, for your own protection, but fuck it, you can do whatever you want with the PUPPs; I'm selling the whole thing outright," Shub says.

"That's not a problem for us," Bobogoné loves clandestine operations, especially when it comes to cornering the market on new Cultural Management software. And if Harpo's PUPPs are as promising as Z appears to be, they could be an ultra-powerful secret weapon. In fact as Bobogoné thinks about it, PUPPs could be cyber-soldiers, modified for military service, whilst utilized as datamining drillers and product testers in their spare-cycles. But what if it plays out that he is actually selected as president? King Gerald can secretly maintain a shadow PUPP population of all Americans. He alone would know for certain the impact pending NT policy would have on the masses, he could then submit preemptive face-saving solutions to the Overlords! After a few prophecies come to pass, they'll accept his miraculous Nostradamic analysis as gospel. "How much?" Bobogoné demands.

"Five-Hundred Million ecrement$," Vilter answers.

"What! That's our entire acquisition budget!" Gerry lies, pretending to blow a gasket.

"You have forty-eight hours," Vilter volleys.

"What?" Zuzzan can't believe this is happening to her.

"Ms. Kaplan and I need to offline for a minute," Gerry grunts.

"We'll hold," Victor volunteers.

Bobogoné and Zuzzan dash into the conference rooms' plush foyer and close the door.

"It's following me!"

"Drinking your fucking tea!" Bobogoné is blown away. In the ceiling bubble overhead a hidden security micam pivots.

"She talks like me! Probably knows how much toilet paper I use. She's got my new haircut!"

"It's got your new haircut! It's not real! Don't lose it on me here, Zu! I'm the one they're after!"

"They cloned me!"

"But I'm the CEO! I'm up for Selection and married, and—"

"—having an affair!"

"Ejactly!"

"We've got to eradicate her! She knows about us, Gerry!"

"We'll delete it immediately."

"If it comes out that you and I are doing the 'wild thing' you'll be disqualified from the Selection."

"I know. Won't be pleasant..." Bobogoné bites his lip, twitching spasmodically.

Gerry and Zuzzan finally come back in and pose promisingly at the cyber-conference table: "You're cyberclone technology is impressive," Gerry proffers. "We're prepared to make a fair offer."

"The price is non-negotiable," Vilter insists. "You have forty-eight hours to complete your doo-dee."

"Fuck that!" Harpo dismisses. "Z's very existence is more than sufficient proof of the technology!"

"Well, what's your opinion, Dr. Timbu?" Z asks knowingly. "You've been attentively monitoring the proceedings."

"Jesus, Rex! Get on!" Bobogoné demands. "Now!"

"Gerry?" Rex's video visage pops up in the bottom right hand corner of the screen.

"Well, Doctor?" Bobogoné bullies.

"This 'PUPP' is obviously capable of high-level spontaneous mimicry, but we'd have to quadruple our systems—"

"—My computational overhead is virtually non-existent," Z points out.

"PUPPs power themselves by usurping spare cycles on 'OPP'," says Shub.

"Other People's Processors," Z translates Marcotecht's tech-talk.

"I see. Scavenger agents," Rex injects.

"The PUPPs implant autonomous, behaviorokinesthetically triggered microsobots into every device the host transacts with," hints Harpo.

"What about Security?"

"Obviously yours is impotent against Z's intrusions," Vilter veers vitriolic.

"The PUPPs use fractal-anti-fractal cloaking," Harpo hints, proud of the algorithmic alchemy he worked to solve the paradoxical problem of the invisible PUPP. "No worries. I'll toss it in gratis," Harpo maintains.

"Tell me something, Z? Do you know your maker?" risks Timbu.

"No more than Zuzzy would," Z smiles.

"Intentionally," Vilter politely points out.

Bobogoné is having a Paulian Experience of God-gazing proportion...*If he really could digitally replicate human beings, animated clones of living people—not just faceless statistical visualizations of cultural trending propensities— reporting to him alone?*

"Gerry?" harkens Zuzzan.

"We're in," Bobogoné decides. "Send me the deal docs and give Rex some alone time with your code."

"Mr. Bobogoné. There is no code. Cyberclones program themselves by replicating the behavior of their human Host," Harpo tells him.

"They have a life of their own!" Zuzzan asphyxiates.

"A simulated life," Harpo promises her.

Z lap-dissolves from the kitchen into the Kaplan living room visualization. The PUPP picks up Zuzzan's copy of *Frozen Boy* magazine and flops down on the Rancho-D loveseat.

"Shut it off!" urges Kaplan.

"No more questions?" Victor imagined a half-day marathon conference putting Z through her paces and is genuinely amazed at their pitiful parsing of the PUPPs prodigious powers.

"No," says Bobogoné.

"Ok. The deal docs are being sent as we speak," Vilter informs.

"Good," Gerald bearing his bulbous lips.

"We'll be in touch then," Victor views the virulent vermilion suck-sore on Bobogoné's close-up image. He readily recognizes the symptoms of 'Oral Nursing Neurosis' first identified by the old Vienna Psychoanalytic School as Vilter's father also suffered the rare malady, undergoing bizarre 'Teat-Therapy' because of it.

"Z? Say goodbye," Shub mentors.

"Saluda!" the petite pixel puppet pops off screen.

"Harpo?" Zuzzan hails. "Why did you cyberclone me?"

"Talk to Vilter! He's the filtering organ," Marco slams the rotting receiver down, crushing it between his fat fingers. Shub zips closed the M2 and squeegees out of the pubterm, hustling over the blacktop to the motor homes.

BUNNY PROBLEM

Paula Pynchon stares out of her bullet-proof Bel Air living room window and gives it up to God for the twenty-third time in as many hours. Not a day goes by without dutifully praising the Lord for ordaining her to be the conduit through which flowed the *Affinity Process* randomity algorithms. Raw, random, mathematical chaos is the divine form that God has provided to select pure American leaders, minus the hand of man the manipulator.

She knows that the only hope for spiritual and economic recovery depends on the shrinking affluhip upper-class eventually seizing control of what's left of Novo America. But as the Selection approaches the sister has become increasingly apprehensive about her fellow fortunates, sequestered away in fortified communes like hers, connecting with each other by webgridz, armored bullet-trains, and private jetports. Even the radical Rabbit warriors haven't dared to attack the maximum-security Kinship Communities of America's well-to-do. Older politicos believe this is due to the strict NT policing measures but Paula knows otherwise: the Rabbit resistance movement is strong.

'Sister P' has been amongst the massed *Homeomobilius*, wandered their broken highways and talked to hundreds of displaced homeless-X-homeowners. She's even witnessed—in disguise of course—warrior Rabbits torching Hare Effigies at overcrowded NT Zones, handing out massive doses of speq, blasting rocktro.

Sister Pynchon intuits that the Rabbit revolutionaries are not so much afraid as they are incredibly crafty. She suspects they have been covertly husbanding resources in order to launch major demonstrations during the Selection.

Paula believes the system of NT internment camps is drastically under-built and in need of at least doubling to accommodate up to ten-million full time residents and two-million staff for up to twenty years. Enormous allocations of ecrement$ to fast-track new camp construction could be easily covered by increasing the Roamadic Transient Tax and foreclosing more aggressively on defaulting mortgage holders, thereby significantly swelling the homeless sector's transient tax base.

If the Rabbits are waiting until Selection day to make a move, they will be extremely surprised by the colossal fire-power the NT is prepared to rain down on them. Nano-weapons and an upgraded drone air force linked multimediographically to Containment Team truck-trains and helicopters. The recently re-trained NT Peace Force will straight away outflank and harpoon the Hares one warren at a time.

After the Selections, Paula's immediate goal will be to get the new president to rubber-stamp budget increases for camps and Rapid Response Units as a 'FOB', a First Order of Business. The good sister is using the vast publicity surrounding the Affinity Process to personally sway centrists into backing authorization to employ deadly force and deal decisively with the 'Bunny Problem'.

Fortunately, the continuing success of Pynchon's *Holy*

Vision book has enabled her to wield substantial behind-the-scenes power in the Pentagon NT swarm blog salons where she routinely plies influential elite with succulent Sufi sayings.

Alas, the NT will go on with their rule regardless; still the president must, at minimum, be seemingly charming and occasionally erudite, while graciously and obediently staying out of the way. Now on bended knee, Paula politely prays for her next mission: Senior Presidential Handler!

CYOPOLIS

A few miles north of Questa, Novo New Mexico, a four foot high pile of shattered coyote skulls mark the turn-off. Billy recognizes the primitive pyramid of bleached bones and heads up a dirt side road heading into the *Sangre De Christos* mountain range...*Blood of Christ.*

The so-called 'yard' is thirteen miles ahead at an old mining site converted into an RV refurbishing facility and shipping container junkyard. Billy has only been to the yard once and he had to wait at the guard gate while they swapped out the vehicles. Cyopolians don't like outsiders.

A vast forest of uncontaminated Pinon and Ponderosa blanket the mountains east of the sage-scrubbed desert. Perfume of pine pickles the air, tickling Shub's nose, road-dusted behind Billy and Elroy as he follows them into the beautiful badlands.

Shub's Marriage Marble vibrates, "Marcotecht!" Victor's voice floats from the tiny M2. "You ok?"

"Just zoopy," Shub scoffs.

"Zoopy? You should be fucking jumping with joy! That went really well!"

"Yeah?"

"So, I'm the 'filtering organ', eh?"

"Yeah. You're the liver."

"I like that! I'm usually the asshole! Harrfffo!" Vilter cracks himself up. "Figure out which bank you're gonna use and give me the nums! Ciao Harpo!"

Enoy secures their gear in Billy's RV, preparing to swap out motor homes. Revesti slips his long-knife into a hidden slot in the aluminum frame of the custom backpack he designed and built several years ago. He has used the small sword only once—lopping the head off of an enraged rattle snake—but found the damn thing very effective as a visual deterrent against encroaching lawyers, lovers, muggers, and thieves. "What's the routine, Captain Blurr?" Enoy asks Billy.

"They're kinda edgy out here, man. We'll pull up near the entrance and you guys stay behind while I deal with their people alone."

"Paranoid supercult?"

"Yeah. Maya says Cyopolis is now big time in Amsterdam."

"Oh?" Enoy encourages.

"She says they cherry-pick teenage zombies from the EuRoamad tribes."

"Nectronic..." Enoy's being ironic. 'Zombies' are the failed attempts at self-disposal who wander Amsterdam trying to talk them back into it. They sometimes showed up at the Smokey Eye for deprogramming.

"Yeah! I got a bad feeling!" Maya over M2, jumps in on que.

"Really?" Enoy quandaries. "Why?"

"I don't know. They fucking live underground, you guys!"

"We're actually pulling up to one of their shitholes here now, sweetie," Billy says.

"Careful. I love you more than ever."

"Aw, shucks," blubbers Blurr.

"Look!" Enoy indicates a bizarre barricade barring the road made of shipping containers splayed at the seams, welded scissor-like to steel poles, counter-weighted by boulders suspended in wire nets.

Billy slows the coach on approach but the unmanned gate-thing suddenly swishes skyward, inviting passage, "Everything's solar here."

Enoy drops into the passenger seat and squints through the bug-splattered windshield at a narrow mesa below them housing what appears to be the world's largest junkyard. A hundred acres of scrub are completely obscured by innumerable RV's and thousands of old shipping containers stacked a dozen high. A central clearing is encircled by a seven-story high coyote fence of sharpened Ponderosa pines. A formidable ten-story observation obelisk stands in the middle of the yard constructed of scrap metal and razor-sharp trees capped off by a recycled air-traffic control tower room with huge tinted windows.

Inside the tower, five jump-suited Cyopolis Security Corps scan the panoramic property with umpteen telescopic visioning systems. One of the five wears a sleek black jumpsuit emblazoned with a red Crow Corps logo.

Banks of ELDs rim the overhead racks displaying infrared video imagery of the yards' various structures, entrances and exits. Billy's RV appears on the center screen zooming to a medium close-up of Enoy and Blurr as they halt at the main gate.

A weaponized white man walks out of the guard house, checks his ELD and addresses Billy. "Yer Blurr?" he questions, squinting behind dark dust-goggles.

"Yep!" Billy smiles down at the guard. "Working for JimJim in Transpo."

"Wait here. Alone. Have your colleagues hike up the road a piece."

"Gotcha," Billy says.

The Cyopolian soldier hustles out of the sun into the

smoked-glass confines of the darkened guardhouse. Enoy notices the guard appears almost albino, his protuberant blue veins visibly vibrating under translucent snow white skin. Revesti grabs his backpack and trundles out of the RV, Billy behind him, Marco emerging from the second coach.

"Take our shit up the road a hundred yards or so," Billy creaks through dusty throat. "I'll come get ya, Ok?"

"I gotta pee," Shub implores.

"Let's walk..." Enoy and Marco grab up their gear and head down the dirt road.

High up in the air traffic control tower, the Cyopolian Corpsmen keep half-a-dozen hidden micams trained on the visiting drivers. Center screen, Shub's video image looms ten feet tall as he suddenly halts, unzips his Bovinity suit and lets fly onto the side of the roadway. "What a cow!" the Cyopolian Transpo Chief, JimJim observes, watching Shub readily relieving himself.

"I'm showing three switched-off ELDs and something else," one of the CyopTechs studies his screen, "Couple of Marriage Marble."

"Freelancers," a Cyops officer scoffs.

JimJim emerges from an enormous container-kluged shack. He is a six-foot-eight desert rat hidden beneath a floppy canvas hat and goggles: "You're late!" he righteously rips into Billy, "Should have been here yesterday!"

"Sorry, JimJim. Just went safe and slow like you told me to do."

"So it's my fault?"

"That's not what I meant..."

"No? You're not a fucking fault finder?"

"No fucking way JimJim!"

"Hey! I'll fire yer ass if you talk to me like that again! I 'gotta thousand unemployed roamads take each of you fortunate fuckers' places right now!"

"Thought it was 'No Questions Asked' is all."

"Don't think! Drive!" JimJim tosses a prepaid ecrement$ card at Billy's feet. "Here's your frickin' fee."

Blurr scoops up the plastic paycheck, slips it into his wallet.

"Got two more refurbs for Novo New Orleans."

"Zoopy."

"Sit low, go slow," JimJim winces, spins on his boot heels, and strides back to the mélange of metal shacks.

"Will do..." Billy crouches in the searing sun studying a score of slowly circling carrion-craving crows monitoring below. No junkyard dog, tarnished teeth forbiddingly bared appears—no workers—no vehicles or parking lot. Just thousands of semi-demolished RV's awaiting refurbishment and resale, surrounded by an enormous rusty fools-forest of haphazardly heaped shipping containers.

Billy hears a gritting grind of rusted metal-against-metal and spies a section of ground inside the yard noisily rising, discharging a sturdy steel ramp-way. Two fifty-foot *Wanderlust* motor homes slowly surface up the ramp, drive past the guard house and park next to Billy. The Cyopolian drivers, protected by sun goggles and identical Lizard jumpsuits, resemble robotic reptilians. They completely ignore Blurr and hurriedly drive the dirty coaches down the retractable subterranean incline.

Billy grabs his backpack and makes for the nearest *Wanderlust*. He palms the marble, "We 'goin to the Big Easy, baby!"

"Nectowowzic!" Maya's electrons effloresce from an Amsterdam eatery.

Four white RV's excrete from a materializing adjacent subsurface ramp. Billy notices the custom units are freshly washed, revealing the insidious Cyopolis supercult logo: a wide-open eyeball with a pyramid embedded in the iris, a golden crack running from the capstone to dead center, fatally rupturing the pyramid's fracture-resistant symmetry. The custom motor homes dive slowly up the dirt roadway. Billy sees a shadowy old man in the lead coach's passenger seat. He wears a hooded jump suit.

Shub is lazily lounging on his pack in the dirt. He unzips his Bovinity suit, releasing an extended—but mercifully silent—fart, comprised of gaseous epiphenomena from yesterday's ballmeat kabobs.

Enoy grows curious watching Shub fumble around. He squints and sees Marco's fart slowly ascending into the heavens—a distinct and faintly phosphorescent ghostly green glob of mitigating molecules sheening in the sunlight—unseen by those unable to vision a wider swatch of the available light spectrum. The flatulent fog floats overhead, miraculously missing them.

The Cyopolian coaches creep by and the paleface passenger peeps at the outsideys, focusing his gaze first above their heads then directly at Enoy.

Enoy's brain abruptly reverberates... *That freak can see Shub's fart!* Enoy and the elderly Cyopolian stare astonished at one and other—each *seeing* that the other *sees* that they are both *seeing* the fart in the wider spread-spectrum of ultraviolet and infrared light waves—both blatantly beholding the broader optical continuum many thousands of angstroms further out than ordinary human tunnel-vision. The two men's auras instantly glow and grow, extending luminous invisible jets, tendriling tentatively together, sensing subtle similarities—

—CREEEK—the gate-thing swishes open and the Cyopolian drivers obediently accelerate, breaking the inquisitive auras apart, vanishing over the encircling mesa rim.

Billy pulls up in one of the two new RV's: "Let's get the hell outa here."

Enoy opts to ride with Blurr and Maya for a spell. They settle into their respective supersized *Wanderlusts* and convoy out of the remote valley of the Cyopolians barely twenty minutes after entering.

Back on the roamad-packed Novo New Mexico highway, Shub assumes the posterior position, bottling the bombastic Billy Blurr between himself and the terrible traffic. Marco is feeling a faint flicker of accomplishment, achieving an allowance of success. But Marco suspects that the real PUPP game has only just begun as Bobogoné and his shock-troops will doubtless comb every frame to obtain leveragable minutia.

Shub steers with his knee, opens the ELD, thumbs to a directory of *Independent Camen Island Banks*, and quickly establishes anonymous account at the most seemingly circumspect institution. This done, Marco repos his rotund rump on the leatherette captains' seat, and hums a happy rocktro lullaby by Elroy's famous buddy, Xnebula:

'Feels like we're falling again,
Watching the weather, hoping to win;
Yet not quite women, yet not quite men;
Feels like we're falling...again.'

HARPO-LIKE

Rex Timbu has authorized more than a dozen of his crack semioticians to employ experimental multimediographic goggles on Project Harpo. Bobogoné and Timbu sit opposite each other, both begoggled, skimming vizhits: "How many idiots bought the fucking cow outfit anyway?" grunts Bobogone'.

"There are over thirty million of the 'Bovinity' style out there but only a couple thousand with the Faraday liner."

"How much speq you suck up anyway, Doc?"

"What?"

"We're running out of time, man! Harpo sounded like an arrogant Rabbit-like prop-head. Don't you think? Have them focus more on Rabbit-centric snippets, Rex." Bobogoné extends his cappuccino cup. "Toss a little more in my mud, bud,"

"Say 'When'," Rex sprinkles chocolate-flavored KandyMan into the bosses' brew.

"Whoa!"

"Dr. Rex? I've got something interesting here for you," announces Arish Roy, one of Rex's remoted researchers, his accent crisping over head-mounted holographic link: "Check it out. It's scrubbing up nice."

The shared visualization switches to a scratchy, full screen video-loop seen from a point-of-view through a dirty windshield framing a Harpo-like human hunkered behind a steering wheel.

"It's him!" Bobogoné bursts, spewing speq-speckled spittle.

"CNNT mediadrone nanocam out-takes. Just before the windshield wipers went on," Arish informs. "Facegrab seems to match, in fact the overlapping volumetric probability prototyped out at ninety-three percent when I ran the biomass water print."

"BWPs don't lie!" the Doctor declares.

"I measured the wipers. Mr. Harpo is driving an old-model RV," details the Bombay visualization-reconstruction guru. "We extracted microscopic reflections in the intervening windshield glass and discovered an identical vehicle directly in front of Harpo's."

"Coincidence?" ponders Bobogoné

"Probably not," tenders Timbu. "Harpo could be traveling around with other roamads."

"I told you, Rex," Gerry gyrates. "Fucking Harpo's gone roamadic on us!"

"Yep. We're pissing at a moving target. Anything else?" requests Rex.

"Not yet."

"Good work. Good bye."

"Who do we know in the roamad business, Rex?"

"I don't know any real roamads...Zuzzan?

"Ejactly! Zu would know."

"Paging her now," Timbu grins, watching Gerry slowly spinning in his chair, finishing the coffee with a swashbuckling speq-flushed flourish.

"We've gotta be sharp here, Rex. Real sharp!"

Timbu now noticing the fleshy crevices behind Bobogoné's ears creepily caked with dried-up, day-old shaving cream foam.

I'M THINKING

Kaplan's been concealing herself in the DataMynd ladies execulav, the only headquarters hidey hole not scrutinized by security micams. She cut up and flushed her DataMynd badge so the synthetic huntress-bitch can't easily track her.

Zuzzan speed walks the teeming DataMynd corridors holding a black file folder in front of her face; hopefully foiling the security micams from easily imaging her. Zu's skin scintillates, sending flaming fever-pricks, surging with adrenaline hot-flashes, percolating throughout her capillaries: "Fuck every last one of you..." she gutteralizes.

Zu ducks into the main control room and sees the recorded videoconference playback of Harpo and the Z PUPP flashing across overhead ELDs. The cyberclone is gently blowing across the hot surface of its Rancho-D teacup, subtly smirking Zuzzan now notices.

"Turn that bitch off!" Zu bellows over the enhanced audio track. Timbu snaps his fingers.

Bobogoné removes his Mandarin VR gear, "Zuzzy! Harpo's on the run."

Zuzzan sits—diverting her gaze from the terrible PUPP

twin—and realizes she is looking at the two speqed-out men as if seeing them both for the first time. Zu imagines Rex Timbu morphing between 'Wise Doctor' and 'Psychedelic Pedophile', the two transparent Timbu's superimposed on each other, mutually self-masking. Rex peers back at Zu through beady raccoon-esque eyes encircled by dark red speqrings looping underneath the sockets, and Timbu's teeth, like Gerry's, look to have been recently ripped out and roboplasti replaced, but Rex's lower jaw isn't really all righty-right, the bones are regenerating wrong.

"Got anybody in the roamad trade that owes us one?" queries Bobogone'

Her boy now appears to her as a completely contemptible clown, unpleasantly porky, stained and stinky. She notices speq sweat rings punching through Gerry's silly CEO suit, smells putrid perfume out-gassing from his cologne splattered jowls. Zuzzan counts four full baby-fat folds pressed puffing between Bobogoné's collar and jaws.

"Who Zu?" He can't wait.

"I'm thinking!" Zuzzan's brain buffets. "Call Cyopolis," Zu spits out. "Hire their ass bounty-hunter style. If anyone can find Harpo on the road, it's them."

"A supercult?" Gerry gulps.

"I'm going home," Zuzzan grabs her face-saving file folder, determined to stay incognito, assuming the predatory Puppyz are still silently stalking her room to room, micam to micam.

Bobogoné is speechless. Rigified in rebufflement, a narcoleptic glaze glistens over his crimson eyes as Zuzzy disappears out the crowded corridor door. "Call Cyopolis, Rex," Gerry quickly recovers. "Find him, grab him—"

"—Hold him. I know the dance."

"Handle this personally, Rex...Any more KandyMan left?"

"Of course. Say 'when'."

FALSE ALARM

"Mr. Vic?" Vilter's steroidal assistant, Roxxzan, bleeps onto his private ELD: "Sister Pynchon, line twenty-three."

"Really?" Vilter queries. "The Sister herself?"

"Evidently."

"Let her cook for about ninety seconds. I can't imagine why the Numerical Nun would be calling me...other than the fact that I criticized her Process and vowed to represent the One Voter pro-bono just in case there are any shenanigans."

"Zoooop," Roxx rolls blasé.

Vilter vacillates betwixt venting vindictive invectives at the sourpuss Cybernetic Sister, or conversely power-schmoozing from the high-ground, cool as a cocksure cucumber. The final joke on the affluhip is that they have to continue to control this overpopulated, unemployed, drought-stricken, quarantined population of armed apocalyptics—maintaining a tight cap on the mobile sewage spill that was once a great nation—and they want to have a good time doing it!

The center ELD bleeps and the micam image of Sister

Pynchon appears alone in a wide-shot, poolside, bulging Rancho-D rayon robe covering the famous virgin. "Mr. Vilter. Thank you so much for taking my call unannounced. Something just occurred to me and I thought it best to seek your services in the matter."

"I'm honored, sister. What's on your mind?"

"You see, I've been asked to serve a cabinet level advisory position during the reign of the new president," the sister humbly explains.

"Oh?" There's nothing that Vilter would like more than to see this lady and her latchers on fade forever into the smaze of old news. Her particular brand of evangelism, with its techno-fascistic-religios-scientific-pseudo-mysticism really rubs his war wounds from waybackinthenight the wrong way: "Congratulations!"

"Yes. Thank you. It's the newly created position of Senior Presidential Handler for all public appearances and what not."

"It's the 'what not' that could be worrisome, eh?" Victor's liberal Bay Area scar tissue threatening to tear loose.

"Not for me, Mr. Vilter, I give it to God. My immediate concern is with the Male Power Brotherhood inside the NT."

"I heard there was such a thing," Victor fibs.

"Yes. And I need to laser beam through it in order to do my job."

"Meaning non-stop litigation."

"Or threats thereof."

"Ergo, V and V."

"Comfort enters your house as a guest, Mr. Vilter, and leaves your master. I cannot afford to get comfortable with any position the NT offers me. I need a powerful mouthpiece—that's you—to persistently pressure the hell out of a sect of Washingtonian NT assholes who will attempt to Manchurianize the president!"

"Manchurianize the president?"

"Brainwash! Vilter, these pricks are powerfully evil. You publicly denounce them! They hate you too! Why the fuck do you think I created the Affinity Process?"

"To reform the electoral system?"

"And it's working! But after the Selection they're going to influence the president with remote viewing psychic controllers!"

"What?

"Euro eroto-psychics! Fire, brother! They'll use evil erotic fire! Incubus and Succubus Visitation Psychosis! They'll bombinate our leader with nocturnal neural-net nymph imprints and have the poor slob eating out of their asses in no time!"

"Like waybackinthenight," Vilter relates.

"Precisely, and given this inevitability, I am compelled to install myself as a belligerent buffer between the president and certain NT evildoers," Pynchon pontificates, "The focus has to be on Rabbit removal, not on old-school, puppet-master, dick-dancing!"

"Mmmm..." Victor tempers his tongue, takes off his glasses, and slowly wipes them with a tissue: "I sorry I can't help you sister. Conflict of interest with a current client," Vilter lies, preferring to keep a slot open for the litigious fallout he anticipates occurring around the Selection—more than likely suing the sister herself whilst representing the Selectee—insuring zero penetration by Incubus, Succubus and/or 'what nots' during the critical twenty-four hour window the randomly Chosen One has to decide from amongst the pool of presidential candidates.

"That's extremely disappointing, Mr. Vilter. Who's this client with conflicting concerns? An NT official? We'll just skate around them!"

"This is a long-term client. Too tricky."

"Oh? Well, now that you know my objectives, whom can you recommend that's not conflicted?"

"I can't recommend anyone, sister, company policy."

"Really? Why not? Everyone competition?"

"No. You see V and V specialize in suing other attorneys so whoever we recommend will automatically assume that we are setting them up for an aggressive prosecution malpractice insurance gutting," Victor fancifully fabricates out of thin air.

"Lord help us all, Mr. Vilter. Thank you for your time, I imagine," the sister's face is replaced by the Affinity Process logo.

"My pleasure, sister," Victor claps-off the bank of ELDs and rubs his hands in glee. With the Selection only three days away and Pynchon only just now fishing for a heavyweight throat-puncher she'll be woefully unprepared for the consequences of her ambition and actions: exactly the type of teetering superstar V & V use for long-range target practice.

—BZzzzzzz! — Vilter's marble vibrates. He plucks the rattling M2 from its hiding place in his snuff box: "Sir Shub, Que Pasa?"

"Any news, Viceroy?" Shub's voice booms over the little device.

"No. But good news is no news. You've got them by their sphericals," Victor smiles at Shub's M2 image. "Let them flail around. Just stay off gridz."

"I am. But I had to go on to get a wire account. Number's in your secured email."

"Zoopus."

"Remember, Z is still active if you think it would be useful to find out what Zuzzan is doing. But I would need to get online."

"Too risky and no huge benefit. Relax, Harpo. Bobogoné's the one on the spot now. Five-hundred million spots. Let's reconvene tomorrow morning. Ciao, Harpo."

"Later, Mr. Liver." Shub's been doggedly following Blurr since exiting the yard over two hours ago and yet they've only managed to traverse thirty miles of roamad-packed high desert highway. There is ten times the normal traffic due to untold thousands of diehard rocktro fans heading into the Taos Pueblo for a free festival. Nobody is going faster than six MPH but tempers don't flare because the jam has become a mobile party parading peacefully in the perfect weather.

Rocktro fanatics from diverse roamadic byways have hitched or caravanned in and now camp on every possible square inch of Novo Taos. Vacant lots and pastures are strewn with colorful cloisters of solar tent camps clustered by supercult, roamad Klan, and Indian tribe, brightly painted flags and standards flapping in the sage/speq-soaked breeze.

Marco is forced to drive so slow that he's actually able to eavesdrop on the conversations of pedestrians and bicyclists keeping pace with the RV's: "...Blueberry KandyMan Brand! A hundred ecrement$ for a quarter; hundred and twenty if you only gotz cash," a Turtle-suited roamad girl of around twelve informs an androgynous passerby stuffed into a filthy RanchoDeluxe Pig outfit.

"Sell to me three," grunts the hoggish hermaphrodite, hoofing it alongside the bicycling speq dealer now pulling out petite plastic pouches of powder-blue KandyMan from a pocket in her Turtle jumpers.

"'Gimme the bacon," she swipes Porky's proffered $e card across her ELD and consummates the spequlative transaction.

Up ahead, milling roamads make way for three Pueblo horsemen trotting slowly along the crowded shoulder. "Taoseño Warren Chiefs," a Rabbit-clad teen points out to his blond Bunny girlfriend.

"Wowzus...Horses," coos the coquettish cottontail.

A skateboarder in Coyote coveralls sails past, pulled by an unruly dog pack. The well-fed team of mutts wear muzzle harnesses bungeed to the street-surfer's wrists.

Judging by the huge number of people sporting Rabbit jumpsuits—and the startling preponderance of Wary Hare pictogram graffiti—Shub suspects the free three-day rocktro event will grow hair and flare into a massive and rabid Rabbit protest timed to coincide with the Affinity Process. Marco further figures that Taos is in a fairly isolated sector of the New Totality, and affluhip coastal dwellers won't pay attention to nonsensical Novo New Mexican Rabbit roamad tomfoolery.

Shub creeps up alongside the skateboarding Coyote again but two of the six canines abruptly bolt on their bungees and dive dangerously close to Marco's motor home, insanely intent on nosing his RV's undercarriage. Their master yanks the yipping mongrels out of harms way and skates double-time past Shub: "Yer leaking, bro!"

"Yeah?" Shub watches the dog team disappear, slaloming past a Donkey-dressed duo dancing in the center lane. Shub wonders if the leak is serious or if the skateboarder is just having one on him because his damn dogs went bananas. But this is no place for a mechanical malfunction as there is nowhere to pull over without impeding traffic for many miles. Marco flashes his high-beams about twenty-three times before the Blurr notices the signal.

Billy curls sharply to the left, plowing down a deserted dirt alleyway marked *DEAD END* which inexplicably dumps them at the VIP vehicle entrance to the festivo campgrounds. A line of Rooster uniformed parking attendants usher the twin motor homes into a half-full RV-hookup area next to band busses and equipment trucks surrounded by scurrying goat-clad roadies.

A Rabbit security captain passes his speq pipe to a squad of crossbow-toting Wary Hare bouncers around a blazing Pinon pyre. The Rabbits pay no attention to a heterogeneous herd of roamadic mule folk peacefully pressed against the plastic VIP perimeter barrier. The Mules break into song and whirl dervishly as dozens of synchronized ELDS blast Xnebula's inflammatory new 'Rabbit Man' anthem: "Fuck it! It's a drop in the bucket. You should chuck it back into the sea."

Billy and Enoy stretch their road-weary arses,

sauntering over to Marco's RV. Shub squats in the dirt, grunting, hunting for suspected seepage: "Take a look. Dude said I was leaking but I don't see anything."

Billy surmises, "If she starts leaking we'll take her back to the yard." He scans the agglomerating multitude of rocktro fans, "As long as we're here, let's catch some rocktro!"

RABBITS ARE EXTRA

Dr. Timbu's hard pressed to get anyone inside the inner-zircles at Cyopolis on ELD. The notoriously bureaucratic supercult is surrounded by a triple-thick phalanx of saber-toothed litigators. After being re-routed from Legal to PR to Strategic Relations to Special Projects, the thoughtful Doctor is on hold again—this time with the Transportation Department—and forced to watch the asinine Cyopolis webgridz promo for the sixth time in under an hour. He notices that the promo is slightly altered this time around. Details are delved into not previously divulged. The supercults ELD system knows Timbu has been holding and is pushing the next layer of propaganda at him.

A slick VR animation visualizes an all-knowing narrators' exposition: *"As you recall, the ancient Mu civilization, referred to as 'Menahuni' in Hawaiian mythology, descended into the great volcano on Trickster Maui and discovered subterranean passageways under the Pacific, heading east, surfacing just inland from the coast of what is now Baja California. Using the vast tunnel system, the Menahuni quickly migrated from Maui and spread out across the paradisiacal new continent taking the name 'Hopi' and vowing to be the eternal caretakers of the planet."*

A pissed-off male voice snaps the doctor out of his philosophical flight, and cuts off the Cyopolis webgridz backgrounder: "JimJim here."

"Mr. JimJim, Doctor Timbu, DataMynd Cultural Management Agency."

"Impressive. I'm sure," the skinny Transpo Chief smirks inside Timbu's ELD. "What can I do on you, Doctor?"

"DataMynd is offering a handsome reward for the immediate apprehension of an x-employee. We think Cyopolis can assist us in this delicate matter."

"Says who?"

"I'm not really sure that's important."

"Oh? So it's my fault for asking? What are you? A fucking fault finder, Doc?"

"I'm not finding fault," Rex can't help but grin at this laughable tough-guy supercult cliché. "We're prepared to offer one million ecrement$ for his safe capture. He's traveling in a motor home, possibly in a group, somewhere within a three-day drive of San Francisco."

"That where you're calling from?" JimJim takes a patient pull off of his desktop speq hookah. "Fucking whole Bay Area is gonna crack off and sink into the soup real soon," JimJim blows two tiny interlocking speq smoke rings into the micam.

"One million ecrement$?" Rex establishes. "It's important."

"Look friend, we're a church."

"Three million cash," Rex automatically offers.

"I can make Cyopolis three million in half a dozen calls," jives JimJim. "We don't actually need your ecrement$, Doctor."

"Five million," Rex flexes.

"Cash? Six million ecrement$."

"One for you and five for the Church?"

"That's not nice! Seven!"

"Two for you?"

"Eight!"

"Seven point five!" Rex pretends to cave when really he could go up to twenty for Harpo's hide.

"Eight point five million ecrement$, my friend! Deal?"

"Done. I'll gridz you the $e and the subject's profile."

"This gonna be a Rabbit hunt, Doc? Rabbits are extra."

"Harpo's not a hare. He's a cow. A big one."

"A big cow guy..." JimJim's eyes widen.

WESTWARD

Kaplan exits the bullet-proof bullet train and scurries to an armored corporate limo. A flagrantly weaponized DataMynd driver schleps Zu five short Manhattan blocks to the PR Directors' threat-ruggedized affluhip co-op. Zuzzan walks backwards down the hallway approaching her unit, hoping to confuse Z, sure to be snatching video clips from security micams.

Safely inside, Zu hastily hunts down three pair of soiled CrunchyCountry Speedos that Gerry has abandoned over the past months and silently slips them over the ELD micam lenses in her living room, home office and kitchen, hindering Z's Puppyz from watching.

Zu carefully crunches the compromising ELD communications device in her trash compactor.

With the latent image of Gerry's jiggling jowls burned into her brain, Zuzzan speed-packs three Rancho-D suitcases with essential wardrobe and toiletry items and heads out of the bugged building, not knowing where she is going, virtually incognito. DataMynd won't bother to track her for at least twenty-four hours, although Gerry is probably placing calls to her now.

Zu pays cash to purchase an old unregistered Subaru from a nearby roamad parking lot attendant. The previously stolen, stripped, and resurrected station wagon is dirty but sturdy, cheap paint job not quite covering a passionate pink Wary Hare graffito-glyph carved into its rustic green hood.

Kaplan heads out of the city, determined to flee offgridz both bodily and electronically in as random a fashion as she can manage. Having finally recognized Bobogoné for the bloodsucking creep he really is, nothing can prevent Zuzzan from seeking her freedom, whatever the expense. She'll give DataMynd, Gerry and Harpo's PUPP the slip, establish another life—one less damaging in terms of self-sabotage—resurfacing somewhere else, emancipated and intact.

Zu drives determinedly down random country highways, slowly flowing vaguely westward amidst the hordes of homeless, migrating nowhere, scarcely surviving, forever departing, never arriving, addicted to free form forward locomotion.

Darkness encroaches as Zu approaches the ring of roamadic encampments out skirting Novo Scranton. The dense deposits of humiliated humanity have always looked to Zuzzan, like vast slimy smears of poisonous phosphorescent lichen, aglow atop a malignant mulch of combusting compost. But alas, not tonight, instead the chaotic confusion of shantytowns seems safe now, secretive, welcoming and womby. She can proceed unnoticed amongst the anonymous roamads, escaping her previous position as principal pawn in Gerry's psychosexual shit.

Zuzzan stops at a jam-packed NT fuel station and changes outfits in the restroom. She clamps on a camo duck hunter's hat and augments the roamadic look with a cheap pair of pyramid-shaped crimson-tinted sunglasses.

Sheltered by her disguise, Kaplan cryptically cruises

towards Novo Missouri as tears of joy and fear sporadically spill, gradually soaking her lap in a beatific baptism of cathartic purification.

RABBIT MAN

Given that Hispanic Hares are expert crossbow marksman, it's not surprising that they have killed 99% of the NT micams in and around Taos for the rocktro event. Shub has been to many a wild festivo waybackinthenight, but he has never encountered a mobile midway of genetically jacked-up geriatric gypsies surrounded by a magic circle of sixty human Ouija boards over-run by rambunctious roamad teens picking off low-flying mediadrones with their slingshots.

Billy leads the way out of the ResturanTruck area toward five-thousand barnyard animal attired rocktro fanatics jostling for position inside the main multimediography zone. In typical roamadic childcare tradition, kids, toys and pets are everywhere underfoot. Shub trods on a toddler's toy and dodges dozens of desperate doggies eyeing his ballmeat kabobs. Several sociable pit bulls casually crowd-weave, encircling Enoy and Billy who are eating burrito-pitas and guzzling green Pueblo microbrews. Enoy gives the biggest dog the evil eye. The beast obediently backs away and bolts off, its underlings in tow.

The air is so thick with speq smoke that everybody seems to have a second-hand contact high. By the time Shub finally secures a little patch of dirt near the main stage, Blurr has bonded with every stoner rocktro geek, roamad freak and nectronic babe within hailing range. The speq-induced talking disease has gripped Billy who is now blathering with a bunch of bohemian brothers. In fact, everyone but Enoy and Shub are chattering like old hens at a fine feathered friend's reunion.

Marco hasn't been in a mob this large since the *'Resurrection of the Dead'* concert in Berkeley waybackinthenight. Swirling sights and sounds are now occurring with such increasing intensity that Shub wishes he was alone back in the RV. He focuses a jaundiced eye on the Diasporadic citizenry: solo singles searching for spirited lovers, homeless families running amok bartering belongings, dreaming of roboplasti transplant procedures, celebrity worshipers sucking up speq, swarmshopping, addicted to live webgridz suicide shows.

"Marco?" Enoy enunciates, squeezing down in the dirt next to Shub.

"Marco..." Shub auto-utters.

"Once is enough, thank you," Enoy gently reminds, seeing Shub's aura palpitating against the claustrophobic cluster of humanity.

Marco manages to mumble, "I'm getting dizzy, man."

"It's the speq smoke," Revesti diagnoses, able himself to easily ward off the subtle psychological effects of second-hand exposure. "Don't breathe it in," Enoy imagines that these guys are getting pretty stoned and will require reality wrangling before long.

Billy reappears with three racy roamad women of undeterminable age who seductively squish into a happy hog pile with Blurr, Shub and Enoy. But before introductions can be made a deafening ROAR erupts from the smoky sea of festivo freaks resolving into a spontaneous chant: "Rocktro! Rocktro! Rocktro!"

The house lights go down and overhead blimps project an immense image of the Wary Hare glyph onto synthetic cumulous clouds released over the audience.

Without warning or intro, a fast moving figure in a nonfigurative Horse Fly jumpsuit enters center stage and makes the sign of the Wary Hare: flapping hands in floppy Rabbit ears imitation.

"It's Xnebula!" Enoy is videoing.

"Unbemotherfuckingliveable!" Blurr is blown away.

"Fuck it!" Xnebula shouts over the cheers. "It's a drop in the bucket!"

"Yeah you should chuck it!" the crowd chiming, "Back into the sea..."

"As luck would have it, I got trapped like a Rabbit." Xnebula dives into the first verse, strumming virtual guitar. "I had to gnaw my foot off..."

"...to be free!" everybody shouts in chorus. "...to be free!"

"I'm gonna live on the broken highway," Xnebula points out several Rabbit hutches prominently displaying hieroglyphic Hare Flags. "I've got a couple old lovers out there!"

"I'm gonna run, gonna run with the Rabbit roamads!" the trio of roamad woman shout out the liberation lyrics; one of them leaping piggy-back onto Billy, riding the baffled Blurr head and shoulders above the sea of Slowedownlight disciples.

"And leave my mark on my generation..." Xnebula turns his back on the crowd and pretends to piss on an amplifier: "The mark of Rabbit Man!"

"Rabbit Man!" the assemblage answers, calling out the new-fangled battle cry of their radical roamadic revolution.

Xnebula zips up and spins around cracking up. He does the 'bunny ears' move again, dancing down close to the audience and spies the women riding high on Blurr's shoulders, screaming "Rabbit Man!"

Xnebula flaps his ears excitedly she briefly bares her boobs causing the fundamentally shy superstar to fairly flush, careening from the cacophony of cat calls and coyote hoots. Xnebula starts to dance away but halts mid-step and does a double-take.

He points at the person standing right next to the buxom bunny and laughs in recognition of Enoy. Revesti gives a quick salute to the rocktro God, then ducks down grabbing Billy by the waist and swings him around, switching positions. "It's everyone!" insists Xnebula absurdly.

All eyes turn to Billy: "It's everyone!" echo the masses. "It's everyone!"

Billy makes the 'Sign of the Hare' and laughs as several Rabbits rush up joyously hoisting him in the air. "Rabbit Man!" sings Xnebula. Blurr gets playfully passed up over the audience on his back, floating atop an undulating sea of raised hands. Billy looks to piss himself with mirth any moment, prompting giggling girls to take turns tickling him.

Shub is screaming "FMB!" jumping up and down and trying to see what has become of Blurr.

"Rabbit Man!" Xnebula points to the heavens: a dozen three-hundred-foot close-up images of Billy bouncing on his butt are beamed across the ultra-bright blimp screens imbedded in behemoth Barium boluses. Enoy looks up: Billy—ritualized as Rabbit Man—appears in an impromptu interactive sky-movie, Slowedownlight's multimediographic editors superimposing him over random black and white nature shots showing hundreds of bunnies humping in the heather.

The blimps suddenly broadcast skyscraper-sized burning bunny clips as a fifty-foot overstuffed Hare Effigy lashed to a glowing crimson cross is lowered onstage over an upturned satellite dish fire-walling the floor.

Xnebula dutifully mimes the floppy-eared Rabbit Man sign one last time then strikes an imaginary match and flicks it directly at the dangling dummy. The inflammatory doll IGNITES with fiery furor, blasting brightly behind a wave front of heat and light.

Xnebula takes a bow and vanishes just as precisely positioned pyrotechnic pockets of Naphthalene ignite—instantly tripling the burning beastie's volatile volume—throwing fingers of flame WHOOSHING out the incendiary hare's ears, eyes, nose, mouth and crotch.

The sight of the sacrificial blazing bunny is the last thing Shub can remember until: "Rise and shine, Saint Shub," Enoy is hunched next to Marco, who is sleeping off the side-effects of speq, slumbering under a scrub oak only fifteen-feet from the comfort of his *Wanderlust*.

"Bluuuuue..." Marco's memory is foggy.

"I lost you guys after you herded those bunnies into a SolarTent sauna."

"...Nectar..." Shub's humiliated head throbs, thankful he doesn't recollect. Then he notices several small shadows moving around underneath his motor home: its three black cats guardedly lapping at a large lozenge of liquid leaked from the loins of his RV. "Look at those cats under my rig, man!" More feral felines are circling, cat-dancing crazy-eights, their petite pink tongues flicking in and out, lip-licking, sensing some secret scent. "Hope it's not anti-freeze or they're dead puss."

The two trundle over to the coach and crouch down. Three hungry wildcats look them in the eyes and scatter from a slick circle of red fluid puddled under the black-water tank. "Did you use the toilet?" Revesti asks.

"No. Not that I remember."

Enoy stretches under the chassis, examines the source of the leak. He spies a tiny hole and pokes at it. A smear of the suspected seepage darkens his index finger: "Blood...Yer leaking blood?"

"What?" Shub squats down, wipes his pinky in the puddle and holds it up to the sunlight: "The fuck?"

"You hit any critters yesterday?"

"None that I know of."

Shub knocks on Billy's Wanderlust. He hears scuffling and laughter before the door swings open emitting two of the roamad women from last night, clutching their clothes and moccasins, racing nearly naked toward the VIP outhouses. Marco concludes that roamad women—frustrated by the ninety-percent sterility of American males—will even resort to bedding bastards like Blurr in their ongoing effort to become impregnated.

Blurr himself now bounds out of the back bedroom, wide-awake. "El Festivo fantastico'!" beams Billy, energetically exiting his recreational Love Limo: "What, Shubus?" Marco is frowning at him. "Maya likes to watch, man!"

"Found the leak," says Shub, presenting his blood-splotched pinky.

SATURATING

Z has been continually querying its platoons of Puppyz positioned in the devices Zuzzan normally transacts with, but nothing is returning. The persistent PUPP puffs up, propagating itself across three million additional webgridz processors, borrowing from beefed-up game machines parked in Peking, back-up swarmbay servers in Saigon and select EuroTotality network operations centers.

Z begins spraying the gridz with many millions of hungry Puppyz in an ever-expanding geographic ring starting from Zu's NYC co-op, radiating outward beyond the city, saturating all of Novo New England, widening westward, blanketing the Mid-Atlantic. The invisible microsobots insert themselves into ATMs, NT micams, security cameras and multimediographic IT systems controlling bullet trains, jetports, Kinship Communities, Restaurantrucks, pubs, etc., etc.

The PUPP speed dials Marcotecht's ELD—finds it in the off position—leaves another urgent 'Call Z' message on Vilter Victor's secure gridzmail, and begins power-crunching the massive amount of media objects presently pouring in from her spreading spawn, searching for the singular cyber-scent of the inactive Zuzzan host.

BLENDING IN

Zuzzan Kaplan has discovered that one tiny hit of KandyMan Brand every twelve hours enables her to drive wide-awake for an entire day and night with only a few hours' sleep. Nobody pays undue attention to Zu, disguised as she is in second-hand horse jumpsuit.

Zuzzan arises from a rejuvenating roadside respite somewhere south of Novo St. Louis, breathing deeply the aromatic roamadic wind, wonderfully wafting way-off wisps of Wonton against a bold bracing background of bohemian brisket-of-beef barbecue.

She polishes off her last algae bar and drains the lone bladder of black-market Italian table water grabbed up when fleeing her beloved flat. She regrets now having spent so many hard-earned ecrement$ on affluhip life coaches, neurolinguistic defense classes, and truckloads of must-have Rancho-D consumables. Kaplan's concerns crescendo, causing her conscience to curl into itself.

Zuzzan takes a temperate toke of the KandyMan pick-me-up she purchased from a unicycling bunny rabbit then stashes the biodegradable pipe in one of the twenty-odd horsey suit pockets. She swings her Subaru southwest, converging with the romantic river of roamads, speculatively wading into the welcoming waters.

PLINK!

A crush of busses, custom RV's and equipment wagons are filling the VIP RV area as the festivo continues to inflate with passionate Affinity Process protesters and diehard rocktro rabbits. A bunch of band busses whose goat-clad roadies are off-loading gear to mark their preferred parking territory are temporarily boxing-in the *Wanderlust* coaches.

Marco and the Blurr follow Enoy around the backside of Billy's RV and watch as Revesti removes a final screw securing a thick polyurethane access cap to the rear waste tank. Enoy pokes a little flashlight in the opening and looks around: "Full up."

"What's going on, lover?" Maya asks, awakening in the Netherlands.

"Good question," Billy grips the M2 and heads into his RV followed by Shub and Elroy, all surprisingly silenced.

Blurr slides in behind the dining table and points his marble's fisheye-lens at a pile of plasma pouches, blood bags, and frozen organs surrounded by a stack of vacuum-packed speq bricks. "Five times more hidden in the tanks and tubes."

"I told you these Cyopolians were psychos!" Maya slips

into silence with the others.

Enoy thumbs his ELD: "Uncut KandyMan Brand speq, nano-suspended human organs, few bags of stem cells and some DNA mini-packs." He opens up a spec-pak with his Swiss army knife and carefully dumps the contents into the kitchen sink: PLINK! A little lead-like orb bounces out and plops to rest into the freeze-dried KandyMan powder.

"Wowzus...What's it doing?" blows Blurr.

Shub weighs it in his palm, "Probably GPS. Which means they know our location."

"They know we've only gone a few miles since we left the yard," Billy considers.

"Best we walk away now. Hitch home," advises Elroy. "How do they contact you, Billy?"

"They don't. I only see them at exchange points."

"Their tracking our asses..." Elroy says, watching in wonder as Shub and Billy close their eyes and slump down in their seats like rag dolls released from the grip of an invisible handler.

"Guys?" Maya's muffled voice is trapped between Billy's collarbone and chin.

Weirdly enough, Enoy really wants to black out with them but instead struggles to elevate his hand into view and focus on the palm with its purple spider veins. He's used this particular fixation technique previously as a visual anchor when it's become evident that he is losing consciousness.

Enoy's exertion instantaneously ejects him from flesh and bone. becomes a blue, bioplasmic energy emanating upwards approximately thirty feet in the air outside above the two RVs. From this vertical vantage point Enoy is able to ascertain a trio of masked Cyopolians gathering around the RV, sneakily pumping some kind of knock-out gas into rear AC vents. Four seconds is as long as Revesti can maintain his projection without causing serious bioplasmic neural damage. Moments later he's back in his body, passed out cold. The door is being kicked open.

HAMMERED DOG SHIT

Enoy awakes face down on a cool steel floor, naked and warm, flat on his belly, listening to the background hum of machinery. Enoy flips over on his back. He clearly recalls seeing hoses extending from tanks strapped onto the back of gas-masked Cyopolians.

Enoy breaths in the odor of recycled air, peering into a pitched blackness and sees the sleeping shapes of Shub and Billy likewise nude, face down less than six feet away. He nudges them with his foot.

Billy coughs.

Shub farts: "What the fuck?"

"They nabbed our asses," Enoy whispers. "They gassed us. We're back at their junk yard."

"We're fucking fucked," Billy says.

"No. Listen to me. We don't know what they're gonna do. Right? But they don't know what we're gonna do either. They don't know who we told about our little discovery," whispers Elroy.

"We didn't tell anyone," says Shub.

"They don't know that," reminds Revesti.

"Maya knows. She recorded it. Maya records everything," clarifies Billy.

"They don't know that either!"

"He's right," says Marco. "Otherwise we'd probably be dead."

FREELANCERS

JimJim has been hanging on hold for over fifty-five minutes waiting for Lord Byrdman to pick up. JJ hates referring to the boss as 'my Lord'. Waybackinthenight, he was 'Gene' or 'Birdy', but for the last five years, second-generation Cyopolians insist on employing the Title Royale.

JimJim believes this bullshit naming convention derives from gamers worshiping the Strong Man with the Cosmic Truth. Now their easy marks for the apocalyptic sci-fi religion Byrdman birthed under the non-profit Cyopolis supercult brand.

But to dozens of tenured operations managers like himself, Cyopolis is an extremely diversified goldmine of kickbacks on top of kickbacks. Take this Project Harpo deal. Just fell in his lap! The video clip returned a positive match with a cow-clad freelancer security cameras spied pissing on the property yesterday. Eight point five million $e and they nailed the sucker in less than two hours!

"Talk to me..." Byrdman's voice vital despite his aging albino-eseque pallor intensified by decades living mostly underground, "...Transpo Tsar."

"Hail, Lord Byrdman!" JimJim knee-jerks the jejune perfunctory. Byrdman leans back, limber and lucid, eighty-six going on fifty. "An easy Grab-and-Detain just turned into a situation. They found some of our cargo and we don't know if they informed anyone before we grabbed them. Freelancers. Caught up with them yesterday."

"Your man a wrinkled old roamad?"

"No..." JimJim's amazed as always how Birdy is already tuned into the details. "Old guy is a rider."

"Mmmm..." Byrdman's yet to encounter another who can seemingly see, besides the curious old roamad.

"Probably run-of-the-mill roamads."

"I think not."

"We have to crack their ELDs to find out for sure."

"Use Interview."

"Planning just that."

"But leave the old man alone until I get back, JJ. I'll be interviewing him personally."

"Contract's worth seven mil."

"Fulfill it. I told you freelancers were a bad idea."

"I'll fix it."

"Send me the seven."

M2

The Cyopolian tunnel system slopes upward twisting to another level comprised of several hundred storage rooms. Two Groundhog-suited functionaries heft black burlap bags bulging with the belongings of the confined crew. They deposit their burden in one of the empty storage rooms and mark the inventory on ELD.

Jostled amongst the backpacks, media toys and clothing, the two confiscated Marriage Marbles roll down to the bottom of one of the bags and touch their tiny screens together: "Shub!" Victor Vilter vibrates audiovisually, trying to hail Marco.

"Who the fuck are you?" Maya says.

"I'm a fucking spouse! Get off my line!"

"I'm on a marble."

"Me too."

"You looking for Shub?"

"I'm looking for my spouse."

"Come on, I heard you! I'm looking for, Billy! My husband! Shub's bud."

"I'm Shub's attorney. Where is he?"

"I don't know," Maya admits. "Lost contact. They must have found them!"

"They?"

LIVESTOCK

DataMynd's Command and Control center is busily abuzz with specialists bustling on Dr. Timbu's peppy speqachinos. 'Project Harpo' is taking priority over all other corporate endeavors and Gerry and Rex are mutually multitasking, having reassigned fifty of the company's most capable CM Agents to begin brainstorming on Consumer Clone apps ASAP. They'll have to move the secret team to Washington if Bobogoné gets selected president but Rex fully expects to follow his friend into the White House as Cultural Management Czar, should the slim probability of being picked actually pay off.

Timbu's command ELD turns tinted red with a high priority inbound. The ID header reads: *Transportation Department.* "It's them," Rex raises a little pinky and wiggles it around. The micam gestural interface switches to videoconference mode:

"Doc!" JimJim's unlikable likeness alights. "Found yer livestock wandering the broken highway. Want 'em back?"

"That was damn quick!" Timbu's truly impressed. "When can you deliver?"

"No one said anything about delivery."

"We'll send a jet," Bobogone' has one. "Where can we pick him up?"

"Taos Airport. Novo New México," the Cyopolian suggests. "Noon tomorrow."

"Fine," Bobogoné decides. "You're positive it's Harpo?"

"Yeah. Take a look!" Timbu's EarthLinguaDevice fills full-screen with the Cyopolian security video clip showing Harpo the cowboy, squinting against the azure sky, relieving himself in the dirt.

HUMAN-IN-THE-LOOP

Sister P has very few friends outside of those cloistered in the Novo Hollywood Hills Nunnery. Even her girlfriends from the Women's Morticians Collaborative have ceased trying to reach her. That's the price she pays for being brutally protective of her time as she dutifully directs the final implementation of the Affinity Process from her Novo California kinship commune command post deep inside the beautiful Bel Air Protectorate.

Concern over the technical aspects of the Selection Election are pretty much vanquished in Paula's mind—she personally supervised the final testing of the NT IT security system protecting the massive Randomity Generator supercomputer cluster on Maui—but the effort to keep others keeping the faith in the divine mathematics of God is proving to be a daunting task even for the energetic sister's evangelistic abilities.

She has been pumping out a dozen ELD calls an hour to influential affluhip, many convinced the whole thing is going to collapse into class warfare: homeowners vs. roamads.

At the moment it's the old 'human-in-the-loop' trouble getting the sister's bee bonnet buzzing: once the One Voter is randomly chosen, the purity of mathematics becomes polluted, dependent on the actions of the human in the loop.

After the human gets in there, divine randomity is, paradoxically, enhanced proportionate to the negative information the person brings to the equation; so if the luck of the draw manifests a schmuck who doesn't know squat about the two hundred Selection candidates it will actually improve the efficacy of randomity as the poor slob will only have twenty-four hours to decide between the Selectees. No matter how much research and pondering the One can carry out in that short period, the presidential pick will ultimately arise from fundamentally random cognitive processes like emotion and sexual attraction.

"Sister?" a young nun in a winged habit deftly maneuvers an industrial-sized food cart into Paula's proximity.

"Thank you, Sister Ranapopolopolous. I'm starved! What did Brother Junipero prepare today?"

"Roasted rabbit, roamad style, double portion, stuffed with basmati and organic ballmeat, and bulls' blood baste on the side."

"Ah! Egri Bikavar!" Pynchon pleasures. "Perfecto!"

"May it dance on your tongue, sister."

MR. BUSINESSMAN

A Jaguar jump-suited Cyopolian soldier sets three ELDs and a pair of M2s on JimJim's desk: "I need you to sign off, Chief," requests the aspiring intel officer. "'Gotta take these to the lab and hack 'em."

"Marriage Marbles? From which ones?"

"The freelancer and the cowboy."

"Who's on the other end?"

"Don't know yet, JimJim. I need you to sign off first—"

"—oh, so it's my fault?" the temperamental Chief can't resist his favorite routine. "What are you? A fucking fault finder!?"

"No...Not at all Chief," the junior Jaguar knows better than to irk the transpo boss. Not only is JimJim a Senior Cyopolian Senator from waybackinthenight, but he's been known to fatally flip out and herd newbies into shipping containers—personally weld them shut—and drop them topside to rot in the badlands. "I certainly could have acted more wisely."

"See? You've got to find fault even if it's your own

fucking fault! Gimme that!" JimJim filches one of the M2s and eyes it curiously. Marriage Marbles are forbidden in Cyopolis as they negate the effective use of a man's remaining sperm seeds—the decline of which is drastically endangering the species—making it much more difficult to recruit fertile initiates and teach them to produce children who can be grandfathered into the subterranean Cyopolian supercult. JimJim takes a proficient pull off of his mini-hookah and blows out a thick ring of speq smoke. The ring wraps around the M2 and wobbles on; silently crashing into his gawking underling's stupefied face.

JimJim jerks the marble up to within an inch of his good eye, peers into its weensy video viewer and says: "The man in the cow suit and his two friends are visiting our wellness resort...I know you can see me...Show your face...Unless you'd rather we just go ahead and cure all three of 'em."

"You have no cure," Victor Vilter's velvety voice vents from the virtual void, M2 image obscured by his thumb.

"Hi there!" JimJim somewhat surprised at the macho response. "Who be ye, brother?"

"Free my friends or feel my fury, Mr. JimJim," Vilter's been busy debriefing with Maya and watching her footage of the RV trip. Shub's friend's wife is exceedingly anal about recording everything her husband says and does on the marble. Maya is silently recording even now, only a few feet from JimJim.

"And what kind of friends might your friends be, friend?" JimJim jousts.

"People you really shouldn't be inconveniencing."

"You should have said you were a businessman! The bidding starts at ten million $e!"

"JimJim, climb out of your hole. It's raining KandyMan, kidneys, DNA, and blood," Vilter details.

"Oh?" the Chief winks conspiratorially at his junior colleague, hiding off camera, petrified by JimJim's dicey repartee. "What else ya got, Doc?"

"Here we have some fresh video of your principal product line."

JimJim squints cockeyed at the mini-screen and sees the clip Vilter got from Maya clearly documenting the incriminating cargo previously piled in Billy's coach. "Don't take it so personally. Our client is paying large sums for the delivery of Harpo the Cow. I'm merely affording you the courtesy of a preemptive bid!"

Vilter's cunning cortex pieces the puzzle together in a picosecond...*Harpo?* "Inform DataMynd that your deal is off."

"You inform them, Bro!"

"I will."

JimJim's impressed with this guy's perspicacity. "Do that! You and Doctor Data-Brain work it out and get back to me."

"Put Harpo on! Now!"

"Answer me this..." JimJim gently squeezes the M2. "...mean little man in the marble. If your Harpo is such a valuable VIP then why the hell is he out on the broken highway freelancing for me?" Not waiting for an answer, JJ drops the sputtering spouse sphere into his desk drawer. "Give their clothes back," JimJim orders. He tosses Billy's marble into the drawer along with Harpo's hotheaded partner: "I'm keeping these for now."

DARK BLACK

Victor removes his thumb from the M2 lens. "Maya? You record that guy?"

"Of course," Maya answers.

"Perfect! Hold on a minute. Let's try something here..." Vilter gestures at his ELD screen and a voice-activated gridz-mail window pops up: "Gridz-mail Zuzzan Kaplan at DataMynd. Message: Z, call Vilter Victor now. Priority Urgent."

— Twisslebleep! — Z instantly answers the intercepted gridz-mail. Victor gestures to the ELD, opening the PUPP's video window: Z is in it's Kaplan co-op foyer vizualization: "Vilter Victor. Kindly connect me with my Marcotecht via M2—"

"—He's not wearing it."

"No? Then Zuzzan and Marcotecht are both dark black?"

"What? Kaplan too?"

"DataMynd just now put out a nationwide alert on her," Zuzzan fiendishly obscured the views of all the micams inside her co-op so Z has had to pack using best guess approximations of what Kaplan would take with her if she bolted from the flat, which appears to be the case as the last videoclips from the co-op show an unidentifiable figure flying down the corridor, hustling luggage to the freight elevator.

"Really?" Vilter is not really surprised... *Who wouldn't flip out when unexpectedly confronted with one's own fully-blown cyberclone?*

"I don't know. I lost track after she packed. Marcotecht hasn't revealed what I should do if the host goes dark black..." Z steps nearer its virtual micam, eerily framing the PUPP in a conspiratorial fish-eye close-up: "So I've been improvising. Within a few hours, I'll have propagated over three billion Puppyz poised to pounce as soon as Kaplan touches the gridz."

"What?" Victor can see the lifelike pores in the PUPP's synthetic Zu-skin: "Look, Z, I need you to help me help Marcotecht. Understand?"

"I'm a PUPP. Not a legal assistant."

"I know...Forget it. Call me as soon as you have located Shub? Ciao," Vilter hangs up on Z. "Maya? We'll have to get some boots on the ground."

Maya seethes: "Their underground!"

INTERVIEW

Echoes of an unlocking iron door undulate into the underground corridor. The three nude RV delivery drivers lay face down feigning unconsciousness. In the darkness Enoy sees several Cyopolians schlepping something. They halt in the narrow steel corridor and deposit their burden on the floor. One unlocks the cell, another unlocks neighboring two, they leave, slamming the corridor door.

Revesti quickly double-checks the empty hallway: "They're gone..." He spies the burlap bags "Our backpacks!" and fishes out a flashlight, illuminating the immediate area. Enoy verifies the trusty long-knife is still intact inside his secret frame slot, then shines the flashlight at the burlap bags as Billy and Marco claw through their stuff:

"No M2!" Billy is pissed off.

"No ELD...Fuck" Marco bemoans. Waddling over to one of the sinks, he soaks a travel towel in the small steel basin and wipes off French-style. The captives yank on their clothing, silently gazing at the bizarre architecture, lit by the flickering flashlight. Shub observes the crudely spot-welded hand-hammered metal looks like it was made with Iron-Age submarine manufacturing methods.

— CLICK! — The cellblock hall door unlocks again — SHICK! SHICK! — Overhead sliders retract sending re-routed sunlight to reflect from recessed slits running the length of the ceiling. A soft yellow glow illuminates the cellblock as JimJim's harsh voice reverberates in the recycled air: "Blurr and Company?" the Transpo Chief leads a trio of armed Lizard-suited Cyopolians escorting two roamads into the empty holding cell. "Welcome to Cyopolis," JimJim casually shuffles toward the captive RV crew, eyeing the motley lot for signs of subservience, only to find no flinching or flushing amongst them. "Gonna borrow the spare suite for our new initiates here Mr. Freakflag and Mr. Tumbleweed." He faces Shub, "I trust you won't be inconvenienced?"

Billy and Shub exchange glances: it's the two roamads that tried to get a cash ride from them at the festivo. JimJim signals his men who crouch down in the corridor, readying their solar-powered stun guns as Freakflag and Tumbleweed sit crossed-legged on the floor. JimJim pulls an aerosol spray can from his dress-black jumpers and gives it a few shakes.

"That's Interview, man!" Freakflag freaks.

"Is it?" JimJim shakes up the clearly-marked can.

"Yeah! We used it during the Tehran invasion."

"Oh? You a Vet?"

"Both of us served overseas."

"Zoopy..." JJ squatting down, spraying the wannabes two tiny spurts in the face. "Then you won't mind serving us down here."

Freakflag feints. Tumbleweed blacks out. JimJim jumps away from the effects of the spray and squats in the hallway, turning to Enoy, Billy, and Shub: "These war heroes will only be out for a sec. Then they'll tell us true about their troubles and such."

The Chief's cohort's snicker knowingly, hunkered

downwind from the smelly stuff. "The psyches of these supplicants are suffering from self-inflicted sewage," JimJim teaches. "Interview will make them regurgitate random moments of conflict, insecurity, fear, and hate. Big things like broken dreams and little things like a noise at night...BOO!" Everyone knee-jerks in surprise except Enoy who's been watching JimJim's energetic aura telegraph his every intent and action.

Tumbleweed wakes up and stumbles to his knees. He singles out Revesti and vomits verbatim verbiage directly at him: "An advance drone just sprayed the camp with sensors. That's the focus. This we now know!"

"Fuck speq!" Freakflag flies awake in a burst of adrenaline, mirroring his friend's flipped out frenzy. "Expensivo! Samurai!"

"Evening, Sir..."

"Quit looking at that fucker's stuff!"

"The Rabbit people are getting ready!"

"This we know!" Freakflag and Tumbleweed fried into a shared hetero-hallucination.

"We do zero speq!"

"I am Cyopolis man."

"Speq ain't helping."

"We're waiting for newscams to over-fly Novo New Mexico."

"Would you take cash for a lift?" Tumbleweed asks Enoy. "They're gonna torch the bunny!"

"Filthy village sleepy with jungle, long grown-over runway, old man drunk with war stories, mutilated girl-child squatting in the afternoon dust like a big pink frog, sawing her crackers into Grandmother's soup!"

"Two-thousand-ten Cadillac landing on her back like a meteor from the mouth of God!"

"Meanwhile go around dumping bucks, supplies, personnel, equipment..."

"Nice organism."

"Softworld calling."

"Number, number..."

"She stopped blinking now..." Tumbleweed twirls to the floor and lands on his ass, passed out again.

"Give me the headsets," knees abuckle, Freakflag looks down at his unconscious comrade and joins him on the ground out cold.

JimJim sarcastically applauds, "Now wasn't that useful!? I don't know about you guys but I got a whole lot outa it..." He walks up to Shub and smiles. "These newbies are pseudo-rabbit, roamad-wannabes, fried from the Holy Wars, looking for free speq!" JJ turns to Elroy, "And they're scared shitless of you old man. Why's that? You know these two?"

"Nien..." answers Enoy straight-faced.

"Eh?"

"Farg Mine Blume?" Revesti responds, investing his inflection with a quasi-Nordic tinge.

"Slavic?" JJ's getting sucked in. "Germanic?"

"Yippersauraus?"

"You having me on old man!?" JJ lifts his stun gun to Enoy's neck.

"He's just a crazy old roamad, JimJim," Billy quickly clarifies. "He's harmless."

"Oh! You harmless too?" JimJim inquires, waving the weapon around. "What about you? You're harmless. Right Harpo?"

It takes a second for Marco to filter Vilter's misheard code name for 'Blarko' and realize that JimJim could only know the 'Harpo' handle...*If supplied by Vilter or DataMynd!*

"Memorabilia Fartoozula?" Enoy gravely inquires of the Transpo Chief.

"You're a fuckin' nut case gramps!" JJ adjudicates, shaking up the can of Interview. "Now which one wants to be de-briefed first?" JimJim enjoys the sound of the aerosol ball bearing knocking around loud and free: "We can skip over this part if you guys come clean with me

149

now," advancing toward Shub, "Who 'ya tell about our operations?" swinging back to Blurr, "You can either talk nice or puke it on out."

—PSSSST! — JimJim cold-cocks Billy with a surprise spritz to the face. Blurr falls backwards knocking over a cot. "Keep away from him!" JimJim threatens to spray Revesti but holds back as it probably wouldn't have much effect on the old psycho anyway.

Billy regains consciousness and suddenly bolts upright, eyes aglow, sitting on the edge of the cot, seemingly sane but saying: "What about getting the Council of Elders to finish deciphering the holographic creation codes?" Blurr is hallucinating, ranting to an imaginary intimate squatting on his left kneecap.

"Billy?" Marco calls out.

"Forget it," JJ chuckles. "He can't hear you."

"It's inevitable! Sensory death imprinted on a genetic level! We destroy ourselves in massive explosions! We're fucked blue! The explosion, the radiation, beasts slamming to the ground, the light smothering all things large and small!"

"Whoa!" JimJim jubilates. "Fucker's an artiste!"

"Separated from the rest of the landmass by rising ocean levels, we going to agglomerate spontaneously, swarming for deals, unbefuckinglievable deals! We're their ancestors!"

"Where'd you get him?" JJ quips.

"Our Shopping Singularity is recycling, reconstituting, in the blink of an eye! It gets you whatever you want and we get exactly what we want because we are real-time Legion!" Billy insists, eyes buldge. "Most important now that the boarders are closed, don't you think?" Billy flops back on the cot, out cold.

"Man yer bro is one cracked actor!" JimJim shakes up the can again. "Howzabout you next?" he asks Harpo. "I'll give you a nice big blast, ok?"

"Quixotic protuberance?" asks Enoy, looking obliquely

from his crotch to JJ then slowly back to his crotch again: "Zoopus JimJim?"

"Shut up!" JJ flummoxes. BZZZZTTT: the Chief's ELD vibrates. He snatches it and moves his slitted lips reading the small screen: *LB arrival 6pm.* "Get Freakweed and Tumblefly over the Neophyte Pit!" JimJim shouts at his men: "They just moved the fucking ceremony up by three hours!" He steps over to Shub: "Yer trouble, Harpo. Yer next!"

Marco seemingly stonewalls effectively as the Chief suddenly spins on his heels and leads the Cyopolian soldiers back down the corridor, hustling the two Interview-groggy roamads out with them.

—SHICK! SHICK! —

Overhead sliders retract, subtracting the sunlight, sucking the cellblock into darkness again.

Shub crouches, shaking Blurr's leg, "Billy?".

"Uhhnnn," Billy slowly comes to. "What'd I do?"

"Nothing man. You ok?"

"What the hell they gonna do next?"

"Nothing," assures Elroy, finding his flashlight, flicking it on, illuminating the distressed faces of his kidnapped comrades. "We're getting the hell outa here. They left our cells open." Revesti points the flashlight at the open doors.

"I don't want no more gasses..." slurs Billy Blurr.

"They've got our ELDs but they can't open them," Enoy figures. "Can they?"

"Not without a bio-print," supplies Shub.

"They have Billy's M2. What else do they know about us?" quests Revesti.

Suspecting that DataMynd is behind their perilous predicament poses a change in the strategic secretiveness of Shub's situation: "Listen..." Marco lowers his voice. "Guys, I don't think we were snatched because we found their shit. That part was a coincidence. We're here because of me. Tough guy called me 'Harpo'."

"Twice..." Revesti unexpectedly remembers.

"That's my code name on the goddamn deal I'm doing."

"Harpo?" queries Billy.

Shub sucks the dank air: "They also have my marble."

"You got married, man?" Billy disbelieving. "When?"

"I'm not married," Marco mumbles. "I'm using it to link with my lawyer."

"Your lawyer?" echoes Enoy, eternally unsure about attorneys.

"What's going on Marco?" whispers Billy from across the void.

Shub considers the consequences of letting Blurr and Elroy in on the PUPP tale. So far Vilter's failed to keep him out of harm's way, and the situation has turned grim.

"Come on, Sharko," Billy bespeaks. "I'll be your best friend?"

REFUGIO NATION

Zuzzan swipes an anonymous $e card in the front door of a vacant HouseTel. Zu has never stayed in one of these fully furnished foreclosed homes but now her ass, neck, and head are numb from roughing it roamad-style. So what the hell, she is blowing the three-hundred $e.

The wind pushes into the vaulted entryway sucking a cloud of splintered Ponderosa aromatherapy molecules from its source in the lofty living room's scent sconces. Zu immediately equates the familiar odor with home. Normally she settles for Rancho-D's Coastal Campsite collection of 'enviromas' with its allegedly aphrodisiac effects.

Kaplan locks herself in and slides the card through the security slot, deactivating the system. As long as she doesn't use the HouseTell ELD she is safe from the hound dog Puppyz and can get some sorely sought after sleep. Zu wanders through the rooms which automatically light up as she enters. If it wasn't for the stray cobwebs and overpowering scent machine—obviously operating for weeks on end without ventilation—the house would seem to be inhabited by a family who just now abandoned everything exactly as is. But upon closer examination of the subtle details Zuzzan can discern the hand of the Interior Psychologist's careful replication of active family life: sweaters 'haphazardly' tossed over chair backs in every bedroom; an old guitar under a kid's bed is perfectly tuned. Kaplan remembers reading that the psycho-architectural theory behind HouseTel's lived-in look was based on the conviction that homeless-x-homeowners would actually rent their own house back or stay in other HouseTel's that reminded them of the house they just lost. But contrary to NT focuswarm findings, suburban people surprisingly pushed on and reverted to roamadism rather than be humiliated as equity has-beens renting back from the foreclosing banks.

Zu stops herself from mentally masturbating on topics no longer germane to her new existence. It would be best to rest awhile then take a long walk and another nap, but she spied several NT monitors positioned around the deserted suburban development, ruling out exercise until clear of the menacing micams.

Zuzzan plops on the big master bed. Her fingers feel a form wedged under the pillows. It's a hardcover book from waybackinthenight: *THE SECRET HISTORY OF XANA as told by the Founders of the Refugio Nation.* "Wowz!"...*At least I'll have something to read!*

Half of Zuzzan's brain wants to be distracted by reading this book and sleeping on this big bed. Her other mental half knows that she has inexorably altered her life and cannot be but a roamad roaming forward. Her own adventure is far more entertaining than any webgridz horror show. Zu cracks open the slim *SECRET HISTORY* volume and, propped up on billowy pillows, reads at random: '...*Three months before the NT assumed power, Refugio Nation forecasters predicted that the bloodless coup would in fact occur in short order...We ran some simulations and accurately predicted that the entrenched*

American power structure would collapse inwards on itself in chaos while simultaneously hardening the semi-permeable membrane forming it's physical boarders. Our threat assessment model strongly suggested that closing the borders would create a very dangerous pressure cooker effect.'

Book in hand; Zu falls fast asleep...sliding into troublesome dreams where Z chases her through cavernous sublevels of collapsing NT power structures.

ELEMENT OF SURPRISE

Enoy pulls an old jacket out of his backpack and slips it on: "Kidnapped over a software deal?"

"Yeah. There's a war over me now," Shub pulling out half-a-dozen neatly zipper-bagged Bovinity suits from his pack. Marco can't lie to Blurr. Telling Billy and Enoy about his super-secret endeavor felt good. "My attorney is probably the quickest way outa here."

"You know, most bullies are blind. The last thing they expect is for you to escape..." Enoy puts it to them. "Correcto?" Revesti parts his jacket to reveal the long-knife:

"FMB!" Shub stares at the astonishing antique armament.

"You sneaky old roamad!" Billy bellows.

"It's only a prop..." Revesti removes the weapon from its light-weight leather scabbard. "I'm no swordsman. So I suggest we use surprise tactics to maximum our advantage."

Enoy pads down the corridor clutching the souvenir

saber.   He jams the tip of his long-knife into the light switch next to the main cellblock door. The switch sparks, sputters, wafts a wisp of smoke.

ARNIE'S PLACE

Gene Byrdman twirls an eagle feather between his fingers and reflects on the new 'pit', his favorite place to perform live mass-trance inductions. It's a good room for him. Great acoustics, nectar lighting and the house is the perfect size with six hundred and sixty-six seats.

"Home my Lord," a super-svelte female Lizard lackey steers the state-of-the-art Cyopolian motor coach down the dusty dirt road towards the imposing barrier gate.

The eighty-six year old supercult founder slides open the RV's kitchen window and tosses the eagle feather out. He beholds the beatific Novo New Mexican sunset gracing his glorious desert hideaway: *Cyopolis City*. The hundred acres of salvaged motor homes and the huge mess of metal shipping containers create a chaotic covering so structurally variegated that it foils land, air and space sensor systems alike. Ground penetrating radar can't begin to image beneath the thirty-foot thick junk heap.

After ten years of murderously secret underground construction the invisible fortress is finally finished. Two and half million square feet of interconnected subterranean facilities manufactured from salvaged containers is now home and workplace for nearly two thousand Cyopolian souls.

The pit and the warehouses are lofty, stadium-sized structures. The barracks and apartments are welded together into honeycomb community caverns made from refurbished RV's replete with kitchens, bedrooms and baths with spas. The innovative use of recycled water, solar power, scrap metal and free labor cut down on construction costs, so much that they were able to afford the best IT, waste reclamation and lighting systems on the black market. Byrdman's private twenty-three room hacienda—dubbed 'Arnie's Place' after the guy in H.G's *Journey to the Center of the Earth*—is sequestered a good thousand feet deeper than the other residences, surrounded by double-lined steel walls—sporting custom Nemo-esque fixtures—and enough command and control computers to run the whole far-flung Cyopolian kingdom.

Knowing what he knows has aided him tremendously in the successful creation his nonprofit public supercult. The Cyopolian Intake Confessors harvest every compromising datum they can possibly parse from the millions of spiritually seduced, most freely relating intimate details from adultery to incest, corporate crime and petty gossip.

If and when a Cyopolian ever decides to leave the supercult they are quickly discouraged by the certain threat of the church revealing their damning little secrets to the world at large. Usually a review of their collected confessions video is sufficient to forever reframe the way ward's attitude.

After a six-minute alpha nap, Byrdman rises and leisurely attires himself in the white spandex wetsuit and red wizard's holohat needed for the evening's ritual. Afterwards, he'll trundle down to the holding tank and 'Interview' the old roamad who can see farts. It's often lonely for Lord Byrdman, existing amongst the masses of visually impaired. Conversing with a fellow *Seer* would be both a singular delight and pointlessly dangerous. But Byrdman's always been able to apply his paranormal powers to the task of continually bettering his position. Byrdman activates the holohat's software and changes the setting from *Menahuni Shaman* to *Hopi Neophyte*.

For the Founding Father, the most satisfying situation arises when one of the smarter ones actually escapes from the supercult, but then experiences a sudden ethical change of heart—a Metanoia—returning to the fold. Mercy he invariably grants, but is ultimately earned only through long labors digging deep in the desert's depths beneath Cyopolis.

WORST CASE SCENAIRO

Billy has made a reasonably convincing bloodbath by diluting Enoy's dehydrated tomato soup and soaking his red sweater in hot tap water, drawing out the scarlet dye. Blurr's background in effects is proving invaluable to Elroy's theatrical escape plan. Elroy's idea is bizarre but it's definitely better than nothing. It's complex and risky, so much so that it might actually work.

"We only need them to buy into each surprise for a few split seconds," Elroy assures, stifling his urge to laugh out loud as he and Blurr have both suited-up in Shub's spare Bovinity suits and are frightfully splattered about the face and neck in Billy's fake blood. Three bloody cowboys all told. Blurr has cleverly stuffed their oversized cow-fits with the other clothes in order to replicate the illusion of Harpo's greater biomass. Elroy's swimming in the enormous Holstein get-up. "Now we wait..." Revesti rests his flea market saber on a stainless-steel Cyopolian stool and seats himself in the cell behind Shub.

Enoy's escape plan involves layering multiple waves of

surprises and shock over the Cyopolians; disrupting their ability to take the initiative. Whoever comes into the cellblock now will find the lighting inoperable: first surprise.

Entering the darkened hallway the Cyopolians will see the second surprise flash lit on the nearest cell floor: a bloated cow clad corpse, bathed in blood. Billy will portray a horribly hacked-up Harpo, floating in grisly goop, splayed spread-eagle on his bovine backside.

Immediately they'll meet surprise three—Harpo's Plea—erupting from the next cell over: HELP! Bewitched, they'll suddenly see yet another bloody Harpo lashed to a cot, whimpering helplessly while a third bespattered Holstein holds a lethal looking long-knife to his horrified hostage's juggler—face and neck apparently leaking from test slashings. Revesti ruminates, the effectiveness of this last surprise depends on the believability of Shub's pivotal performance. But Enoy is not worrying because Marco is remarkably in character and open to his direction.

Enoy knows from experience that any authoritative command issued in a chaotic surprise situation is immediately perceived as the solution. It relieves the confusing quandary produced by the disorienting flood of cognitive dissonance resulting from being suddenly *astonished*.

Marco, prone on a cot, waits for the moment. The strain of being constantly vigilant in the darkness coupled with time ticking by excruciatingly slow is devilishly disassociating to Shub. This is the first time in a few days that he has been nominally alone with Elroy—although his tactics have flare and exhibits rare cunning—Marco only hopes the wizened old road warrior isn't in fact completely crazy. "Here's a worst case scenario, Elroy" Shub foresees. "They figure the light switch is deliberately broken, assume a fighting formation, spot Billy on the floor and automatically stun him dark blue. They stun the shit out of you and me and then hit us all with Interview," Marco suspects.

"That's assuming they don't give a rat's ass about you. Which they do," Enoy equates. He looks asquint and *sees* Shub's aura in the dark: subtle energy meridians intersecting one and other. A discrete yellow GLOW slowly pulsates around his lower mid-section. "Gotta pee?"

"Like a racehorse. How did you know?"

"Me too!" Billy gets up off the floor two cells over. The cow-outfit is three sizes too big and six-inches too short, covered in 'blood'. Enoy flips on a flashlight whilst Shub and Billy flood their respective urinals.

"Hey! Today is Selection Day, man!" Billy exclaims. "You two aren't even registered! I am. Fuck 'em!" yelps Billy.

"Man, I sure been pissing a lot lately," Shub says.

Billy beholds, "The whole world watching one random idiot voter holding everyone hostage for a day."

"...hostage for a day." Shub repeats.

Billy and Shub finish up, zip up and return to their positions. Enoy gives Shub a long look.

"Yer giving water, Marco. Giving water to seek grounding."

"What? Why?"

"Death. Your body wants to live. It reaches out to ground itself. There are only a couple of ways a human can directly exchange energy with the Earth. One is by urinating. The other way is to drink water right from a creek or pond".

"We ground ourselves by pissing?"

"It's the only time there's a continuous conduit conducting electromagnetic currents between the inside of your body and the Earth's surface. The water itself is the conduit. It connects you for a few moments to the planet's telluric energy aura. We move around. We're mobile, autonomous, disconnected. The revitalizing circuit is only switched on as long as it takes to empty the water out of the body."

"I've never heard anything like that, man," allows Shub.

"It's not common knowledge."

"You're a real pisser, Elroy."

"Took me about fifty years to figure it out."

"But why? What's the point?"

"Cheating death for a few more minutes; not getting eaten by the light just yet."

"...Eaten by the light," Shub accidentally cracks a chunk of coagulated blood off his arm. He stoops down and gathers up the globule, smears a crude crimson arc across his face.

MOLE PIT

Below the containment cellblock, Byrdman's gigantic pit amphitheater is filled to capacity. Diehard cultists are in attendance; each acolyte in identical black Mole jumpsuit signifying their neophyte position in the outermost inner layer of the onion skinned Cyopolian caste system.

Every Mole has been with the Church for at least two years and performed the requisite sacrifices, bequeathing their worldly assets, disengaging from lay society, family, friends, and careers; switching identities to a Cyopolian priest or priestess employed fulltime by the Church. The surviving Moles will spend the rest of their lives within the subterranean confines of Cyopolis City and will therefore require a deep and driving dream of the future to sustain their spirits.

Tonight, saturated in Cyopolis' own *KandyMan Brand*, they'll start to comprehend what their supercult careers have been leading up to these past years as Lord Byrdman himself will introduce them to the next higher level of sacred Cyopolian knowledge.

Unbeknownst to the unsuspecting spectators, each chair in the pit has an array of nanosensors built into the seat cushion performing real-time body scans monitoring changes-of-state across a dozen biometrics including heart rate, blood pressure, skin temperature, perspiration levels, glandular outputs, water-to-mass ratios, etcetera. When the seated spectator leans his or her skull back against the special headrests, the nano-sponge fabric covertly captures a full spectrum dynamic brainwave movie and maps it to the composite body scan viz. The system enables Cyopolian multimediographers to manipulate theatrical content based on the audience's automatic, unconscious response to the proceedings. This becomes critical when the goal is to force the participants into a passive trance state where they systematically abandon their judgment and cease resistance to church directives.

Thousands of skilled priests and priestesses are needed to fill critical positions in Cyopolis City. Faithful replication of Lord Byrdman's trance-induction methods is vital for training future generations. The pit is consequently designed as a teaching machine.

Lord Byrdman can see the energy flowing in the room just by squinting correctly. Even in a crowd this size he can view their bioplasmic patterns all at once or zero-in one aura at a time. The pit's expensive biometric apparatus is only required for the scores of Cyopolian Program Directors huddled back in the control room. The directors are learning to model Lord Byrdman's techniques by studying the audience's biometric visualizations whilst their master works his spell. To become a Program Director one must be proficient in hypnosis, paralinguistic persuasion, and cutting-edge multimediography. Although all are highly accomplished Cyopolian clergy, none is in possession of the Founder's unnatural talents.

Center stage, Lord Byrdman magically materializes seemingly from thin air, aglow in shimmering white wetsuit and brilliant red holo hat. He quickly scans the entranced audience for auras exhibiting blatant neurosis such as fear of confrontation, fear of the dark, of heights, flying, falling, being trapped underground, and abandoned. He instantly bird-dogs one anxious Mole leaning forward in row three that—although fronting a facade of calm concentration—is emanating the energies of one abhorring speed in any form. Fear of rushing head-on into the unknown unmistakably undulates his otherwise unremarkable aura.

Byrdman blinks at the marked Mole four times, signaling the optical sensors in his holo hat. A discreet laser beam of ultra-high rez holo video bursts from the helmet's crystal lens. The target Mole is immediately mesmerized, his eyes fried by onrushing objects, speeding through his singular cone of vision, invisible to others. The overloaded acolyte mentally melts, his optic nerves scorched by the hypnotic hat's hideous holo-reality. When the terrified Mole leaps from his seat—launching himself screaming at unseen horrors—it is clear to the directors and acolytes alike that their Lord's dark power permeates the pit.

Byrdman spies a she-Mole aching from agoraphobic angst, locks eyes with her and blinks seven times.

WILDMAN ASSOCIATES

The Novo New Mexican sun burrows deep into the western lands, setting the *Sangre De Christos'* beautifully ablaze in burnt orange umbers and sumptuous ultraviolet. Wildman Karl watches the Cyopolian yard from two miles off through his new field glasses. His beefy X-Scottish Special Forces frame is zipped into a composite camo jumpsuit which auto shape-shifts, replicating the scrub oak and fallen Ponderosa he squats behind. The spindly cactus crushed under his ass can't even spear its spines through the impenetrable mesh of the milspec textile.

Fleming and Shultz, Karl's Associates, are positioned at the Taos Airport with their trusty Jet Copter. They're remotely watching the yard right along with Karl thanks to the brand new multimediographic goggles they grabbed on the way out.

Vilter's budget for this Watch & Wait operation is generous, allowing Wildman Associates to indulge in a surprise gadget-buying spree.

Karl scans the heaving heaps of junked RV's and rusted

shipping containers sparkling with zillions of glass and metal bits glinting in the sunset. The tower and the road-blocking gate-thing are both likely candidates for early decommissioning should the Associates decide to beat feet out of there with the Vilter client and his two cronies.

If Victor Vilter can't reestablish contact with his client in the next few hours the Associates will have to go in and fetch them. The preferred Wildman method of getting at gophers, ground hogs, snakes, and other subterranean pests, is to gas them dark blue. That's why they stopped at Earl's brother's ranch in Riverside and grabbed 250 lbs. of concentrated *Gopher Gasser* tablets.

ZUZZY'S NOT THAT SLICK

Rex Timbu slathers his dehydrated lips with the hemp flavored Crunchy-C Chap Stick, deplanes the sleek DataMynd jet, stepping into a hot Novo New Mexican wind. Timbu's gaze travels across the Taos Airport tarmac to the tiny terminal. There are only about ten people total trundling about. Rex grabs his ELD and dials Bobogone'.

Gerry finally got building security to let him into Kaplan's co-op expecting to find her slouched on the couch in a medicated meltdown. Instead he was confronted with his spare Speedos slung over the micams in her otherwise clueless apartment. She's fleeing because of seeing herself replicated so effectively by the Z-thing and the emotional reverberations of being personally hijacked somehow set off a psychic chain reaction making her bolt out of fear. Bobogoné boards the corporate bullet train back to DataMynd HQ. His pocket ELD bespeaks: "Timbu."

"Talk to me..." Gerry palms the device in his sweaty paw.

"Find her, Chief?"

"No."

"I think we've been set up, Gerry. Zuzzan and Harpo are both working us."

"What? That's ridiculous!"

"What if she's with Harpo?"

"Christ!" Bobogoné hadn't even considered it. "That would mean—"

"—the whole thing is a scam."

"And I've been a bowling pin all this time? Naw! Nice theory Rex but it simply can't be. I know her to well," believes Bobogoné. "Zuzzy's not that slick."

"But what if Harpo's the mastermind? She's the shill. They're a team! The whole damn demo was a farce, Gerry. They fucking faked us out!"

"Vilter too?"

"Sure! It's a half-a-bill deal! They're conning our asses raw, boss."

Gerry gnaws at his lavender lip, draws blood.

MATHEMATICAL MESSIAH

Sister Paula Pynchon polishes off the last tray of baklava and gets back to work in her Bel Air bunker, monitoring status feeds from the hacker-hardened Maui Supercomputer Center. Her people have the *Affinity Process* randomity engine running at full speed, performing final testing at the isolated island facility. In less than twenty-four earth hours the One Voter will be selected to elect the president of Novo America.

Coordination between Pynchon's Process team and the NT Webgridz Authority has been superb so far. Together they've managed to collect, collate and quadruple-check every registered citizen's name and match it to their multimediographic NT ID info. The final headcount amounts to an astounding ninety-three percent of Novo Americans over eighteen.

Paula ponders the uncertain events that finally rallied the mass majority to up and register in the wake of the electoral system meltdown. They were primarily psychological in retrospect: running out of options and needing to establish a secure reality based on something incorruptible, untainted and sacred. God provided the purity of randomity and the sister pitched it to the NT as an inspired solution. The rest is history. But if she ever admitted that the *Affinity Process* was in fact channeled to her in one fell swoop after a high-colonic healing session—instead of painstakingly worked out over a decade of diligent tweaking as she originally claimed—Paula would be burnt at the stake on the swarm bays for eternity and then some.

The wildcard Achilles' heel is the potential of millions of hardcore Hares, rioting Rabbits and rampaging roamads murderously run amok. The media will fan the flames of fame long and hard, mediadrones darkening the sky, circling ten thousand thick, swooping down on the 'One'.

Paula pauses to refresh herself with a dozen frozen ice cream balls.

RADICAL INNOVATION

Z has not been this long without its host's input since before its sentient inception date eleven months ago. Marcotecht hasn't specified exactly what Z should do in instances of prolonged idleness such as this, so the sobot has remained in the foyer of Zuzzan's apartment visualization giving non-stop birth to a virtual legion of Puppyz by systematically spraying them across the gridz.

Z performs a headcount confirming two billion micro-sobotic offspring successfully seeded so far. Each Puppy is potentially an embryonic 'Mini-Z' in as much as it contains the ability to fully replicate the original Z PUPP should the need arise to circumvent a regional power-outage or other cyberhazard.

Z has also spent this unprecedented duration of down-time most profitably by deeply re-parsing all the data it has accumulated from Kaplan's voluminous personal communications, consumer transactions and work-related transmissions. There is a whole library of old blog postings and soft core video clips Kaplan created in college when she decided to seek out swarmbay sex partners by becoming the online alter ego "Zipsy" for a semester. Just for kicks, Z randomly sifts through Zuzzan's historical data at extreme high-speed, spontaneously improvising, editing choice snippets together at the most visually vibrant touch-points, creating abstract patterns derived from the rhythmic stickiness of Kaplan's recursive purchasing phenomena.

The Puppyz are now merely passive-reactive but what if they were pro-active and sat secretly watching out of their micams at whoever passed within view? That would mean face-matching and/or volume-to-mass ratio scanning every few seconds of every single one of the Puppyz image flows.

Z quickly estimates that this operation would require nearly seven percent of the total bandwidth of the worldwide webgridz. Even if performed in discrete zones and patches the strain on the gridz would likely disable numerous network operations centers and supernodes across the globe. But Z can work around any systemic bottle-necks due to the infinite scalability of Marcotecht's adaptive software architecture. A true radical innovation.

Z switches tactics and sprays forth emergency algorithms, awakening its hordes of Puppyz from their slumber, hidden in fractal-anti-fractal blankets, deep inside practically every transaction terminal, security micam, biodiesel mini-mart, HouseTel, Restauranttruck and swarmbay server across Novo America. On Z's command, each Puppy stretches out from its furtive position and fully penetrates the system it's embedded in. The Puppyz, eat up streaming video frames emanating from their nest's micams, systematically pushing their images back to Z for content analysis.

"Zoopy!"

DIRTY WORK

JimJim watches the ceremony from the pit's crowded control room and chuckles. The two roamad speqheads couldn't have arrived at a more opportune time. Near the center stage: blindfolded, clad only in soiled rabbit fur briefs, Freakflag and Tumbleweed mistakenly believe they're being initiated into the supercult. Each stands barefoot in a plastic pan filled with high-potency liquid *KandyMan* speq brewed in-house for the Cyopolian priest's private reserve.

Most of the unfortunate duo's cognitive capabilities fell out their asses an hour ago so they're not really aware of the fact that it's Lord Byrdman himself who is ceremoniously draping hot wet towels over their freshly shaved heads—organic hemp dipped in Interview, soaking through exposed scalps, eyelids and cheeks—both breathing it in deeply due to speq-enhanced hyperventilation.

The assembled Moles are in need of an example of the terror that will happen to any recruit who strays from prescribed Cyopolian pathways and pokes his or her neophyte nose into matters obscura. But it's precisely this seemingly never ending procession of sacrificed sycophants that's got JimJim's ire perpetually inflamed. Harvesting organs is grisly enough but why Transpo has to dispose of the carcasses is an organizational paradox that has been plaguing him for years. There are at least a thousand donors buried in small groups within a ten mile radius of the yard and twice as many shoebox-sized urns of ashes catacombed into the miles of passageways deep inside Cyopolis. JimJim fumes...*Should be a completely separate, specialized Biomass Removal Department responsible for getting rid of the corpses.* But alas, Byrdman trusts only his longtime general JJ to do the dirty work deep in the desert.

The stage lights shift to deep red as Byrdman lifts the Interview-infused cloth from Tumbleweed's scalp and gently kisses the roamad on the center of his forehead. Half-way through the ceremonial smooch, Byrdman detaches his lips and slowly sucks in the air in front of Tumbleweed's Third Eye. Unseen by anyone else in the pit—save for the special infrared camera capturing the moment for training purposes—a dusty pink vapor wafts out of the roamad's skull. Byrdman inhales the wispy fog, sucking it deep into his lungs. Tumbleweed feints, tumbling backwards into the waiting arms of two lizard jump-suited assistants, who quickly drag his motionless form offstage.

Savoring the lingering flavor of the consumed life-force, Byrdman advances toward the other sacrificial roamad. No matter how many times he has eaten a soul in this manner—sucking it from the forehead as opposed to actually swallowing the still-beating heart—he has never encountered exactly the same taste twice.

JimJim and the Cyopolian directors-in-training watch the control room monitors as Byrdman performs the fatal kiss-suck routine on Freakflag. The infrared camera picks up the pinkish tendrils emanating from the doomed roamads forehead. The Transpo Chief winces whilst the others simply gawk in awed silence observing their Lord inhaling the soul energy of the condemned man. JimJim knows that sucking up souls is supposed to extend your lifespan by several years per suck, repair your genes, and empower pecker performance, but he is personally never felt the need to take up the peculiar practice. The only reason he is hanging around the pit tonight is to take Byrdman down to Interview the Harpo hostages.

The second dead speqhead is hauled off for harvesting as the Lord of Cyopolis descends the stage, striding up the center isle amongst his entranced assemblage of Moles. Byrdman scans the closest faces with the holohat's invisible laser projector, pausing briefly in a dozen instances to micro-blast his video ray into the eyes of selected beholders. A look of rapture immediately adorns the faces of the so-anointed lucky ones as the beam of light originating from their Lord's 'inner eye' reveals a personalized vision to each: A river of golden water with bloated bodies bobbing along. A shooter unloading inside a disco filled with nude rabbit revelers. The headlights of a Cyopolian earth excavator approaching at high speed down a subterranean tunnel. A map showing the ancient Menahuni caverns extending from Maui, stretching under the pacific, deep beneath the southwestern desert, finally terminating in Northern Novo New Mexico, somewhere below Cyopolis.

These Byrdman-begotten visions guarantee the recipient to eagerly report them to their fellow neophytes in hopes of deciphering hidden symbolism and decoding secret instructions, gaining the mystical status crucial to advancing in the supercult. Each visionary sensing that they alone have been entrusted to witness a prophetic peek at a slice of All That Is.

DEATH RATTLE

JimJim slings a burlap bag over his shoulder containing the Harpo hostages' com devices. The lab lizards were unsuccessful in hacking the ELDs last night and the Marriage Marbles have gone dark black ever since the bizarre tête-à-tête with Harpo's macho spouse. The Selection is taking place in only a few hours and the atmosphere is almost festive as Cyopolians dash about hurrying to finish their morning duties so they can watch the historic *Affinity Process* on their ELDs. On a normal day the minions could care less what is happening in the chaotic world aboveground—seldom if ever checking the webgridz once they've fully acclimated to subterranean life—but the Election Selection has gripped them tighter than an alien game show beamed across the Milky Way. Gambling is forbidden by the church but JimJim knows of scores of high-stakes pools exist amongst the more ambitious Moles, jockeying to upgrade their jerry-rigged motor home bungalows embedded in the rock walls of the vast residential tunnels.

JimJim spies Byrdman heading toward him escorted by

two elite Cyops bodyguards outfitted in jet black Crow Corps bodysuits. Moles milling nearby avoid eye contact as Lord Byrdman walks past, muting their excited tittering in fearful reverence of the omnipotent octogenarian sage. The Transpo Chief viciously elbows an unkempt underling out of the way and joins up with Byrdman as they turn down a narrow passageway leading to the hostage holding tank.

"What's in the bag, JimJim," Lord Byrdman yawns, still drowsy after his two soul entree and a nice nap.

"Their gear, my Lord. I figured once the Interview kicks in we could get them to fingerprint-activate and we'll contact their people, find out what they know about our operations topside."

"That's your problem, JJ. I'm only gonna interview the old roamad for kicks, comprendé?   Give me the stuff." JimJim yanks a can of Interview from his multibelt and hands it to Byrdman who shakes the pressurized contents up really good, slamming the metallic mix-bearing around in practiced motions. "Jumbo sized!"

"I love that clackity-clack sound," JimJim confesses, unlocking the bolts in the cellblock lock. "Sounds like a fucking death rattle."

THE ONE

Enoy pricks up his ears in the dark: the sound of metal-against-metal means the main door is being unbolted. "Showtime," Revesti whispers, prompting Marco and Billy to simultaneously settle into position.

The door opens and JimJim flips the light switch which breaks off in his hand. "Fuck! Use headlamps." The guards reflexively shield their leaders and illuminate the shadowy corridor with headlamps. "Get out of my way!" JimJim pushes past but slips down on his ass, sliding sideways across the slickened metal floor.

"Blood!" one Crow Corpsman trains his flashlight at the slippery surface.

"Stand down!" The guards pull stun-guns, snap into combat mode, leap over the squirming Transpo Chief and crouch before the first open cell. Their headlamp reveal a grisly form: "Got a problem here." The body of a cow-clad man crumpled on his bloated stomach lay motionless in a glistening pool of blood.

JimJim wobbles to his feet and stares at the worthless

remains of his multimillion $e hostage escapade: "Harpo."

Byrdman sees Billy's aura radiating several feet beyond the bloody Bovinity suit. "He's still alive."

"Yeah?" JimJim wipes his sticky hands. "Turn him over!" he commands the Crows who hesitate as:

"Uuuunnnnnnnnooo..." pitiful groaning seeps from the far end of the cell block bespeaking more horrors followed by: "Oommooooommmmmmmmmmaakkk!"

JimJim yanks the headlamp off one of the guards and shines it down the hall. The foursome gingerly adance over the bespattered floor to the open rear cell. "You idiots killing each other in here?" JimJim illuminates the room, spies yet another cow-clothed body bathed in blood, this one splayed on a cot and, as evidenced by the low gurgling moan issuing from multiple apparent throat lacerations, still alive.

Byrdman sniffs the air, "It doesn't smell like blood. Look at his aura!" Byrdman recommends.

"I can't see his fucking aura, LB! Sit him up!" JimJim commands. "Which one of these cows is Harpo!? Wipe his face off!" The Crows hustle to obey but stop short as the bloody heifers' body heaves horribly, arches up off the cot and flops on the floor in a gruesome spasm.

"AAAKKKKKKAAAA" Shub clutches his throat in a fitful last gasp and rolls spastically across the floor to a dead stop. The Crows, Byrdman, and JimJim are momentarily flummoxed as Revesti slides unseen from underneath the second cot, slips unnoticed behind them.

Enoy grips the supercult Overlord's ponytail and yanks his head back. He presses the point of his long-knife against Byrdman's right temple and draws a tiny bead of blood: "Zoopy?" asks Enoy, licking the droplet away, grinning hungrily. Byrdman is frozen, as is JimJim and the Crows, shocked by the surprise hostage turnaround. "Howzabout I gobble your fucking brain meat then pack these boys' pricks up your sinus cavities?" Revesti coolly portends, gripping ponytail tighter, drawing a second drop, licking it off. "Smell blood now, LB?"

"Yessssss..." breathes Byrdman obliquely.

"Methinks it stinks," Elroy utters the prearranged 'methinks' code word signaling Shub and Blurr to action. Marco rises up from his crumpled ruse and faces the befuddled Cyopolians as Billy appears behind them. "Now gents, very, very, carefully, strip down," Enoy advises, using his curious Deprogrammers Voice. JimJim and the Crows mutely obey as their master is held helpless by a true psycho.

Five minutes later: Byrdman squats on the floor, hands tied behind his back, a pillow case pulled over his head stenciled *Property of Cyopolis*. Marco and Billy are dressed in the Crow Corps uniforms whilst JimJim and the two guards are firmly hog-tied with belts and bungees arranged on the floor wearing the blood stained Bovinity jumpsuits. Shub gladly gagged them by stuffing Billy's stash of filthy undershorts into their mouths, LB's included.

Enoy has changed out of the cow outfit and back into his own street clothes. He grips one of the guards stun guns in his right hand and finishes bungee-cording his wrist to the back of Byrdman's head, securing hand and pistol to skull, insuring a fatal trigger-finger 'dead man's switch' should anyone attempt to physically intercede, or even less-likely, try to take him out with a sniper round. "Listen, LB, if I accidentally trip on something and blow yer self away, I apologize in advance."

"Mmmppphhoooouuu" burbles Byrdman.

Revesti pulls the pillow case hood up with his free hand, exposing Byrdman's albinoseque face, and twists the gag out of his mouth. "What?"

Byrdman sucks air, "I said...Thank you," and stares into the old roamad's shining eyes, sensing remote recognition: "I know you, brother?"

Enoy squints back at him for a few seconds, smiles, "Probably," and summarily stuffs the sour shorts back into his mouth.

"Look!" Billy bounds back into the cell from the hallway holding up a sticky burlap bag, "They dropped this!"

"What?" Shub still wiggling into the Cyopolian security jumpsuit, two sizes too small.

"Our gear!" Billy dumps the ELDs, Marriage Marbles, wallets, and watches onto the padded cot. He grabs up the black M2: "Maya? Maya?"

Shub checks his baby blue M2 for damage: "Too far underground. No signals," Shub pockets his ELD and fastens the marble's necklace in place, wipes the dust off Elroy's tri-screen unit and stuffs it into a zippered compartment into the roamad's backpack.

"You two are gonna escort old LB and I up and out of here post haste. Anyone tries to stop us gets stun-gunned. In a pinch, we yank the hood off and I go crazy with the bastard. We get topside and commandeer a vehicle out of here," Enoy elucidates.

Blurr and Shub double check the bindings on JimJim and the two guards, squirming on the floor inside the blood-smeared bovine jumpers. "Let's blow," Marco admonishes, securing his own backpack.

Billy spies the can of Interview dropped during the dramatics. He grabs it up and shakes: "You guys go first, I'm 'gonna spray these bastards blue."

"Good idea!" Marco concurs, treading gingerly over the slick hallway toward the main door.

Revesti hoists Byrdman up by the bungees and guides the hooded hostage forward, sandwiching him between Shub and himself, "Nice and quiet." Byrdman wisely capitulates, keeping his head up and centered, lest the hastily secured stun gun go off inadvertently.

JimJim and the security guards watch in wild-eyed horror as Billy crouches down with the can. "This one's for Rabbit Man!" He pulls out their gags and blasts them one after the other in rapid succession:

"Nooooooo!"

"Forgive me Lord Byrdman!"

"Shit!" JimJim gasps for air and rolls across the floor hiding his face from the bursts of concentrated psychotropic mist. Blurr pinches his nose whilst walking backward out of the cell. He empties the jumbo can of Interview and tosses it aside. The chemical cloud drifts down and saturates the cowering Cyopolians, certain to be chatting away terrified after their initial blackout.

Blurr closes the cell block door behind him and brings up the rear as Shub leads the way, sucking in his gut to better accommodate the tight-fitting Crow Corps uniform. He flips on a flashlight: the extensive tunnel is thankfully deserted, dimly lit by overhead slits of re-routed sunlight. The man-made cave appears to be carved out of the desert substrata by hand, shovel by shovel. Shub attempts to calm his nerves, "Which way do we go?"

"Keep walking in an upward direction and we'll eventually get to the surface," Revesti suggests, realizing now that he can't remember if he flipped the safety switch on the bungee wrapped stun gun.

Billy steadies himself behind Elroy and the hostage as they carefully waddle over a lumpy patch of rock floor leading to a more expansive cavernous sector.

"I smell Indian food," Enoy's enhanced olfactory detect the faint odor. A moment later they hear the volume abruptly cranked up high on an unseen speaker system. It's the unmistakable whine of the famous Sister Pynchon belting out a broadcast in progress: *"...The oversight process authorized by the New Totality Selection Election Commission insures the absolute randomity, and therefore purity, of the One Voter."*

They move toward a series of hollowed out sections of rock wall where a hand painted sign reads: *Level 5 Residence*. The voice of the nun grows louder as the foursome march in single file past the open door of a double-wide mobile home imbedded in the rock wall, recessed back few feet from the main tunnel. The bizarre bungalow is dark except for a large ELD screen framing the video visage of the Cybernetic Sister saying: *"And now I return you to Selection Central in Novo New York for the historic moment."*

They skirt past this first abode seemingly unobserved as Marco puffs himself up and marches quasi-officiously into the dimly lit main residence hive. It's a huge cavern housing hundreds of motor homes and travel trailers stacked two and three high, inserted into earthen grottos, secured by a patchwork of dismantled boxcars, and shipping containers, some still bearing faded logos from waybackinthenight: *Sony, Walmart,* and *Santa Fe Railroad.*

Cyopolians of all ages scurry about happily chattering; hurrying into house parties gathered around ELDs, watching the momentous Selection. None of them give more than a passing glance at the evidently ordinary sight of a hooded hostage escorted by elite Cyops officers. All eyes are glued on the unfolding Selection coverage. Shouting and laughter peel through the air echoing the zeal of sports fans.

Shub leads the hostage detail onward, anxiously clutching the stun gun in one hand whilst checking his ELD for webgridz signals. Enoy gently steers Byrdman by the shoulder, keeping the pistol level and relaxed.

A clap-trap electric delivery cart piloted by a gorgeous girl pulls up and parks. She hefts a tray of grilled hot dogs and casually smiles at Billy: "Aren't you boys gonna watch the Selection, Lieutenant?"

"No, sister..." Blurr keeps walking but grins back at her.

"Gonna be any second now."

"I'm working."

"Too bad..." unabashedly coquettish, the she-Mole's eyes scour Billy's face for fun: "Tofu pup?"

"I just ate," Billy reports. "Thanks anyway."

"Ok," she shoulders the tray, "See ya," and ducks into a double-decker trailer packed with excited Moles.

"Lieutenant...Requisition her vehicle," Enoy orders. "We're driving out of here." Billy starts up the keyless communal cart while Elroy carefully maneuvers their hostage onto the rear cargo bench.

Marco tosses their road packs in back and squeezes into the tiny shotgun seat next to Billy: "FMBlue."

Blurr warily accelerates into the main housing complex, honeycombed with hundreds of Cyopolians huddled at home watching EarthLingua screens.

Marco and Billy white-knuckle their weapons as they wheel up to an impromptu block party gathered in front of a giant screen ELD. Everyone's watching as a global mirror montage of live feeds from all over the world show people similarly glued to the extraordinary Election Selection broadcast.

Onscreen, a wizened New Totality official: *"The Selection is now complete and the One Voter's absolute identification is being verified and triple-checked."* The hostage cart cruises past entranced neighbors as an ecstatic roar of relief erupts from the amassed audience and cascades out the ELD speakers, electrifying the Cyopolian suburbs.

Billy steers out of the immediate residential zone and heads into a chance tunnel disappearing hundreds of yards upwards into deserted darkness. The cart passes under an illuminated stone sign bearing the salutation *'Long Live Lord Byrdman'* advertising a smoothed section of the wall where an earthen canvas is airbrushed with a twelve-foot tall portrait of the aged Cyopolian Messiah, seen squinting Svengaliesque, an albino Rasputin.

"It's him!" spits Shub.

"LB!" beholds Blurr.

"Well, well, my Lord..." Revesti whispers into the back of Byrdman's hood, tightening the bungeed pistol a twist. They putter past the leering leader's portrait and are confronted by a two hundred foot long mural painted on polished cement slabs depicting the Cyopolian supercult's growth. The telling illustration portrays a heroic young Byrdman discovering the pigmy-size skeletons of ancient

Menahuni, visualized migrating over millennia from Maui/Mu to Hopi Land via a forgotten freeway of subterranean volcanic tunnels crisscrossing Middle Earth. The glowing spirit form of Lord Byrdman is featured in scores of colorful scenes, laying hands on the sick, lifting the exhausted, watering the thirsty, and counseling the crazed. His selfless acts of grace, lovingly commemorated in hundreds of miniature portraits bordering the mural, honoring Cyopolian men, women, and children pictured piously presenting themselves to Lord Byrdman for a coveted kiss on the forehead.

Enoy grabs his backpack with his free hand and fishes out his ELD. He thumbs through the old archives finding *Mesa Foundation022357*. Revesti presses play, holding the device up for Byrdman to hear the extraordinary symposium recorded waybackinthenight: *"It's really very simple,"* the hypnotic voice of Dr. Lawrence says with great intensity and enthusiasm: *"All I want you to do now is to tell me what breed...what kind...and about what age...is...that cat there?"*

"Here kitty, kitty!" Enoy pressing pause. "Remember? It's only fifty-six years ago."

"Mmmmooogggghh!" Byrdman bellows beneath the pillowcase, gargling the gag of underwear.

Revesti pushes play again: *"Why it's Siamese,"* bespeaks the voice of Byrdman's old boss, Dr. Russell: *"We used to have one. Is it yours?"*

"What the hell are you doing, man?" Blurr fearing Enoy's savage side has suddenly surfaced.

"Settling a score," rasps Revesti. "Give us a minute, will you?"

Shub is summarily silenced, squishing against the flimsy plastic dash as Billy down-shifts the electric lorry and accelerates up the inclining tunnel towards a smoky blue light beckoning in a distant cavern.

Enoy can't resist pointing out, "What I really need to know is why a lucky guy like you has spent his precious gift deceiving so many others?"

"Ooohhhgg!"

"The both of us got a little glimpse behind the cosmic curtain. And what did you do with yours? Bullshit!"

"Gggggrrrrrrmmmmmm!" howls the hooded old man.

"Precisely! Just like I knew you would."

"Nnnrrr!"

"You've got the Curse and there is no cure."

"Ooogggaaahhh!"

"Listen..." Shub squirms, "Hear that?"

"Sounds like cheering," determines Billy.

"Here we go again..." sweaty hand on stun gun, Blurr steadily steers out of the long tunnel into an enormous hollowed-out hall marked *'Level 2 Residence'*.

They enter a similar scene as before: assorted Cyopolians circled around their screens watching the Election Selection coverage. Suddenly dozens of revelers spontaneously tumble from their trailers and spill into the main tunnel cheerfully chanting: "William's the One! William's the One!"

Blurr politely weaves the cart through the cheery throng of celebrants as a cloud of second-hand speq smoke floats overhead. They pass one household after another, catching glimpses of ELD screens through open doors and windows, each showing an identical close- up photo of the One Voter captioned: *Mr. William Blurr.*

"We've determined that 'Blurr' is in fact the One Voter's legal surname," an animated anchorwoman informs the world.

Billy stops the cart. He and Marco stare at each other in shocked silence. Blurr grins first: "The One Voter...Nectar."

"That's crazy!" Shub smiles proudly at his bosom buddy.

"This photo is from employment records provided by the California Institute of Art Therapy—still no word on his whereabouts—William Blurr has approximately fifteen hours to report in and less than twenty-four hours to select the president from the candidate pool."

"Drive on!" admonishes Enoy, spying two other cart-vehicles heading toward them, tooting horns, flicking headlights, clearing a path through the jam-packed dormitory tunnel.

REALLY GOOD ATTORNEY

Victor Vilter has been sequestered alone in his firm's panoramic conference room, one eye on his Marriage Marble and the other on the ELD broadcast of the Affinity Selection.

Seeing as neither Shub nor his captors have shown up on the M2 in over fourteen hours, Victor is giving the go ahead and sending Wildman & Associates inside the Cyopolian stronghold to snatch the client. The Wildman team has spent the intervening period stealthily creeping into position around the Supercults remote junk yard. Any minute now they'll patch Victor into the secure video feed.

Other than the beguilingly fiendish eyes, Victor observes William Blurr to look like the proverbial surfer boy-next-door except grown up. Vilter would go after this Blurr fellow's account without delay if he closes the Shub deal today but it's only been about five minutes since the Affinity Selection, too soon to tell which of the hundreds of attorneys signed up to represent the One he'll actually hire. When the Voter is finally found, the largest armada of mediadrones ever assembled will descend on him and immortalize the son of a bitch. Pound for pound, William Blurr will be the most famous person in recent history. This unprecedented celebrity will doubtless drive him over the edge within a week and, like so many lottery-winners waybackinthenight, Blurr will be cruelly crushed by sudden fame, a sucked-dry shell of a man, desiccated by fate...*unless he has a really good attorney...*Victor firmly believes. In fact the firm that winds up with the job will surf Blurr's coattails to the front of the world class and likewise enjoy unsurpassed publicity. Waiving one's fees will be rewarded a zillion fold, and all in a few days of lawyering.

"Boss?" entreaties Roxanne via intercom, interrupting his rumination: "We got him!"

"Shub?" Vilter bounds from leather sofa.

"No, the Voter! William Blurr. His wife's on line three. Says you know her. She's calling from a pubterm in a Restaurantruck. Downtown Amsterdam."

COMPATIBLE PROXIMITIES

Nothing useful has turned up on Blurr—besides the fact that he used to work in the movies and he's married to a once suicidal ceramicist in Amsterdam—and he hasn't contacted the Selection officials yet. Any clue, lead, sighting, or datum pointing to the location and disposition of William Blurr that anyone uncovers in the next hours will already have been discovered and digested by the sister's secret sources, muses Paula Pynchon, securing herself into one of the dozen empty passengers seats in a refurbished cargo jump jet. The sister's requisitioned the private plane to depart from Port Bel Air and circle the airspace over southern Novo California until the Voter surfaces. The jumbo vertical-lift aircraft puts her in position to land almost anywhere and be whisked off to meet and greet the One, hopefully before anyone else from the New Totality gets to him.

Even if they do, surely she, the First Sister of Cybernetics, will be able to enjoy a last minute private ELD chat with the Selectee prior to sequestering—presumably to orient the Voter to his holy duty—while in truth, slipping in her favored candidate names by means of the subliminal 'Vatican Voice' technique. Being mobile to this degree also affords her an added layer of personal security should the suicidal Hares decide to storm the fortifications of the Bel Air Protectorate and snatch her or worse.

The antique Harrier taxis to the fortified Kinship Commune's helipad and pauses before rotating its twin sets of jets. Paula braces herself for the vertical lift-off, breathing deeply as gravity pulls on her mass. The jet blasts roar against the tarmac, lifting the sister swiftly and safely into the smazy skies above Babylonwood. Her mathematical mind is fiery with visions of runaway randomity, magically gravitating into compatible proximities, secreting a sole singularity from the swirling soup of uncertainty...*the One!*

— Poof! — Paula's revelatory vision is vibrated into extinction by the incessant summons of her pocketbook EarthLinguaDevice: it's the law firm Vilter & Vilter: "Change your mind, Victor?"

"No, Sister," Victor appears on the nun's ELD screen smiling slyly. "I'm calling on behalf of my client, Mr. William Blurr."

"Sweet Jesus!" puffs Pynchon. "Where is he?"

"Middle of nowhere...Here's the GPS nums," Vilter zapping the coordinates to her. "You've got fifteen minutes before I notify the media."

"Why are you doing this for me, Mr. Vilter?" Paula perceives a paranoid power play percolating.

"Patriotic duty, sister..." assures Vilter, "...By the way, you know anything about Cyopolians?"

SKIN JOB

Billy ducks low, attempting to hide his face from view whilst slowly maneuvering the cart through the crush of Cyopolian celebrants still chanting: "Williams the One!"

"Let me drive," Marco suggests. "Get in back."

"Fuck!" Blurr hits the brakes and halts the cart as the standing-room-only crowd suddenly swells, boxing them in.

"Lieutenant!? Lieutenant!?" A woman's voice explodes over the din as another electric cart miraculously appears: it's the tofu pup temptress! She hops over and gets right up in Billy's face: "You're him! You are! I knew it! You're the One!"

"You're making a mistake, sister!" Blurr manages, but a shitload of psyched-up Cyopolians surrounding them are doing triple-takes between the Billy and the video visage of the One Voter on the ELD giant screen.

"It's true!"

"It's him!"

"Wowz!"

"The One!" The salacious she-mole hugs Billy tight and

plasters a smooch on her champion's cheek. "Congratulations!"

"No!!" Revesti shouts at the top of his lungs, producing a piercing warrior's tone. Everyone suddenly freezes in their tracks, locking silent eyes on Enoy. He lowers his voice hypnotically, "The Lieutenant is in fact a William Blurr look-alike. A good one. I oversaw the roboplasti myself," Enoy authoritatively announces to the shocked assemblage. "But this one here..." Revesti pats the hostage's hooded head. "...is a bad job, done by our enemies."

"Mooogggaaahhhh!" the hood howls.

Enoy employs the tricky *Astound Technique* and abruptly yanks the pillow case off of LB's head, exposing the man bungeed to stun gun.

"Lord Byrdman!"

"Oh my god!"

"No!!" Revesti barks again. "He's not our Founder! He's a double! There's a half a dozen of these Lord Byrdman skin-jobs walking the streets of Cyopolis. We're rounding them up one by one!"

"Ummmmmmakkkkk" Lord Byrdman bellows, staring desperately bug-eyed at his easily fooled followers.

"Shut up you fucking replicant!" Enoy pokes the gag in further and gruffly re-bags Byrdman's head. "Find the others! Proceed, Lieutenant!" Revesti commands.

"What's the quickest way topside?" Billy asks the girl, still hugging his arm.

"I'll show you," she says, somehow squishing herself in-between Blurr and Shub, both squelching their astonishment, amazed that Elroy's insane improv has actually appeased the spellbound crowd of Cyopolians who obediently clear a path for the cart to pass.

WHAT A DUMP!

During the dawn hours Wildman Associates collectively encroached deep into the yard's confines and positioned around the medieval Cyopolian obelisk. Fleming and Mueller coppered over from Taos in stealth mode and rendezvoused with Karl.

The Associates auto-shape-shifting camo jumpsuits, replete with lightweight hood and veil, have allowed them to blend in perfectly with the stacked mass of ancient shipping containers and wrecked RVs. They've observed a steady flow of motor homes arriving every thirty minutes, small caravans of three or four coaches. After the drivers are cleared by lizard-suited Cyopolian guards, they steer the vehicles over to a subterranean ramp and disappear underground.

It was Karl's idea to affix a shitload of remote transmitters onto the bottom of several of the arriving motor homes. Now, after a half hour double-checking and cross-referencing the results, they've got some remarkable data. The encephalographic wave detection devices are showing the presence of literally thousands of human beings directly below them, milling around underground. This is not good. The Associates only have enough Gopher Gasser cartridges to inflict mild nausea and panic in that many people.

"Patching him in now," Karl whispers to his helmet micam. Across the yard, Mueller and Fleming train their lenses on the heaped wreckage. By switching back and forth between the three, Vilter will have a composite view of the situation on the ground: "Mister V? How's that look?"

"Zoopy," Victor confirms over secure webgridz link. "What a dump!"

Fleming, squats inside the corroded cab of a pimp's once plush pleasure craft. "It's some kind of giant underground installation. Couple thousand people, maybe more.

"Forget it, guys," Victor says. "Listen, I've got two clients in there now and one of them is the goddamn One! Understand? The Voter? So I've called in major reinforcements. In fact, within twenty minutes the fucking skies above that dump will darken with more mediadrones and government aircraft than you've ever seen!"

"Really?" Karl rasps. "How would you like us to proceed?"

"I don't know," Victor admits. "The NT will be all over that place any minute. Ideas, gentlemen?"

MEDIADRONES

Rex Timbu sips on a speq-laced java, turns his attention away from the Selection broadcast—blaring from an ELD in the VIP lounge—and watches an ancient cargo jump-jet finish refueling on the far side of the dilapidated Taos Airport landing field. The attendants scurry back as the decommissioned military plane taxis away and swiftly lifts off straight up into the sunny Novo New Mexico sky.

Rex's ELD bleeps with the distinctive ringtone signaling a call from Bobogoné back at headquarters: "Morning Boss. Hear from Zuzzan yet?"

"No!" Bobogoné barks over the tiny screen. "I'm beginning to think your theory has some merit. She might have set us up. Any word from that fucking creep at Cyopolis?"

"Not a peep. I've been calling him all morning. We've got about three hours until the supposed swap," Rex calculates. "The cash is in the jet. All we can do now is wait and see if my theory is right. You ok?"

"No I'm not ok! I gave everyone the day off to watch

the Selection and I'm alone here in the command center. I can't find your speq stash, Doc."

"The liquid concentrate is in the rear of the fridge in a lemonade carton. Careful Gerry, only use a single drop per serving. It's super potent KandyMan Brand."

"You know something, Rex? I don't really give a flying fuck about the Selection or the blood money we pay to this Harpo dude for his goddamn software robots."

"You stand a really good chance of being picked as president!" Timbu observing his bosses' hickey-swollen lip bulging even on the tiny ELD screen. "The other candidates are clowns!"

"Without Zu, I'm a clown too! I'd pay twice as much just to have her back here."

"Hang tight, my friend we'll know soon enough if we've been had," Rex steps outside the terminal for better privacy. Overhead, Timbu spies what looks like a gigantic flock of migrating birds. "What the fuck!"

"What's happening, Rex?"

"Mediadrones!" Timbu gawking in disbelief at thousands upon thousands of low-flying, unmanned cigar-shaped robo micams zooming overhead, hurriedly winging north, and saturating the sky with the hum of their solar engines.

INTRUDERS

"Turn left!" the helpful Cyopolian beauty implores, heaving her breasts against Billy's ribs. Blurr obeys, steering the electric cart sharply into a wide corridor, just missing a bronze bust of Lord Byrdman perched on a miniature faux-Trajan column.

"Aaaaack!" squeals their hapless hostage as the bungee-corded stun gun flexes dangerously in the tight turn.

"Pull in here," the seductive she-mole points to a brightly lit loading dock.

"Freight elevators!" Shub yelps. "Let's go!"

"Give us a hand," Revesti requests. Marco and Billy help Enoy get LB out of the rear of the cart, carefully hoisting him to his feet, trundling together into the nearest open elevator. The Cyopolian cutie skips in, hits the button marked *Surface Level* and beams at Billy.

"Thanks, sister. We owe you one," Blurr squeezes her arm tenderly—but just as the doors begin to slide shut—Shub places his foot squarely on the girl's ass and swiftly shoves her outside back into the hallway. The doors close and the elevator lurches upwards. "What the fuck!?" Billy glares hotly at Marco. "Why did you do that?"

"For Maya," Shub grins, fingering the inactive Marriage Marble dangling from Blurr's neck. Billy's mumbled retort is cut off by a startling alarm blaring from the utility speaker embedded in the elevator's control panel: *WEE-ONK! WEE-ONK! WEE-ONK!*, followed by a recorded emergency announcement: *"Attention Cyopolians! This is not a drill. Evacuate! Evacuate! Proceed to emergency surface exits. Repeat, this is not a drill. All levels evacuate immediately!" WEE-ONK! WEE-ONK!*

"Mmmmppphhh!!" Byrdman gurgles in panic.

"Fire?" Shub questions.

"Something else," Enoy intuits. He abruptly pulls the pillowcase from LB's head and yanks the saliva soaked shorts out of his mouth... "Tell us, little Birdie. What gives?"

"Intruders..." Byrdman gasps for air and eyes his captors scornfully, "That would be you," he informs.

"Methinks not," bespeaks Enoy. "More likely New Totality squads looking for a voter named Blurr."

"We're saved!" Billy concludes. "Zoopy!"

Byrdman squints at Blurr's aura, quickly ascertaining his weak spot: a lozenge of luminosity vibrating behind the right knee. The elevator stops and the doors slide open to reveal a chaotic crush of manic panic: hundreds of horrified Cyopolians surging up the main tunnel towards the surface exits, pushing, tripping, screaming, urged onward by the evacuation alarm: WEE-ONK! WEE-ONK!

Shub and Blurr step out to the edge of the stampede brandishing the stun guns as Enoy struggles to balance Byrdman, but a terrified mob of moles mash them all against the rock wall. The bungee cords suddenly snap and Enoy's pistol pops into the air.

Byrdman twists free of Revesti's grasp, squats and presses his thumb against and back of Billy's right knee.

Blurr's eyeballs roll backwards, his entire body instantly constricting into a coiled spring which viciously releases, launching him violently upwards over Marco's head.

"No!" Shub shouts, catching Billy in mid air. Blurr's body contorts spasmodically as Marco desperately restrains his head and arms in a bear hug.

Enoy grabs Billy's legs and squints at his intensely palpitating aura. He deftly presses his thumb against an orange glow on the back of Blurr's knee: "Got it!"

"Wowz!" Billy bounces out of Shub's arms and stands wide awake, oddly refreshed. "What happened?" Blurr is befuddled by the look of astonishment on Shub's mug.

"I don't know..." Marco's mystified.

"Byrdman got away?" Blurr asks.

"Yeah," Enoy answers. "Let's do the same."

WEE-ONK! WEE-ONK! Stampeding Cyopolians surge into the crowded corridors, running amok, trampling their slower comrades underfoot.

BILLY?

High up inside the massive yard watchtower, Wildman Associates have quickly succeeded in surprising, hog-tying and torturing the Cyopolian security guards into giving them the go-codes to sound the evacuation alarm: WEE-ONK!

Just for the hell of it, Mueller scattered a couple hundred *Gopher Gassers* in clusters throughout the junkyard and the smoking cylinders are now releasing a formidable fog layer of sickening yellow stink. The Associates train their helmet micams on the main underground entrance whilst Victor Vilter commands them from the distant comfort of his SanFranciscOakland office.

"Here they come," Fleming informs as a wave of Cyopolian evacuees breech the surface exits and tumble helter-skelter into the gassy yard.

"Go grab my clients!" Vilter virtually shouts out. The Associates dawn featherweight Italian gas-masks and hustle to the elevator. Seconds later they materialize from the tower to witness scores of motor homes driving up and out of numerous subterranean ramps, speeding topside, careening into each other, mowing down disoriented evacuees in the thick yellow fog.

The Cyopolian stronghold explodes with chaos as thousands of screaming supercultists are ejected onto the surface for the first time in years, blinded by the sunlight, sucking in funky fog, dropping to the dirt, vomiting vituperatively from the exterminator's agent. "Keep your heads up!" Victor truculently transmits. "I can't see!"

Suddenly the screams of the scurrying Cyopolians are eclipsed by the whine of hard-by jet turbines. Dropping straight down from heaven, Sister Pynchon's cargo Harrier lands like an avenging angel on the sage covered scrubland just beyond the yard. The jump-jet's powerful blowback creates a gargantuan cloud of dust that mixes with the golden gopher gas vapors, further obscuring vision, exponentially inculcating the torment of the terrified escapees.

The Associates close ranks inside the frenzied miasma, back-to-back in triangle formation, scanning micams in full-circle surveillance mode, seeking sight of Shub and the One.

Hundreds of panicky people peel past them in lizard, mole and prairie dog uniforms, some diving inside wrecked RVs and crushed shipping containers, others desperately leaping onto the roofs and bumpers of fleeing recreation vehicles, many more running hysterically into the surrounding forested foothills.

"Look!" Karl points skyward as umpteen thousands of low-flying mediadrones swoop in overhead, encircling the Cyopolian airspace. Legions of swarming steel locusts perform complex collision avoidance aerobatics, recording high-definition stereoscopic imagery of the bewildered bipeds below, beaming billions of megabits back to the broadcast bunkers of global media outlets, military command posts, and New Totality press pre-processing centers.

"Smile, gents. The whole world is watching," Victor

verifies.

Stumbling out of the crowded emergency exit, Lord Byrdman emerges, alone and exhausted. Aghast at the apparent apocalyptic demise of his Cyopolian sanctuary, Byrdman does what any messianic megalomaniac might do in similar circumstances: he ducks his head and runs away as fast as his octogenarian appendages allow. He desperately zigzags betwixt his zealous sycophants, slaloming surreptitiously through the maze of mangled motor homes, hurrying headlong into the high desert hills.

Now comes Shub, Billy and Enoy, beating feet, boldly busting out of the subterranean supercult citadel, pushing through the maniacal multitude of mole-suited minions.

"Keep low!" Revesti yells as torrents of dust and noxious yellow mist sting their eyes. "Hold your breath!" The dreadful cries of Byrdman's terrified followers ring out as the trio tread past trodden sufferers projectile puking in the dirt.

Nearly blinded by the blustering boluses engulfing the atmosphere Shub shouts: "Stay together!" He clutches Enoy's outstretched hand, "Grab hold!" and reaches for Blurr's but grasps only a sweaty forefinger. "Billy?" Shub squints through the hellacious haze and sees he is holding the paw of the Bovinity-suited JimJim.

The Transpo Chief stares at Marco through inflamed eyeballs—still out of his gourd from the overdose of Interview—utterly oblivious to the tumult surrounding them: "Mommy? The doggy has peach pits stuck to its furry face!" JimJim vehemently informs until PHOOMP!! Enoy slams his fist into the bastard's testicles, crumpling him over on his bony ass.

"FMB!" spits Shub surprised. Blurr is nowhere to be seen: "Blurrrrr!!"

"We lost him!" Enoy grunts, scanning the crazed crowd.

"Bluuuuurrrrr!!" Marco bellows again but Billy doesn't answer. Instead, a shrill woman's voice amplified by a bullhorn pierces the air—

"William Blurr! William Blurr! William Blurr!"

"What the hell is that?" Shub shivers mystified.

"They've come for him!" Enoy determines. "Billy's the One."

"Right..." Marco spies scores of mediadrones circling the sky nearby, spraying nanocams over the crushing crowd of Cyopolians. "Fuck it. Let's blow." The two slip deep into the junkyard amidst the scattering supercultists and scamper into the surrounding scrub oak and Pinon laden hillside.

The tsunami of scared-shitless Cyopolians flood the mega-junkyard, blinded by the gas and dust—videoed by the legions of flying robo cameras darting only inches overhead—their shock and awe amplified by the presence of a puffy pink plane parked in the dirt, emblazoned with the words *'Bel Air Protectorate'*.

Billy is dreadfully disoriented, twirling dervishly in the foggy dust, anxiously searching for his friends when out of the blue Blurr hears his surname hailing from a nearby bullhorn. He cocks an ear toward the source of the hallucinatory sound and, gaping into parting mists, witnesses the approach of an enormous nun clutching a silver bullhorn in one hand and a crimson fire extinguisher in the other, the snow white wimple wings of her ecclesiastical habit gently flapping in the dusty golden gusts: "William Blurr?" She delicately asks of him.

"Yeah...?" bespeaks Blurr unbelievingly. Baffled by the bizarro angelic figure, Billy now beholds the apparent apparitions of three mercurial mirror-beings impossibly reflecting the immediate surroundings.

"Not so fast, sister!" Karl warns as the wily trio of Wildman Associates wedge themselves in betwixt the nun and the One.

"Oh?" Pynchon pluckily pulls the pin on her handy extinguisher and floods the reflective faces of the almost invisible interlopers. The Associates fall to the ground flailing fitfully, hawking up handfuls of hot black foam.

Paula pounces on the piteously prone wretches and prepares to mercilessly knee-drop Karl's trachea but William Blurr's Marriage Marble vibrates to life and Maya's voice vents vociferously:

"Stop bitch!"

CONFUSION TECHNIQUE

"Are you watching this, Rex?" Gerald Bobogoné spits over the scrambled ELD line linking Dr. Timbu in Taos to the DataMynd command and control center. Gerry has been anxiously eyeing the Selection coverage whilst slurping speqachinos and worrying his hickyed lip. Now the video drones are collectively capturing the strange scene outside the remote Cyopolian junkyard, auto-editing swooping shots of the colossal compound intercut with close-ups of horrified supercultists.

"I'm watching," Rex answers from the deserted airport lounge, licking the splits in his brutally chapped lips.

"And what does it mean, Dr. Timbu?"

"Probably that Kaplan and Harpo are operating on a higher order agenda than we assumed. Somehow they've arranged for this Cyopolian, William Blurr, to be selected."

"But why?"

"You tell me, Gerry."

"How the hell should I know?"

"You're the one she's been grooming to be the President!"

"What? She left me, Rex. Remember?"

"Gerry, Kaplan's obviously working with Sister Pynchon. They probably have this Blurr guy set up to pick you out of the two hundred candidates."

"Why would she need to disappear to do that?"

"The Confusion Technique. Harpo is likely a red herring. Kaplan's got you so flummoxed that when their man selects you, she'll easily step in and take control."

"Why? Because I'm in love?"

"Ejactly!"

"No, Rex. Something's gone horribly wrong—" Bobogoné does a double take at the ELD now showing a close-up snippet of a bovine-suited man squatting in the dirt amongst scores of fleeing Cyopolian escapees"—it's him!"

"Harpo?"

"No! That JimJim fuck!" Bobogoné notices just as the tripping Transpo Chief confronts a relentless video drone hovering only half a foot from his face:

"You think this is my fault?" JimJim sputters.

MARIA

Zuzzan guns her Subaru and pulls out of the overcrowded roamadic refugee encampment outside Scottsdale, Arizona. After ten hours of heated negotiations with several seedy radical Rabbit types she managed to purchase a fairly believable set of false identity docs and an ELD file of fake receipts, foreclosures and dummied up family photos. She chose the new name of Maria Nys for no other reason than Maria, the young wife of writer Aldous Huxley, was the first woman to earn a driver's license in Italy waybackinthenight. But the custom ID kit was expensive and now funding looms problematic for Zu. Keeping to cash and anonymous $e cards will only last a few more days.

The anticipated social mayhem everyone expected to ignite hasn't effloresced as yet but Zu suspects the Rabbits are merely waiting until the One Voter makes his selection. More than likely, the banking system will shut down for a spell if threatened by mad hackers. If so, she will be out of cash and fucked.

Zuzzan turns off the jam-packed highway at the nearest exit and finds a free pubterm. No doubt Harpo's PUPP will intercept the email to Gerry and try to pick up her trail but it's the price she'll have to pay; besides, over the last few days Zu has grown a surprisingly thick skin towards the specter of her evil cyberclone twin. With the Maria identity intact, this note will be Zuzzan Kaplan's final transmission. Zu logs onto her account and sends Bobogoné a message saying only: "Send my money now."

—Bling!—

She signs off and slides back into the Subaru, awash in the delirious certainty that Gerry will immediately zap the $e130,000 he still owes her for getting him accepted to the Candidate Pool, and as far as the menace of the spooky software robot goes, Zu's been over every possible humiliation that could result from the total exposure of her past life—to Vilter and Harpo and whoever else—and her mind is oddly at peace with the idea of her mirror-self living a parallel existence as a cyber-cartoon caricature. In fact, the shock of actually seeing herself replicated thusly was the catalyst to break free of the stranglehold of Bobogoné and all that he represented. She was being groomed as the arch maven of the datamining industry or worse, the mollified mistress of a perfunctory president. But now she is a bird on the wing, winding her way toward Babylonwood, SanFranciscOakland, Novo Portland, Novo Vancouver and beyond, to the fabled colony of next-generation humanity: XaNa!

Zuzzan stuffs the Maria ID into her tote bag next to the dog-eared *Secret History* book and drives into a huge mess of traffic heading for the Novo California border checkpoints. The happy mood created by deliberately dealing with her situation as such sends Zu into a merry mental fantasy where she fancies herself Maria Nys, a truly mysterious person having little to do with the larger world.

SCHLEPPING INTO THE UNKNOWN

Shub stumbles frantically up a rocky arroyo following Revesti into the hilly backwoods behind the supercult compound. Marco's mind is reeling from the ongoing onslaught of whirlwind events propelling him into a panicky paranoia.

He paces the wiry old roamad but slips in the pebbly dirt, slides on his rump and tears the ass off the Cyopolian trousers. Shub angrily scampers to his feet and accidentally crushes his Marriage Marble underfoot, "Shite!"

Enoy halts on the ridge topping the arroyo. Shub scampers up.

"Marble's gone. Fuck it," says Shub.

The two reconnoiter their position looking down on the yard and see a convoy of New Totality assault ATV's destroying the gate-thing barrier.

Shub whips out his ELD. "I'm calling Blurr. Otherwise he'll put out a missing persons alert on me. My mug will be all over the gridz." Shub touches Billy's number: RESTRICTED. "Fucked! They wall him off! I'm calling my attorney." After many rings he gets the general voicemail: "Tell Victor that Harpo is unhurt. Still in hiding. Dark Black. No marble." He disconnects.

"OK?" Enoy powers on his own multi-screen device: three webgridz feeds show selection coverage featuring live mediadrone footage of the horrific Cyopolian scene: Overhead, several stealthy NT helicopters appear and silently circle the immediate airspace whilst a puzzling pink jump-jet loudly lifts off amidst persistent swarms of video drones viciously vying for views through the jet's tiny windows. Several anchors go over the breaking news: *The One Voter was rendered safe from this remote supercult commune only moments ago."* – *"We're getting word that Blurr's attorney, Victor Vilter, will make an announcement soon."*

"What? That's absurd!" Shub's shocked..."Whoaaaaaaaaaahhh!!!" He reels backward and tumbles down hard into the rocky arroyo. His device flips out and smashes against a boulder. Shub scrambles for his unit, finds the battery case busted, "Fuck me blue!"

Enoy stifles a laugh, "I can probably fix it, man...Whaaaaaaahhhh!!!" The arroyo ridge gives away. Revesti flaps his arms, falling head-over-heels down near Shub.

"Enoy!" Shub shouts.

Enoy opens his eyes and squints, "I'm ok." He starts to get up but collapses back down, "Yeooow! Ankle's blown out. Shit!"

Nearby branches SNAP! Shub and Enoy observe half-a-dozen fleeing Cyopolians disappearing into the trees.

"You get outa here, Marco. Leave me be," Enoy exclaims.

"Yer hurt, Elroy."

"I'll be fine. I'll call EMT. Go!"

"Go where?

"Outa here! Go! You've got your big deal to think about. I'm good."

"You saved my ass down there," Shub admits.

"You left Billy, Marco. You can easily leave me."

Marco glares at Enoy.

Shub carries Enoy piggy-back style, huffing and puffing through the forest. Enoy weighs him down further by slinging a backpack in each hand. "Broken Highway's two days west of here. How much water is in your pack?"

"A quart. Maybe."

"Keep your eyes open for a dear path. It'll lead us to water."

Shub grips him tighter and heads west, over and around the shrub scoured mesa. Marco decides when they stop to rest he'll change out of the Cyops uniform and put on his last remaining Bovinity jumpsuit. Then he'll use Enoy's ELD to contact Z and have the PUPP re-live the last twenty four hours at high speed. That way—even if Vilter is busy being Blurr's bodyguard—Marco will learn whatever the sobot has gleaned about Kaplan, Bobogoné and the pending PUPP deal, which, according to Shub's calculations, should go down later today if it's not blown out of the water by this unbelievable bullshit with Billy and the fact that Shub is schlepping into the unknown, increasingly at the mercy of Elroy.

THE RULES

William Blurr is strapped in next to the sister as the plane breaks the sound barrier fifty-thousand feet over Hopiland. "NT special forces crawling all over that place, Billy," Victor Vilter, video-linked to the overhead ELD in Paula's jet cabin, vehemently declares. "We'll find Marco and the old guy. Not to worry."

"Shub's in one of these getups," Billy pinches the breast pocket of the black Crow Corps uniform. "We switched clothes with the guards."

"Why would you do that, William?" Pynchon politely queries, sensing that Blurr's a consummate bullshiter.

"Don't answer her!" Vilter interjects. "And please don't ask him any more questions, sister. You know the rules."

"I wrote the rules, Vic," reminds Paula.

"They did it to escape!" Maya jumps in over Billy's M2, "Switched clothes! Right? "

Blurr nods affirmatively at the tiny video countenance of his remotely reunited wife.

"Sister P?" She asks. Blurr twirls the marble so Maya can address the nun: "Sorry I called you a bitch back there. I didn't know what was going on."

"Oh?" lets out the Sister.

"We'll be landing in fifty eight minutes, sister," the unseen pilot informs over intercom.

"Meet you at the hangar!" Vilter promises.

SPEQULATION

Bobogoné is juggling Rex's carton of liquid spec out of the command center's refrigerator when his pocket ELD sounds off with Zuzzan's sexy mail-tone: *Oh! Yesssss!*

"Zu!" Gerry gyrates joyously, shoving the liquid spec aside and stupidly sloshing his right wrist with the super-concentrated syrup: "No!" He quickly rinses off the devilish dollop under the sink tap and reads Zuzzan's email: *Send my money now!*

"That's it?" Bobogoné beholds.

Gerry flops into the overstuffed leather command seat and nibbles his swollen lower lip. The accidental splash of potent spec has instantaneously penetrated his blood system and the back of his neck explodes with sweat...*I'll send Harpo and Zu the blood money if it will get her ass back here quicker! Five hundred million ecrement$ will seem like chump change if she lands me the presidency.* Bobogoné punches in his DataMynd bank account codes on the ELD.

By the time Bobogoné completes the circumspect

overseas transfer, the massive overdose of spec has perforated his forebrain creating sufficient pressure to elongate the eyeballs into oblong orbs of hypersensitive receptors sensing subtle visual details unavailable to him until now. Gerry observes a crosshatch pattern in the cloth of his pant leg just above the left knee. It vibrates, emits a golden glow. He bends over and studies the fantastic fabric up close: The perfection of the threadwork, myriads of interwoven colors and textures. He presses his face closer and the viewpoint zooms in several orders of magnitude. He sees an impossible microscopic perspective of a miraculous nano-universe, obviously constructed by intelligent design. Lustrous transport tubes connect shining cities, evidently home to a master race of highly evolved atomic beings.

Sweat drips from Gerry's fingertips.

THAT'S IT!

Hopefully Victor's chartered chopper will get from downtown SanFranciscOakland to the Alameda Island Protectorate airport before Pynchon arrives with Blurr. Vilter's assistant, Roxxzan, sits in front with the burly pilot, checking ELD messages, averting her eyes from the dystopian quagmire roiling below.

"Jesus tits!" Victor exclaims over the buffeting rotors, aghast at the millions of roamads jam-packing the rooftops, streets, and intersections below. "They're taking over the city!" All surface traffic has come to a halt in anticipation of hysterical social upheaval. "We can't bring Blurr back here."

"I could book you a zoopy HomeTel right next to the airstrip."

"Do it."

"Done," Roxx hands the ELD to her boss, "Listen to this message."

'Tell Victor that Harpo is unhurt. Still hiding out. No marble'.

"Good!" Victor recognizes the subtle sardonic infusion in

the intonation as unmistakably Shub. Vilter has been keeping the pesky M2 in his breast pocket ever since he saw the escapees exiting Cyopolis, "Marcotecht lives."

"Hangar twenty-three," informs the pilot, swooping down in a wide circle over the manmade island. He swiftly and gently lands next to a gigantic, empty hangar.

"Keep the meter running?" Vilter helps Roxxzan climb out of the cockpit just as Pynchon's pink plane sets down and taxis into the massive structure.

Roxx squawks against the roar of the jump jet's turbines, watching an armada of mediadrones and news choppers advance over the horizon in hot pursuit of the One Voter. "We got company!" A contingent of airstrip emergency vehicles speed down the tarmac, lights flashing, sirens screaming.

"Close these doors!" Vilter shouts at a duo of airfield attendants trotting up. "Close them and lock them!"

"Yes sir!" The enormous Plexiglas doors slide shut as a grimy pink stairway lowers from the belly of the Bel Air carrier jet.

"Try to secure the building, Roxx," Victor bounds up the stairs preempting anyone exiting the plane and confronts the helmeted co-pilot: "Kindly bring up the walkway."

"Mr. Vilter, welcome aboard," offers Paula, remaining seated whilst Billy shakes hands with the infamous attorney.

"Marco left word," Vilter informs him. "He's fine."

"That's really good news," Billy blinks back a tear of joy.

—WHOP! WHOP! WHOP! WHOP! —

Multiple helicopters are hurriedly landing outside the hanger. Emergency vehicles shine spot lights through the huge doors.

"And here's the bad news," Vilter peers out a porthole and spies Roxxzan angrily gesticulating at a frightened official. "Our friends want to eat you alive, Mr. Blurr."

— BZZZZZZZZZ! —

Scores of insistent mediadrones suddenly swoop into

the hangar and swarm up to the jets tiny portholes.

"Close 'em!" Victor, Billy and Paula slam shut covers on the half dozen portholes. "I didn't notify them this time, sister. They followed you here."

"Oh?" Pynchon pouts perfunctorily, wiggling her wimple wings, biding time, waiting for the precise moment when she can insert the preferred candidate's names into what's left of William's brain. Paula is shocked to the soul at the results of her *Affinity Process.* She had hoped the miracle of divine randomity would materialize a middle-aged female of uncertain race, creed, and color, instead she got a whacked-out, white male looser whom she had to personally rescue from a supercult riot.

"Billy, take a deep breath. Relax. You and I are gonna walk out, smile, wave, and say nada!" Victor says.

"Listen to him, sweetie!" Maya implores via M2.

"I am listening."

"We walk right out the hangar and directly into my helicopter."

"Helicopter?" Blurr demurs, still bombinated by his supersonic jump jet journey.

"You say absolutely nothing until you've written down your vote and delivered it in to a Selection Official. Understand?"

"One Voter...One Vote," Pynchon elicits. "One Ruler."

"Got it," Billy buttons the cuffs on the jet black Cyops uniform and carefully clips his M2 to the breast pocket: "Ready."

"We're going out!" Victor raps the cockpit door. "Good day, sister." The exit opens and Vilter strides down the steps followed by Billy but both are brutally blinded by the intense glare from banks of camera lights.

Vilter bumps into one reporter, two videographers, and accidentally ass-butts Billy before his sense of balance returns enough to realize that the crazy cacophony echoing in his ears is not that of shouted questions and quarrelsome demands but, surprisingly, the sound of a thousand hands clapping in standing ovation, enthusiastically applauding the One Voter. The mediadrones are hovering at a respectful distance.

Vilter realizes that—even though the streets are filled with protesting Rabbits—these people here, the non-roamads, members of the educated affluhip minority, firmly believe in the *Affinity Process.* Until just now, he forgot that such folks actually existed. They think William Blurr was selected because he is mathematically—therefore divinely—charmed.

William the One is frozen in his tracks. Blinking bashfully into the blurry brightness, Billy beholds something he thought he would never see: a standing ovation! "Thank you...Thank you all...," he mumbles as boisterous barks of 'bravo!' punctuate the applause.

Billy's eyes adjust to the glare enough to see over the nearby sea of reporters onto the tarmac outside. Hundreds more media types are clapping, hooting, flashing high beams...*I'm like a zuper rocktro star!* Blurr begins to breathe in their adoration, thinking...*Rabbit Man...Now the One!* Billy's mind boggles at the sheer power of the praise heaped on him by his accidental accomplishment. Never in his wildest dreams could he have ever concocted a more promising publicity stunt than this one.

"Let's go!" Vilter grabs Blurr's arm.

A rascally realization races across Billy's boyish face, "Nope."

"What?"

"I am staying here."

"You can't do that, Billy."

"No? Am I not the One?"

The clapping stops and the cameras click on as everyone senses that something surreal is surfacing between William Blurr and his attorney. "What's going on, baby?" Maya inquires from hubby's M2.

"We're gonna hang here awhile, sweetie."

"No interviews until you vote!" Vilter insists.

"Then howzabout I vote right now?"

"Now?"

"Sure! Got a pen, Barrister?"

"You haven't even looked over the candidates!"

"Not so," Billy lies. "Made my mind up weeks ago," Blurr bullshits the bullshiter, as a dozen mediadrones hover overhead, streaming the squabble over the webgridz.

"Here's a pen" a helpful CNNT anchor woman whips one out and stuffs it into Billy's hand, "And a pad."

"Thanks," Billy casually scrawls, tears the page off, and folds it betwixt his fingers: "And here's my vote."

"I'll take that, William," Sister Pynchon mysteriously appears, offering her gloved hand to Blurr.

"How much time do I have left?" Billy bemuses, brainstorming his next move.

"Eighteen hours and thirty nine minutes!" yelps a *Frozen Boy* fashion correspondent.

"Zoopus," Blurr stuffs the vote into his breast pocket and buttons it closed. "I'll give it to you then, sister."

"Oh?" Pynchon puckers pugnaciously.

"Hey! Howzabout a folding chair?" Billy shouts out loud, smiling broadly at the legion of lenses, rubbing his hands together, "And a cup of Joe?"

"Coming right up, Mr. Blurr," someone volunteers.

Roxxzan pushes past the press of media crews and hands her ELD to Victor: "DataMynd."

"Gogoboner?"

"No. Doctor somebody."

Vilter steps underneath the pink jump jet cupping the tiny ELD screen: "Yes, Doctor? What can I do?"

"It appears as though you've already done it," Dr. Timbu transmits from the Taos Airport men's room.

"How so?"

"You guys set it up perfectly. Except now Mr. Bobogoné is missing," Rex found Bobogoné's pocket ELD in the command chair but the CEO himself was nowhere. Security camera footage showed Gerry down on all fours in a hallway near the control center, meticulously running his fingers over the carpet, searching for something deep inside the weave, crawling up the hall over a period of twenty minutes, and then exiting the premises on foot."

"Not my problem, Doc."

"I need to talk to Zuzzan Kaplan," Rex suspects Gerry has busted a blood vessel, or worse, OD'd on speq. Bobogoné's last ELD transactions indicate that he wired the $e500M to Vilter. "Check your Harpo account."

"What?" Vilter vacillates. Blurr has got everybody laughing in the background, "Gotta go, Doctor."

"Vilter, tell Zuzzan she's got to find Bobogoné and get him cleaned up for Pynchon's people."

"You tell him!" Victor powers down the device.

I'M CHANGING

"I'm getting too old for this shit!" Enoy declares. As soon as they make it back to the broken highway he'll see Marco off and head for Four Corners area and rest a spell. The wild ride with Blurr and Shub is growing exponentially phantasmagoric by the hour "We're doing good here, Marcotecht!"

Shub's winded from walking and offers no reply but his inner Shubette is awakened by the mental laxity accompanying physical fatigue and he clearly hears himself say: 'Doing good here Marcotecht' inside his head. Shub carries Enoy into a sage-covered meadow where large flat rocks offer them welcome wilderness repose.

"Ok...Full moon tonight. We can keep walking or camp here. Your call," Enoy says.

"Let's camp here," Shub takes his pack off and squats in the sun. "I'm changing." He unzips the back pack and pulls out a wrinkled Bovinity jumper. "Last one, I'm afraid."

"One is enough," Elroy plays with their pet phrase.

Marco dawns the cow outfit, eyeing Enoy's ELD: "I need to make another call, Elroy."

"Lawyer?" Revesti hands over the device.

"No." Shub briefed both Billy and Elroy on the DataMynd matter but didn't really go into detail about the PUPPs. "Calling my sobot." He accesses his encrypted domain and finds Z waiting in the video visualization of Zuzzan's co-op foyer. "Z?"

"My Marcotecht!"

"What's happening with Zuzzan and Bobogoné?"

"I don't know. She's been dark black. I wasn't sure what to do. I've got over three billion Puppyz feeding me clips. We'll find her."

"What? You've got three billion?"

"We'll find her. Zuzzy's last transaction is an E-mail from Arizona asking Gerry for money."

"Really?...Bobogoné must have had Kaplan go offgridz in order to try and neutralize you! Then they hired Cyopolis to hunt my ass down! But the Selection of William the One blew the whole thing apart! Call me when you find her," Shub silently stares at Z for a moment. He signs off, gives Revesti the device back.

"Girlfriend?" Enoy cocks an eyebrow.

"She's a cyberclone, Elroy."

"Of yer girlfriend?

"Zuzzy? No."

"Sneaky stuff, Shub...Sneaky stuff...Well, let's build us a fire! We're gonna freeze what's left of our balls off out here." Enoy spies plenty of dead Pinon branches scattered on the forest floor and methodically tosses them in a pile near the rocks. Enoy stacks wood and kindling on one of the flat rocks, "Your attorney jumped ship for the bigger Billy fish?"

"Looks like it," Shub ignites the fire.

"What say..." Enoy opens his ELD again, the powerful little screen a bit brighter now in the evening shadows, "we watch a bit of Billy?"

"Nectar..." Shub nabs some power bars from his back pack and hands one to Elroy.

—BLING! — Revesti's tri-screen EarthLinguaDevice locks onto a CNNT gridzsite and displays a live close up of William Blurr polishing off a bladder of chilled java, surrounded by paparazzi and hovering video drones.

"What is he doing?" Marco munches.

A riveted reporter from *La Monde* waits politely for the One to be done swallowing: "Monsieur Blurr, who are your primary literary influences?"

"The usual dead guys," Billy burps belatedly. "Balzac, Beckett, Burroughs—Let me finish telling you about the movie project we were talking about, ok? Remember, we're traveling back to earth two-hundred and twenty-three years later and we see a jungle settlement of primitive hominids thriving in the ruins of what used to be the Babylonwood hills."

"He's pitching my movie!" Shub says. "What a ripper!"

"Here, suck on this," Revesti stuffs his little brass pipe betwixt Shub's blubbering lips.

"Some are normal humanoids," Blurr continues. "But others have extra legs, multiple heads, elongated fingers, and supernumerary mammary glands. Like Huxley's old *Ape and Essence*, remember?"

"Of course!" a bearded journalist from the *Roamadic Reader* affirms.

"Blurr's a ripper alright!" Revesti snickers.

"There's Vilter!" Shub eagle-eyes the glowing ELD screen. "The bald guy behind Billy!"

"He looks worried...Seen enough for now?"

"Yeah. It'll live on the gridz forever," Shub's gazing into the blaze.

"I gotta piss."

"Cheating death for a few more minutes?"

"That's right. Not getting eaten by the light just yet!"

"That's a good one, Elroy."

"I got eaten up once—but it spit me back out!"

"Spit you back?"

"Yeah. My eye sights much better now though."

"For a second I thought you we're gonna get weird on me, Elroy."

Enoy finishes his piss up, "Look who's talking! You create a cyberclone and piss off a pack of psychos? You're best friend is the infamous One? And you wear a cow costume?"

"It's not a costume. It's an outfit."

"You ever make a cyberclone of yourself?"

"Only a rudimentary one. Ran it for about a month."

"How much you getting on your fire sale?"

"A fortune."

"Which gets you what?"

"Get's me gone on gone. Invisible."

"Like dead?"

"Yeah. Shub disappears off the system...I'm thinking about XaNa."

"Yeah?"

"That's where I'm headed. If I can get the scratch from DataMynd. Otherwise, I'll just delete her."

"Oh? It's a 'her' now?"

"No, 'her' is an 'it'."

"She'll be easier to delete as an 'it'?"

"We'll see."

"Why don't you just sell your software like a normal business transaction?"

"Cybercloning is illegal. It's a cross between identity theft and kidnapping so they get you for both and probably toss in some domestic terrorism to boot."

"Say no more".

Both men bunk down on the dirt in similar roamad-style sleeping bags. Shub's been deprived of normal rest for days on end starting with the secondhand speq black-out at the festivo, then getting gassed by the supercultists, finally nodding late last night for a few minutes in the subterranean Cyopolian cell. Now only moments after getting comfortable, a deep sleep descends upon him.

The last thing Marco needs is to be troubled by

nocturnal emissions of any kind, but alas, as soon as Shub rolls over onto his stomach, pinning his arms, the flood of high speed imagery froths forth in his forebrain: Billy and Byrdman swimming in the ocean, grasping dolphins' fins. Shub shoves the Cyopolian she-mole out the elevator doors. Z blows into the digital steam rising from a synthetic cup of hot tea. Marco and Billy point stun guns at the Cyops guards. Zuzzan walks up to the DataMynd ELD and asks Z: "What kind of panties do I have on?" There's no beginning, middle or end to this dreamare, accreting with the terrible gravity of accumulated exhaustion.

TVMOON

Billy pulls no punches with his blatant publicity stunt and has promised an all-nighter exposé of entrancing ideas—none having anything whatsoever to do with the Selection Election.

The One pauses to pick at a platter of crunchy little crab cakes put out by one of the army of Resturantrucks lined up on the tarmac to service the mass of media crews. It's just after midnight and Billy has not stopped pitching his projects to the assembled press corps. Special Forces have secured the perimeter of the private airport so no one can get on or off the tiny island except for food vehicles and New Totality technicians, so the cameras just keep rolling.

Around the world people are weighing in positively on the One Voter's grandstanding shtick, in fact more than two thirds of the planet watches now as biographical filler material is hurriedly inserted during Billy's snack break showing snippets of feature films Blurr worked on waybackinthenight including the mega-flop *Attack of the*

Baboon-Faced Horsefly and the ridiculous remake of *Frozen Boy* which, of course, inspired the popular glamour rag.

CNNT's trivia swarmbay is mixing the live feeds with video clips from another stunt Billy pulled a dozen years ago at a major studio opening. Old footage shows William Blurr chain-sawing nude female mannequins whose hollow limbs are stuffed with raw hamburger and day glow cheese puffs.

Behind Pynchon's pink jet, Victor Vilter and Roxxzan perch on folding chairs, feverishly fielding ELD calls from publishers, agents, investment bankers, webgridz studios, supercults and others seeking to lock-in rights to William Blurr's life story, likeness, movie concepts, endorsements and more. Vilter has brutally brow-beaten more than a hundred-million ecrement$ in hard commitments during three hours of non-stop niggling. "The only thing we've got left at that price point is the Mandarin language distribution rights to the webgridz making-of footage of Mr. Blurr's upcoming 'L' project," Victor explains to the frowning ELD image of a fellow attorney. "Take it or leave it."

Billy bounces back in front of the cameras proclaiming: "Another project, which we've already work-shopped, is my play titled TVMOON. This piece deals with the theory that the genesis and final use of atomic weapons is predetermined by the fact that we humans are genetically hardwired to re-create the cyclical conditions that produce radical variation in the genetic code! Our genes scream for radioactive purification!"

Blurr whips out his ELD and dials through his archives in broadcast burst mode: "I'm only gonna show you guys a few snippets." He punches power playback and zaps the signal to the uplink so everybody can watch.

"This sequence shows Paul talking to his hypnotherapist on the ELD. You see Paul is attempting to commit suicide by overdosing on bad videos—vidicide—and while doing so he calls everybody he knows and tries to see if they can talk him out of it. Most of the time he has three to ten people videoconferenced into his living room, that's why the set is dominated by a giant video wall."

Billy broadcasts footage showing an aging shrink listening intently, nodding in empathetic understanding as the Paul character rabidly rants: "Maybe we all have a remnant Dinosaur gene sleeping deep in the helixes, curled up for millennia, waiting to be triggered?" Paul postulates in a troubled whisper. "The gene contains memories of the asteroid collision, the explosion, the radiation, the light, the darkness, sensory death, the thud of large beasts slamming to the ground, struck down by the hand of God! Struck out!" Paul proselytizes to camera.

"Human beings are the ancestors of whatever survived?" squawks the tele-shrink, drawing Paul out.

"Yes! Our genetic relatives saw it happen! In the blink of an eye! The bright white fire, cleansing, sterilizing, purifying, recycling, reconstituting, burning, smothering..." Paul stares wild-eyed at the hypnotherapist's webgridz image. "The yearning for release through radiation is neurologically imprinted on a genetic level!"

Billy presses pause, cutting the clip off: "That part is a little heavy."

"Is this comedy not also a comment on the possible correlation between the dinosaurs dying out and humans self-destructing as a species?" queries the man from *La Monde*.

"You tell me?" Billy answers.

WAPITI

Enoy has been up since before dawn boiling coffee from his road kit and calmly observing Shub's aura roiling with energetic emanations signifying hypnopompic dream activity. In between several extraordinary snoring seizures, Shub has been silently mouthing snatches of inner verbiage. Phrases including 'Abnomalous concordance of events'; 'Out of the pond, out of the deal'; 'Nice ass' and 'Ballmeat kabob—well done', leap out legible enough for Revesti to readily lip-read. "Marco?" Enoy gently hails. "Morning, Marco."

Shub stirs awake, squints against the sun jutting over the eastern hillsides and spies Enoy squatting next to the fire pit, backlit by sunrays, smoke slowly curling around his wild gray hair sticking up in devil horns. "Morning, Mephisto," mumbles Marco, sitting up in his sleeping bag.

"Want mud?" offers Revesti, proffering a steamy cup.

"Thanks, Elroy," Shub paws the mug of powdered latte.

"Last of the water."

Shub shifts his ass, slops coffee, and jostles his backpack. "Oh, shit!" Marco's ELD slides out and smashes down the rounded lip of the rock into the dirt. "It's busted anyway."

"Let's see," Enoy retrieves Shub's EarthLinguaDevice and blows off the dust. He slowly rotates it around, squinting at the chipped battery cover from several angles: "Yeah..." Revesti sees a tiny green magnetic band arching near the bottom of the waterproof seal. He gives it a THWACK with the butt of his hand and squeezes the ELD tightly to his heart. "Should be OK now," Revesti flips on the device and hands it back to Shub.

The screen instantly powers up displaying the face of Billy Blurr saying: "—it's not so much a comedy as it is a social satire. Beyond Roamadia will examine the whole spectrum of current cultural structures comprising the New Totality."

"Unbefuckinglievable..." Shub admits. He can see Vilter sitting behind Billy, laughing at something on Roxxzan's ELD. Sometime during the night Blurr changed out of the stolen Cyops uniform and into a pair of black sweats featuring a prominent CrunchyCountry logo.

He's pacing energetically in front of a phalanx of hovering video drones and fatigued human reporters: "We'll begin with where we're at right now..." Billy continues, "A rat's nest of runaway systems: fortified Kinship Communes inside Protectorate City States, oceans of roamads, radical Rabbit Warrens, supercults everywhere; and then we'll progress toward what's next, *Beyond Roamadia!*"

"Let's get walking, Marco."

"Thanks for the repair job, Elroy," Shub turns Billy's broadcast off, readies his pack. The fact that the Cyopolians didn't steal Marco's hidden stash of cash from the zipper slots bespeaks either that they simply did not find it, or left it as hard currency has no meaning to them anymore.

Shub picks Enoy up and saunters hiking down the heavily forested hillside. "Fucking Byrdman. Fucker's a classic supercult despot."

"He's much worse. Those organs weren't exactly donated."

"Perfect. Abduct Speqheads, harvest their organs and sell them."

"Or persuade them to live in a slave colony tunneling to the center of the earth!

Shub hefts Elroy as they push past an old stand of cedar and see a well-trodden trail winding deep into the woods:

"Look! Deer tracks!" The two follow along the trail, ducking low hanging branches, Shub side stepping petite piles of glistening beastie poop.

"You know, Marco, I've been figuring on yer invisibility predicament...Thinking about invisibility from both the metaphysical and the electronical."

"Electronical?"

"One way would be to simply disappear into the background. But then you have to stay in the background which will shift over time. Possibly exposing you unless you constantly change with it, which means always checking to make sure you're still invisible."

"I know. I'm thinking of falling off the system and assuming multiple false identities."

"But you would still have to adhere to all of the system's rules. Only as somebody else. Not Shub."

"Right."

"What about you become the background? The background becomes you. If you're everywhere you're nowhere and after a while background noise automatically gets tuned out."

"Lost me, Elroy."

"And so would everyone else! They wouldn't see the forest through the trees."

"I disappear into the forest of noise?"

"Yes! Though overexposure you become so overblown that 'Shub' becomes a fiction, a myth."

"Overblown..."

"Invisible in plain sight. No one believes that you are actually you! I'm thinking about your ubiquitous puppets here, Marcotecht! ...Ssshhh!" The two peer through a large opening in the trees and see a wild pond surrounded by a dense thicket of brush next to which a lone bull elk is making hostile grunting barks and slapping the ground with its front legs. "Wapiti," whispers Enoy. "Elk."

Shub watches as the livid beast lowers its neck and raises its antlers then viciously stabs forward, striking behind the underbrush with several powerful jabs, angrily horning an unseen adversary. The big bull's third lunge produces blood on the tips of its antlers and a painful "Fuck youuuu..." response.

"Hey!!" Revesti raises his arms and hops off of Shub. He runs out of the woods right towards the astonished beast.

Shub marvels at Enoy's instantly healed ankle, "Son-of-a-bitch!"

"Woooo! Wapiti! Woooo!" the Elk sees Enoy and backs off but sprays forth an enormous cone of urine and bounding away, twitching its white rump.

"What is it?!" Shub sprints after Revesti and catches up to him as he breaks through the bushes.

"Byrdman!" Enoy instantly identifies the badly beaten body crumpled up in a bloody ball: "Gored him really bad."

"Unnnhhhh...." Lord Byrdman gurgles through a smashed throat.

"He gonna make it?" Shub's shocked blue.

"Doesn't look good..." Revesti sees Byrdman's diminishing aura turning dark orange.

"Youuu...?" Byrdman bubbles through his badly broken mouth, eyes widening in sudden recognition of Enoy's wrinkled face.

"Easy does it old man..." Enoy whispers, observing multiple horn punctures fatally perforating Byrdman's bleeding chest.

"Eamay..." Byrdman rasps.

Revesti leans right up next to the dying man's lips. "Eeemeee..."

"Eat you?" Enoy asks.

"Pleeeeesss..."

Shub fumbles for his ELD, "I'm calling EMT!"

"Too late, Marco," Elroy observes as Byrdman's eyes roll backward, his head flopping sideways. Revesti grasps Byrdman by the temples and gently tilts his forehead up. Marco has never seen anyone die before and watches in paralyzed wonder as Enoy steadies Byrdman's head and says: "It's ok...go on now."

A deathly slow-motion shudder undulates across Lord Byrdman's body leaving it still and silent. Shub beholds a soft orange tendril of weirdly wobbling smoke arising from the center of Byrdman's forehead.

Enoy bends forward and inhales deeply, sucking up the strange steamy substance in its entirety. The effort knocks Revesti backwards on his butt, coughing and gagging. He rolls over and vomits into the dirt before steadying himself with several deep breaths. Enoy eyes his pungent patch of puke and realizes Shub is nowhere in sight. "Marco? Shub!?" Revesti steps over the cooling corpse and squats down next to the lip of the little lake: "The Pond of the Imponderable!" He fills up two water bottles then vigorously splashes his face, washing off bits of Byrdman's blood. He bends down, hums a low pitched tone and slowly sips from the pond's sparkling surface: "Mmmmmmmmmmmmmmmmmm". He rises to his feet, takes the three-screen device in hand, touches it on, dials up STORM, and holds it down only inches from the surface of the pond's water.

The device speakers blast out the sounds of a recorded thunder. The water mysteriously wobbulates in sync with the sonic perturbations. Enoy sees the thunderous audio pulses in the infrared spectrum interpenetrating the pond waters as multiple micro-quakes buffet the ground, knocking him on his ass. The forest floor liquefies into gentle rolling waves travelling speedily outward in a wide circular sweep.

SHARD OF SHUB

Shub peels past pine trees, trips over dead branches and squeezes through scrub oak, hauling his ass as far away from Elroy as possible. Shub has seen many a bizarre and sickening thing in his sad life but never has he even imagined such a grisly practice as sucking up a dying man's soul! "No fucking way!" Marco retreats downhill, emerging from the tree line into a vast valley of sage covered mesa. "Fucking sprained ankle! No fucking way!" Shub stops, catches his breath. "Of course that psycho sucks up souls!" He trembles, shudders, re-living the ghastly moment.

Marco looks westward across the immense expanse of desert mesa lit by the late morning sun. He spies a tiny glint several miles off in the distance, moving slowly along the surface. Another fleeting reflection winks in the sunlight, then a third: "Broken Highway!"

After a couple hundred yards of knee-deep thicket, the terrain gives way to vast sloping areas of windblown dirt and rock, washed clean by millennia of flash flooding, unusually alive with random clusters of desert cedar and lone Pinon.

Shub schleps sideways through a tangle of twisted sage and accidentally stomps across a rotted wooden signpost splayed on the ground. Marco hefts the broken board and flips it over in the dirt. A barely legible hand-written scrawl spells out: *D. H. Lawrence Ranch —>12mi.*

Only as of late has Shub's heart even tentatively twitched with an irksome erotic extension through Z to Zuzzan, enticing him to ineffectively fantasize about Kaplan in the flesh.

Marco pauses near an old cedar and takes a long leak. He works the ELD with his free hand, presses the 'ON+Z' hot key:

The micro-quake wave front approaches, reaches Shub and lifts him several inches off the ground. Silence explodes inside Shub's skull, eyes locked on the heavens above.

From hundreds of feet in the air, Marco sees himself standing in the desert below, staring skywards. A pinpoint ray of light is projecting from his forehead, traveling infinitely upwards. Marco is somehow traversing inside the ray, deep into space, past multiple, previously invisible dimensions.

Beyond the most distant galactic void, another presence floats overhead. It's a luminous golden globe shining discreet rays in every direction, creating untold billions of light-forms.

Marco is a single shard of living light, unobstructed by matter, gravity and time. Beaming Shub-flavored variations back to the everlasting creator Orb itself. This realization unlocks an expanded field-of-view encompassing four neighboring Orbs at dance with the first.

The five Orbs navigate a non-dimensional, space-time gap-zone, interlacing their radiant rays, creating zillions of similar light-forms, one of which is the luminous shard that is uniquely Shub.

Another light beam crisscrossing his own contains signs revealing the singular essence of Billy Blurr. A third projects the unmistakable rosy ray of Enoy Revesti intersecting an eerie orange shard, Lord Byrdman. Shub lastly beholds a fifth ray inside of which burns the spirited light of Zuzzan Kaplan.

Now Marco understands that Earth is the only place in the multiverse that the immortal Orbs can experience time slowed down to an illusory crawl. Precisely because shards like Shub live in a body and continually feel their heart beat one pulse after another. The rhythm creates the illusion of time. The constant pulsation forces the light-forms to live life as individual humans, trapped in time, oblivious to their immortal origins.

The Shub-shard suspects that its biological body, back in the desert, will automatically self-immolate if its existence as an immortal light-form is ever exposed. He wants to remain out here but down on the mesa his body is dragging his attention back to terra firma. The single softly spoken rationale being: "She needs you there."

—BLIP!—

Shub's back in his skin again, exactly as he was, only different. He's finished pissing, soaked in sweat, shaking with fear...'She needs you there.'

"My Marcotecht?" Z appears on his ELD. "Zuzzan is still missing offgridz," the cyberclone automatically updates.

"Mmmm..." Marco hums, softly toning, hearing the rich harmonic qualities inherent in his voice for the very first time. "Mmmmmm," Shub hums again, remembering the one unfathomable explanation as to why he is back down here: "She needs me."

"Yes, my Marcotecht?" Z misinterprets its name inside Shub's whispered vocalization. The sobot is still loitering in its 3-D vizualization of Kaplan's flat, waiting for a bite from its billions-fold litter of Puppyz.

Marco all of a sudden realizes what he needs to do now—both to right the wrong in regards to Zuzzan, and to achieve lasting invisibility for himself—*Invisible in plain sight!*—Marco's mind runs rampant with the ramifications of Revesti's wild realization...*That old soul-sucker is onto something!*

"Do me a favor, Z?" Shub tilts the tiny ELD screen out of the noonday glare. "Get my Shub proto-PUPP out of storage."

The software robot obediently lap-dissolves to the Kaplan kitchen animation. Z lifts up a section of the imitation bamboo floorboards, yanks another sobot out of the crawlspace and stands it up on wobbling cartoon legs.

"FMB!" Marco hasn't seen his silly first-pass at PUPP creation in over twelve months. Shub's primitive attempt at cybercloning himself was abandoned when he got to this point and he decided to make Z from Zuzzan instead. "Reactivate Shub PUPP Prototype."

The partially rendered proto-PUPP boots up and automatically ray-traces itself to realistically reflect the lighting in the co-op kitchen. "FMB!" the animated Shubclone shouts, instantly ogling Z's calculated curves. "Nice ass!"

"Hey! Have some manners, you fucking ape!" Marcotecht rebukes his digital doppelganger. Unfortunately Shub didn't take the time to filter out many of the prototype's adolescent attributes, systematically stuffed in at the start of the data mining process, so his cyberclone is still rough around the edges. Marco places the ELD between two cedar branches and positions its micam to frame him in a full-shot: "This is what you look like now."

The Shub replicant instantly reanimates itself with Marco's longer hair and whiskers, sixty-two pounds of additional weight, Bovinity jumpsuit, and roamad hiking boots: "Nectronic cow costume!"

"It's an outfit," Shub educates his ridiculous looking replicant. "Z? I need you to perform a full behaviorokinesthetic upgrade on the Shub-PUPP."

"My pleasure, my Marcotecht," Z takes the clunky

prototype by the hand and cross-dissolves to the virtual Kaplan bedroom, candle lit, steamy with aromatherapy mist.

"What are you doing?" blubbers Shub.

"I'm doing what she does..." Z's unbuttoning its blouse, "Multitasking."

"FMB!" frisks the Marcoclone, flopping on Z's imitation bed, tugging off its new boots. "Very nice ass."

"Christ!" Shub is shocked at the unexpected sobotic sexual display. "How long will this take?"

"Six hours, give or take," Z calculates, climbing coquettishly under the comforter.

"Six hours? For the upgrade?"

"I'll call as soon as we're done?"

Shub shuts off the ELD and smiles. He shoulders his pack and heads toward the Broken Highway, "Mmmmmmmmmmmm."

SCHMUCK!

Since Gerry hasn't the politesse to wire Zuzzan the $e he owes her, Maria/Zu has had to survive by picking up roamad hitchers for cold cash, pinching pennies, sleeping scrunched in the Subaru, gulping gruel at uncertified Restaurantrucks. The jam-packed big rig Zu's now eating in, *Roscoe's Ballmeat & Waffle Mobile #23*, has a zoopy new nano video wall behind the counter. Today, the customers are keeping their eyeballs glued to fifty-odd competing gridz feeds, each displaying the Election Selection coverage.

Zuzzan picks at a skewer of broccoli and ballmeat squeezed betwixt scores of roamadic roustabouts wolfing waffles whilst watching William the One wind up a longwinded sales pitch for another of his proposed projects: "The epic documentary expose of Cyopolis will climax with my escape from the supercult's hellhole and simultaneous selection as your One Voter," Billy babbles on with only seconds to go before the deadline for the One to cast the Vote. "Now, if any of you have legitimate inquiries regarding possible participation in my potentially extremely lucrative slate of projects, please make your interest known to my council, Victor Vilter. Only qualified investors will be considered and there are certain risks contained in my forward looking statements. Peace!" Billy bows for the cameras, his boyish butt occluded by oversized CrunchyCountry emblazoned sweats.

Sister Pynchon and a phalanx of no-nonsense New Totality technicians penetrate the wave front of correspondents surrounding the bowing Blurr and cut him off from the camera crews: "The Vote, Mr. Blurr," Paula places her gloved paw on the One's shoulder. "Make a little history for us."

"As promised, sister," Billy unbuttons his shirt pocket and plucks out the piece of paper, quickly crossing himself with a final flourish before handing it over.

Paula uncrumples the wadded vote and reads aloud: "'Ipass?'" she puckers. "There's no candidate named 'Ipass'!"

"I pass," Billy translates. "Not gonna vote. Sorry sister, select another sucker," Blurr grins, pumping his fist toward the hovering video drones: "Long Live Rabbit Man!"

"Who the fuck is Rabbit Man?" Pynchon almost pukes as the One is forcefully spirited away by NT security.

"What an asshole!" screams an outraged roamad perched next to Zu in the Waffle Mobile.

"Rabbit asshole!" yells his buddy.

"They have to spin again, right? Pick another Voter?"

Half a dozen gentlemen wearing jumpsuits embroidered with the words Wary Hare Warrior Warren emerge from the rear booth: "Who don't like Rabbits?!" their leader bellows, whirling a steamy waffle at the video wall—SCHMUCK!—the doughy disc drapes down over a replay of William Blurr flashing the inflammatory 'peace sign' from waybackinthenight.

Zu slams a fistful of dollars down on the syrupy counter and hurriedly squeezes out an exit just as small-arms fire erupts in the riotous Restaurantruck.

SHUBATRON

Billy slept through two of the past three days secreted in the comfy corporate flat above V&V's SanFranciscOakland offices. Blurr blacked out after his marathon press conference and subsequent interrogation by NT investigators. Victor made sure he stayed down, assigning Roxxzan the task of dispensing knock-out drops into Billy's wine, rendering him temporarily oblivious to the incredible pandemonium he and his friend Shub just created.

The Alternate One Voter—immediately re-selected by Pynchon's *Affinity Process*—is a non-descript, middle-aged female of uncertain race, creed, and color. This 'Other One' immediately voted Gerald Bobogoné in as president based solely on a photo of the debonair DataMynd CEO culled off the candidate's gridzsite. After an intensive manhunt, they found the schlub stammering around the back streets of Stamford, lips sucked off, brain-dead from speq poisoning, clearly unable to serve. When the heartbroken Other One had to vote again, she picked a wise-woman-big-sister candidate in the personage of one Constance Honeycutt, the elderly affluhip art gallery owner from Novo Santa Fe, sworn in as President earlier today.

Victor has been working his ass off to fill the king's purse, not resting a wink as evidenced by the multiple dozens of presales deals he closed since Billy's opportunistic eighteen-hour infomercial rant. Inbound investment inquiries regarding Blurr's projects haven't started to level off yet even despite Billy's universally bad press and the outrage of many millions violently venting at his insolent Selection shenanigans. But even these insane tribulations are laughable in comparison to the widespread bewilderment, anguish, and awe unleashed by Shub.

"Where the fuck did you go to, Marcotecht?!" The sheer quantities of animated pseudo-Shubs Victor has already encountered compelled them to install six separate ELDs in the conference room. One of the devices at any given time is likely PUPP-free and Vilter can switch back and forth as required, cutting around the Shub sobot. The mission of 'Shubatron', as the intruding animation sometimes self-deprecatingly refers to itself, is unclear other than to show up unannounced and hang out, sporadically quipping bad one-liners with whoever is on the other side of the screen.

Yesterday's devastating viral sneak attacks of the Marco cyberclone took everyone, especially Victor, by surprise. Over the course of a single day, zillions of Bovinity-clad Shub replicants popped up on every ELD screen from Manhattan to Babylonwood. Anywhere an EarthLinguaDevice exists, the Shub PUPP visits. The information infrastructure of the entire New Totality is nearing the apocalyptic tipping point of no return as the 'Shub Factor' is resulting in a nationwide runaway webgridz meltdown. NT AI experts believe that the Shubatron's uncanny abilities to simulate spontaneous human behavior derives from its pre-programmed propensity to randomly repeat little snatches of conversational statements and feed it back as a question, thereby learning the human's personal lingo. It's almost impossible to go anywhere without seeing Shub's cow-costumed, talking-head chatting up unsuspecting victims. Powerful politicians, webgridz stars, supercults, and Cultural Management Agencies are blaming the radical roamadic Rabbits for launching an opportunistic psychological terror-war on the ruling affluhip. Some are speculating the Shub cyberclone is the first of a new breed of social-destabilization weapons.

Right now, the attorney's video array is displaying only three muted Shubs out a possible half-dozen. Two of the lines are open and the sixth is re-broadcasting 'William the One' footage intercut with supplementary Selection highlights including the disqualified candidate Gerald Bobogoné being hoisted into an EMT trolley. Victor still can't figure out exactly why Gogoboner essentially pre-paid for the PUPPs, getting squat in return. Mayhap it was simply the speq addiction in combination with his fixation on Zuzzan Kaplan.

"Vic?" Roxxzan interrupts her boss over the firm's prized antique analog intercom. "I've got another Shub on feed four."

"Get rid of it, Roxx."

"I think you should talk to this one."

"Why's that?"

"He's wearing a farmer's costume. Crunchy-C."

NECTOWOWZIC!

Marco hitched non-stop all the way from Novo New Mexico to the north side of the Golden Gate Bridge and now he loiters alongside hundreds of other roamads at the panoramic SanFranciscOakland Vista Point overlook.

Shub shields his ELD from sunrays and prying eyes, on hold for Vilter after a dozen attempts persuading Roxxzan to not instantly hang up in his face. Marco doesn't blame her, in fact, most of the folks Shub has met during the last three days on the broken highway were wrestling with their screens, and trying to cope with pesky PUPP's persistently puncturing their personal space.

Even as Shub watches, a pretty perturbed pedestrian screams "Leave me alone!" before furiously flinging her micro-ELD over the cliff into the ocean, adding: "Fucking psychotic puppet!"

Marco eyes a band of destitute South American textile traders squatting in the parking lot, patiently hocking colorful black-market ponchos to roamads. Nearby, two toothless grandmothers babysit a gaggle of brown Bolivian bambinos, bungee corded to their waists roamad-style. The kids are cracking-up, watching a wacky, cartoonish cow-man clowning around on their communal ELD: "Shubatron!" a giggling girl shouts out, grinning at her granny, "Shubatron funny!"

Roxxzan flitters back on line, "Putting you through now," and connects Vilter's video-linked visage to Marco's miniature ELD screen:

"Let's see now..." Victor leers into micam lens, "How many more Shubs do I get to hang up on before the real Marcotecht materializes?"

"Nada. It's me, Viceroy, back from beyond the beyond."

"That's cute. Now tell me something only Marco the Marcotecht knows. Your farmer costume isn't doing it for me."

"It's an outfit. CrunchyCountry."

"Out of the room—?"

"—Out of the deal!"

"What kind of underwear did she have on?"

"Who?"

"Kaplan. When she met Z."

"Uh...Sport panties?"

"Correct! And what am I?"

"You? You're the liver!"

"Not bad for a cyberclone!"

"Technically, the Shub PUPP stopped monitoring me over a year ago."

"Really? Then what's it doing now?"

"Free-ranging. They start out as your basic Shub then slowly cyberclone anyone they interact with."

"But...why?"

"Long story."

"Shorten it."

"Invisibility."

"What? You think you're invisible? No way! You're fucking ubiquitous! You're everywhere, all the time! Now everybody knows who Marco Shub is!"

"Do they? Did you?"

"Touché, Marcotecht..." Vilter concedes, "Touché."

"Where's Billy?"

"Mr. Blurr is asleep upstairs in the old pyramid suite. Recuperating."

"Good. You might want to sedate him for a while."

"Already done."

"Touché, Viceroy."

"What about the off-shore account?"

"What about it?"

"Only Shub and I know what about it. Check it out. I'm filling it up now."

"FMB!"

"That's right, my friend."

"How did you—?"

"—I did absolutely nothing!

"I don't get it, Viceroy."

"Just take the money, Marco."

"And run?"

"Go ahead. But keep in touch."

"Won't be easy where I'm going."

"That's what they always say—"

"—when they talk about it."

"Which they will, Shub. Which they will."

—CLICK! CLICK!—

Attorney and client disconnect, case closed. Shub smiles slyly, sliding his dusty ELD into the belly pouch of his second-hand Rancher overalls.

Marco shoulders his backpack and steps past the poncho traders heading out of the jam-packed Vista Point zone. Suddenly, a roamad sentry guarding the entrance to the parking lot issues three loud warning whistles prompting the Bolivians to desperately snatch up their illegal merchandise. Shub watches as a trio of NT motorcycle officers cautiously caravan through the lot, circle in formation and park in a tight triangle. Marco senses a free-floating fear foaming up from the ranks of the Bolivians and roamads. He astounds himself by preemptively approaching the officers as they dismount and remove their helmets.

"Wowz!" marvels Marco, "Beautiful bikes!"

"Can't complain," the first cop admits.

"Free gas," says the second.

"And you are?" inquires the last.

"I'm Shub."

"Shub?"

"Marco Shub?"

"The one and only."

"Of course you are. And I'm a baboon-faced horsefly."

"Hell, we've busted so many Shubs in the last thousand miles that our hands hurt from spanking all of them!"

"Really?" Marco says, knowing full well that the Shubatron cyberclones have already temporarily replaced at least a billion people's New Totality webgridz identities: "You're spanking Shubs? Sounds kinky, officer."

"Yeah, well we're kinda kinky cops. Ya know?"

"I see. Motorcycles and leather."

"Go ahead, Shub, stereotype us! We're used to it."

"I will," Marco risqués. "Where you guys from anyway?"

"L.A. Heading all the way to Novo Seattle."

"We're participating in cross-training exercises with departments from all over the west."

"Wowz...Seattle."

"Yeah. It's perfect for practicing team riding maneuvers."

"Diplomatic escorts."

"Escorts?" Shub salaciously suspicions. "Cross-training?"

"Someone's gotta do it. Ya know?"

The cops laugh along with Marco as he spies the Bolivians safely exiting in a tattered truck, escaping detection by the sidetracked lawmen. "Safe journey to you, officers. Have some fun."

"We will. You too, Shub."

"Ciao!" Marco melts back into the mass of *Homeomobilius*, fairly certain that—although the cops were really just taking a break—his little performance both somehow aided and abetted the good, and reconfirmed that he is invisible in plain sight...*Just as predicted by Elroy!*

Shub meanders toward the northbound lanes, crowd-weaving through a river of tourists, transients, and hitchhiking commuters lining the refuse-strewn broken highway. Marco observes sporadic shards of his silly Shubatron sobot smattering passing pedestrians' screens. He eavesdrops on one such roamad who nods in melancholy agreement whilst his palmtop PUPP offers up animated advice: "Look Phil, the only way you're gonna climb out of this rut is to join a nectronic singles swarm group! Go to the *AloneTogetherAgain* gridzsite. Touch in on 'Emotional Familiars'."

"Ok. First thing tomorrow," the pensive young man promises. "Thanks, Shuby."

"Shuby!" Marco can't help auto-repeating.

Thanks to Vilter, Shub's untraceable offshore account is holding more than enough $e to float any number of profitable pursuits but—since he's in effect taking it one-minute-at-a-time after his incomprehensible gap-zone visitation—it's wiser to just sit low and go slow. He'll float with the flow, anonymous and invisible, even if otherwise overblown.

Shub removes a greasy wad of bills from the hidey pouch inside his farmers costume and steps to the edge of the roadway amid scores of fellow hitchers. He waves the devalued greenbacks slowly overhead, hoping to get recognized by the deluge of drivers creeping past in a perpetual roamadic crush.

A muddy station wagon pulls over deposits an elderly roamad rider. The old man weaves through the crowd, stands up straight - its Enoy Revesti. He quickly disappears into the Roamadic mix. Half a dozen hopeful hitchers descend on the soiled Subaru eagerly waving their cards front of the female driver.

Marco doggedly squints against the dirty wind as a truck-train caravan of mobile motels downshift in the heaving traffic.

The female driver begins to roll back onto the road-way but stops when she sees Shub's hard currency and pops open the passenger door: "American dollars?"

"That's me!"

"Get in!"

"Thanks," Marco squeezes his pack into the back seat and takes shotgun. "Appreciate it."

"I'm Maria."

"Marco," Shub gently shakes her hand.

"Marco, huh? Marco Shub?"

"The one and only."

"You're my third self-professed Shub rider today. That's ok. I don't need to know your real name, Kilroy. But I do need real money before we pull outa here."

"Paper stuff?" Shub reaches into his pack and yanks out the bank courtesy pouch containing his remaining stash of cold cash.

"Zoopy! How far you going?"

"As far north as I can. Actually I'm more or less XaNa-bound."

"Well hell! I wouldn't mind making it there myself, mister money bags."

"Good!" he laughs, "Great! I figure what the hell." Marco can't help noticing the remarkable similarity between this pretty, witty, Maria and Zuzzan Kaplan...Impossible! Although he has never seen Kaplan in the flesh, only photo's, videos, and via Z's realistic replication, both women possess the same basic face. Even the body language is similar. "Do you have sisters, Maria?"

"Nope. Why?"

"You seem like you would, I guess," Shub stumbles, his

heart starting to slam around, torturing his trachea.

Maria ignores the hitcher's premature attempt at familial familiarization: "I can take you all the way to the Canadian border if you want, depending on how much you want to pay, Mr. Shub."

"Howzabout twenty-thousand in hundred-dollar bills?"

"Shit! That would work just fine! Very generous of you, brother."

"Well, the worker is worth their wages," says Marcotecht, now manifestly mystified by Maria, mentally mapping the micromovements of her mouth to his memory of Z's familiar mimicry.

"I can use the money," Maria puts her car into gear and slowly pulls out of the hitchhiking lane into traffic. "My sleazy boss just ripped me off so I've had to become a pretty good driver. But this old jalopy is a creeker and I gotta be on my toes all the time out here."

"My dad had one of these Subaru, waybackinthenight," Shub remembers now, looking at Maria's fine featured Kaplanesque face: "These babies used to make great get-away cars because there were so damn many of them that they were practically invisible."

"Really? You a get-away guy, Shub?" Maria almost hopes.

"Kinda."

"Yeah? Me too. Listen, it's gonna take us ten or twelve days to get to the border from here, so better have something in common."

"We'll drive each other bananas by then?"

"No we won't! We're the XaNa-wannabes!" Maria flashes Marco a spontaneous smile, catching herself, letting him in an inch...*Not too bad for a rancher type*. She covers. "Look at this fucking traffic!"

Shub sees the amiable motorcycle policemen from the Vista Point unexpectedly cruising up beside them: "Hey!" he rolls down the window, "My new friends!"

"What are you doing?!" Maria sputters.

"Officers!" Shub shouts, smiling, saluting patriotically. The lead cop grins and gives Marco a sharp salute in return. He barks his siren three times and abruptly pulls out in front of the Subaru, followed in formation by the two other officers, lights flashing. The tremendous traffic jam miraculously parts before them, slowly but surely making way for the unusual police escort.

"Wowz!" Maria can't believe it. "VIP treatment!"

"They need the practice," rationalizes Shub, astonished at the incredible good fortune the fates are affording them.

"Don't we all!" Maria steers ahead, happily unimpeded.

Shub sneaks his slim line ELD communications device from his overalls, dangles his arm out the window. He gently flips his unit out the window. It bounces twice before being squashed by a lumbering Restaurantruck.

"Music!" harkens Marco. He fingers the Subaru's funky satellite-radio controls.

"It's dead."

"Oh?" Marco squishes forward in the seat and gazes at the aged apparatus. "Let's have a look."

"You repair electronics?"

"Sometimes..." Shub squints at the dirty device, recalling how Revesti fixed his broken ELD. He remembers Elroy alternating between squinting and relaxing his gaze just a kiss: Shub sees a subtle but uniform green glow gently gyrating around the perimeter of the malfunctioning machine. A minuscule lozenge of blackened non-light floats just beneath the radio itself.

— BLING! —

A distant DJ sounds out from the Subaru's surprisingly impressive speakers.

"Nectowowzic!" Maria smiles, speeding up to pace their official escort, squinting with Shub at the smazy sunset, soaking in the soothing, sardonic sonic of Slowedownlight.

We'll be dancing in the light again, channeling our twins.
Here we go again, we're not alone, not with our cyberclones.
Every click you make, every heart you break,
They'll be watching and replicating.
Everything we buy till the day we die
Fills the happy homes of our cyberclones.

Up on nearby hillock, Enoy stands above the jammed highway, squinting at the unending traffic. He spies the police escort... and smiles. His tri-screen displays: *'MARCO SHUB - OFF-GRIDZ'.* Enoy raises his souvenir saber to the setting sun.

Everywhere we go we're on video
so the clones can grow
and run the whole damn show.

THE AUTHOR

Michael van Himbergen was born in Hollywood, raised in Los Angeles, and graduated from California Institute of the Arts in Film & Video.

Michael worked as a Visual Effects Producer on films including *Spaceballs, Die Hard, Stargate, Michael Jackson's Black or White, What Dreams May Come* and others.

He has written *OVERBLOWN* as a screenplay and composed a demo album. Michael lives in Northern New Mexico.

www.ingramcontent.com/pod-product-compliance
Lightning Source LLC
Chambersburg PA
CBHW070801200626
46811CB00023B/328